Cathedral of Christ the King

714 KING STREET WEST
HAMILTON, ONTARIO

THE
CASTLE
AND THE
RING

BY

C. C. MARTINDALE, S.J.

P. J. KENEDY & SONS · NEW YORK

CUM PERMISSU SUPERIORUM
Library of Congress Catalog Card No. 55–9612
Copyright 1955 by P. J. Kenedy & Sons, New York ©
Printed in the United States of America

To
the Society of the Holy Child Jesus
and
in loving memory of my time spent in its
Settlement at Poplar (London Dockland)

FOREWORD

WHILE these chapters were appearing in *The Pylon* (the missionary magazine of the Society of the Holy Child) I was often asked, "How much of all this is true?"

Well, it is a story about the Magi's gold and a castle in northern England. We have to assume (rightly or wrongly) that gold is imperishable, so that this might possibly have been the story of what happened to the gift offered at Bethlehem. Further, the castle is my version of a real castle. The outline of the Saxon house can still be seen from the terrace where the yew trees are planted; the first stone tower still stands. The Ferdinand Medd I write of did put heart-shaped windows into the walls before La Colombière came to St. James's. The water still falls behind the rock face (despite my last chapter!) and can be seen through the two lance-shaped openings. As for the scenery, there is nothing, save in two chapters, that I have not watched and loved.

As for the history. In Part One I fear that experts may find a flaw in it, though I hope not. Of course it is extremely simplified, but I should like these vignettes (what more are they?) to introduce readers, young and old, to parts of our Catholic life to which they may not have given much attention so far. When conversations of historical personages are introduced, I have tried to use documentary evidence for what they say, or could have said, even when, by exception, an encounter between St. Bernard and St. Hildegard cannot be shown to have taken place.

In Part Two certainly the history becomes more allegorical, and the constant interconnections with the episodes of Part One may, I hope, not be too obscure. I hope also that the conflict between the perishable and the sole indestructible, between time and the everlasting, will be discerned without any underlining. I so much dislike explaining! And if the preternatural continues to interweave itself with normal experience, well, that is certainly what happens.

I know this may seem a very pompous preface to a story written, at first, for my own recreation; I continued it because I feel at home in various parts of the long Catholic life and like to move about there. I certainly never meant to write a "cautionary tale," but I would not know what to make of the world if I could not see a heavenly gold shining across the glitter and the promise of a heavenly home for us exiles that never has been broken.

I wish to thank the editor of *The Pylon,* 120 via Boncompagni, Rome, for the infinite pains she took in seeing the original pages through the press.

C. C. Martindale

Burton Hill
Petworth

CONTENTS

Contents

PART ONE

PRELUDE / *SOLI INVICTO*

THE two soldiers, Favo and Marcus, sat on a high ridge in northern Britain and looked down upon immeasurable forests. The day would have been hot even in Rome; bees murmured in the heather, but neither trees nor bracken stirred. Down there you could just catch the glint of a brook and hear the clink of steel where Roman soldiers were building a stone bridge.

At last Favo said, "Where there are bridges, men will build houses. There will be a town down there, and up here perhaps a camp."

"The world," Marcus replied, "grows greater, and yet smaller. How quickly we move — roads, bridges, everywhere. Soon the world will be one Rome."

"Man of dreams," said his friend, smiling, "here for once is a dream I can understand! Our unconquered armies draw all distances together, and yet our empire goes on spreading. Yes, one Rome, eternal Rome, Rome everywhere!"

"I should certainly like to have a house here," said

· 3

Marcus. "Just down there, above the stream, sheltered by this ridge."

"You think of houses; I, of empires."

"I think of both," said Marcus, who was a Christian. "A little ring for my body's life and a circle without frontiers for my soul."

"I am no philosopher," said Favo rather brutally. "I am a citizen of Rome; where I can eat and find the wife of the hour I am at home."

Meanwhile, he had been chipping away at a large flat stone and had engraved the words *Soli Invicto* quite deeply on it.

"We must give something to the gods," he said. "To the Unconquered Sun! There is no room to write 'Mithra,' but he will take it for granted that he is meant."

Marcus smiled to himself, because after all the words could equally well mean "To the Sole Unconquered"; and next day he came up alone and carved a cross above the words. He then carried the stone down to a cave not far below and left it there, for now it was no more Mithra's, though Mithra, it is true, was worshiped in caves. Then he went lower still, to where a source poured incessantly behind the rock face; you could see it through two lance-shaped openings and it was sacred to the genius of the place. People threw offerings down where the water disappeared, and Marcus, half-laughing, threw in a small gold coin.

"Lord," he sighed, "baptize this place and all the world! Thou Road, Thou Bridge! Carry me from these small and passing things to my eternal home. And build for Thyself, too, here, an imperishable house."

He laughed at his own words and at the taste of melancholy they had left. "Up with your hearts!" he cried, and crashed down through the incense exhaled by the trampled heather and through a golden air to the place where the arch of the bridge was already taking shape.

1

THE GOLD IS GIVEN

AND now," said the old doctor, "I will give you my greatest treasure. Life has become very uncertain for you, but then death must be very near for me, and you are my dear nephew and I have no one else." He placed an oriental casket on the table and unlocked it. It contained three little bags.

"This one," he said, "had the myrrh in it; it is almost all powder by now, but you can still feel a solid crumb or two. This one contained the frankincense, but that, long ago, is dust. This one is dust, too, but the gold dust. See how heavy it is!"

"Did *she*," said Helkias, trembling, "give you this?"

"Yes, when I was composing my first treatise and asking her so many questions. She was by then no more young, but it all seemed to her like yesterday. Did she not wish to keep these treasures? Yes; but still more, no. She *was* keeping them, as she kept everything, in her heart. In fact, she had already given a few grains of myrrh, a few shreds of frankincense, to friends who were

u myself, and your ill-bred Bishop Sagaris as well. Do
imagine you can give your gold to *him*." And she ran

The night grew cold. He was alone, and felt the near
proach of death. He was terrified of pain, and saw, red
ough the shadows, the arena and the fire. "O Christ,"
wailed, "help me, your unfaithful servant."

oubtless Chio had managed to unlatch the cupboard
r, for just then it swung open. He could see the casket
a cloudy lamp. He took it out and opened it. He
tied the dust of myrrh into a goblet of water.

t least she shall not have that," he whispered. He
k it, and his very soul seemed bitterness. "Nor this,"
ighed, and poured the shriveled spices on to a dying
ier, and the whole house became sweet with the
rance.

t the gold? He did not know what to do. "O Christ,"
id, "I give it back to you! Take care of it." His spirit
me full of golden light; he prayed, and slept.

xt day he and the bishop were arrested, examined,
tortured. They were faithful, and were killed. Chio
delighted she had not had to waste the gold dust on
be. She had it melted down and shaped into an
ent like a knotted snake, and she wore it at fes-
and had great success when relating its origin. Un-
y, having divorced two more husbands, she was
f divorced by the fourth, who naturally took posses-
f her jewelry, including the snake.

---

sailing away; and even some of the gold she had given
to the poor. After all, it had been given to Him, and they
are He. But I could not resist keeping what she gave to
me. However, now I give it to you, with my love and
blessing and, I am sure, with hers."

Helkias knelt down and took the casket. "Dear Uncle
Lukas," he said through his tears, "even should this gold
be lost, thanks to *you* her Song is still sweeter than any
music; and all generations that shall call her blessed will
be grateful also to you."

2

A.D. 165

THE GOLD ASTRAY

Helkias was martyred not long after the death of St.
Luke but had given the casket to his son who had settled
in Bithynia only to be martyred there himself in 112, under the conscientious governor Pliny. He had time to en-
trust his treasure to his own son, Meliton, a mere boy,
who did not realize what the box contained or know much
more than that he had been baptized a Christian. After-

ward he married a pagan girl called Chio; they lived in Laodikia.

When Marcus Aurelius began, in his turn, to execute all who were denounced as Christians, Meliton became much bewildered. Chaos was returning; the barbarians were restive; the very army was mutinous and the Tiber overflowed. Pestilence followed and then famine.

"You *must* see," said Chio, exasperated, "that it is all the fault of you Christians. I never thought much of your intelligence, Meliton; but even you should have grasped by now something of our stoic wisdom. And yet you others — you cannot even keep your own laws! Your deacon Phaidon who only last week ran away with all the money belonging to your widows . . ."

Meliton muttered that the poor man's wife and little girl were ill and that he was sure to repay the money when he could; God was merciful. "We have heard that before," said Chio. "Neither you nor I see God; but we see him in his works, and in what work of his is he more visible than in the empire? It is his spoken word. And in whom is the empire recapitulated if not in our emperor? He is the father of us all, so serene, so wise. Yet when you pass his statue you will not so much as throw a grain of incense to it. You are enemies of the human race itself!"

Meliton, obstinate rather than strong in faith, repeated that he was a Christian, though he couldn't answer her arguments. And indeed he could not deny that the Christians seemed to be splitting the empire into halves — were at war with society. They must appear as bad as atheists. Remembering his background of many martyr-

doms, he could but say that he hoped t
here.

"Oh, but there will!" Chio retorted
men like that so-called philosopher J
cuted, and that widow Felicitas an
Rusticus, a personal friend of the E
serenity would never allow mere fr
with justice. And there have been pl
even here. Well, if you are denoun
off."

"But, my dear, where would yo
can hardly pay for our dinner as it

She nodded wisely. "Leave it to
ing straight to the bank before it
would lend *you* anything, but ban

"But, my dearest Chio, what h

"Gold dust," she said triumpl
I've never looked into that dirt
secret? There's gold dust in on
There's quite a lot."

He felt as if she had struck hi
had always been in his family.

"What is the sense of that,"
family for it to be *in?*" And ind
careful to have no children.

She rushed toward the cuph
kept. He seized her wrists. "You

"Let go!" she screamed. "You
He let go suddenly, and she
"Beast!" she shouted. "Enou

3

THE MAKING OF THE RING

THE golden snake passed through various hands till it was picked up by a young Roman officer stationed in Macedonia. He was Constantius, nicknamed Chlorus, the Paleface, as his skin was pale as parchment. He had sick leave for a month, so he sailed round the end of the Euxine and along its southern coast to a small town named Drepanum. Here he disembarked for a spell of sea bathing. It was quite fashionable — a lovely beach, medicinal baths, good hunting in the hills behind the town. He could not afford grand lodgings, so he stayed in a horrible inn that even the police were shy of — sailors, broken-down actors and petty criminals lodged there. He did not care; he would be out all day. But he fell in love with the stable girl, Helena; and anyhow, girls went down automatically on the bill. Helena fell even more deeply in love with him; perhaps out of sheer surprise that anyone should be really in love with her; perhaps the very pallor of the man appealed to this black-haired, aquiline girl, vivid in her dress of scarlet and orange and emerald-green scarf. He at once gave her the golden snake.

Roman soldiers were forbidden to marry but could form lasting associations not regarded as dishonorable. Helena went back to Europe with Constantius, and they had a son called Constantine. Helena's volcanic temperament swept Constantius from glory to glory, and power was evidently latent in this bleached and bloodless man. In fact, when the Emperor Diocletian — tired of tyranny and already looking forward to the cultivation of prize cabbages — divided his cumbrous empire into East and West and entrusted each half to an Augustus with a Caesar under him, Constantius, to his amazement, found himself Caesar in charge of Britain, Gaul, and much more. And thereupon he was ordered to get rid of Helena and marry Theodora, stepdaughter of his Augustus. If he were tied up in a family alliance there would be less chance of jealousy and political intrigue. Young Constantine was sent to Asia, to live in the silken prison proper to princes who could not yet safely be assassinated; and Helena, flinging her jewels behind her, yet clinging to that first golden gift of near twenty years ago, went out into the dark.

Constantius ruled prudently, making roads and bridges, improving the postal services and agriculture. He built a vast palace by the Seine, close to the island that contained the town of Lutetia Parisiorum. But he was lonely, and when he felt himself dying he sent to Asia for his son Constantine. The young man, sure he would be murdered if he lingered, raided the imperial stables, stole the best horses and hamstrung the rest, and rejoined his father. He crossed with him to Britain and was with Constantius when he died, in 306, at York. Instantly the soldiers acclaimed Constantine as emperor and in only a few years it was clear that he must be sole master of the West. In 312 he entered Rome triumphant, and ten years later had conquered also the Eastern Augustus. The son of the Paleface and the stable girl was world emperor.

Meanwhile he had summoned his mother to Rome. How would she succeed — this old exile — as mother of an emperor, of *the* Emperor? No one who knew her could doubt it. Compete with the calm patricians and neurotic millionairesses of a Rome still majestic in decay? Not she! Arriving with but the one jewel on her breast, and next day smothered in pearls, her haggard features being imprinted on coins that would wander across the world, she still refused to do her hair in any but the outmoded way that *she* preferred. There was now but one Augustus in that world. Constantine entitled her Augusta, and thus she, too, became unique among women.

Constantine was convinced that Christ had proved himself stronger than all the pagan gods taken together, though by now they were all, even Mithra himself, fused in the golden haze that surrounded the Unconquered Sun. The Emperor was not, in fact, quite clear whether he was not himself, somehow, that Sun whom his father had adored up there in the rolling moors of northern Britain. Certainly he felt himself Giver of Life; certainly the Sole Unconquered, and without the change of a single letter *Soli Invicto* could mean the Unconquered Sun. He

· *13*

had to hold together an empire of which all the great hereditary officers were pagan. He put baptism off and off; he retained and enjoyed the title "Pontifex Maximus." "I," thought he, "am the supreme Bridgemaker; none can travel anywhere save by way of me." Still, he propitiated Peter and Paul with unimaginable riches; he made over his Lateran palace to the Roman bishop. He convoked the other bishops that they might unify dogma, and then, awestruck by these venerable presences, bowed low before them. He was both servant and master of the Church.

Through his clouded mind lightnings of intuition could flash, and in it thunderclaps of decision would explode. It was hinted that Crispus, the brilliant son of his first marriage, was plotting against him. In a mad fit he had him killed. Helena, who adored Crispus, came rushing back from Asia, where she had gone on a journey, to confront her son. But meantime Constantine had become convinced that it was his second wife who, out of jealousy, had inspired those rumors and he had had her suffocated in her bath.

Helena saw clearly that she must become an anchorage for this man, tossed by tempestuous and conflicting moods — this Roman emperor with ruddy cheeks and yellow hair and chained with barbaric ornaments, ordering pagan rituals but standing by to jeer at them and raising everywhere the cross. To link his Christian self to her, he caused that old golden snake of hers to be melted down into a heavy ring surrounding a cross with Christ's initials graven on it.

He had been shocked to hear that Calvary, the place

where Our Lord died, still lay buried under pagan ruins. "We must excavate!" he cried. "We must build a basilica!" He wrote to the bishop of Jerusalem a letter combining piety with finance and architectural details.

Helena alone grasped the situation, the imminent delays and confusions. Though now eighty years old, she resolved to go and see for herself. The imperial treasury was already open to her; and she, who had loved to go to Mass and stand among the people in her widow's dress, unadorned save for the golden ring beneath her tunic, who had invited the destitute to meals and had served them in slave's costume, now made the tremendous progress of a Christian empress throughout Syria, all but worshiped by the thousands who flocked to see her pass.

In Jerusalem she inspected the work of removing the accumulated debris on which the pagan temple had been built; but she shrank from the noise and the crowds and felt too awestruck to remain in the city. The lonely slopes of Olivet attracted her. These, at least, were unchanged since the divine feet had trodden them. Nonetheless, she planned a basilica there — left to haphazard devotion, the Mount might well be desecrated by the crowds. But she preferred, even so, to go to Bethlehem, and planned her second basilica there.

She spent her last night there in vigil before the cave where the Son of God was born. She was in peasant's dress but still wore the jewel which had wedded her now to Christ. Other jewels she heaped up for the new basilica, but as for the ring: "Keep it," said an old priest, "it will remind you to pray for the salvation of your son, for the

Church of God, and that no man of a place and an hour may seek dominion over her."

Left alone, she laid the ring upon the sacred rock. Many little lamps flickered in the humble shrine, but then to her eyes the ring began to glow with its own radiance and illuminated the waves of incense that rose from two bowls where spices smoldered. Even to think of imperial splendors at such an hour would have been bitterness, though the memories of her tragic life seemed to have had the bitterness drained out of them. "O Christ," she said, "though I take back this ring, it still is yours, and to your keeping I commend it." Peace enfolded her.

Next day she began her return. Populations poured out to see her, hailing her as Mother of the Empire and of the universal Church. She was very tired. She smiled, waved, let her hand be kissed, but moved as in a dream.

Instead of going straight to Nicomedia, she made a difficult circuit to Drepanum. The town had grown, but away from the inn where she had served. It survived, therefore, but she could hardly recognize it, so had the habit of palaces made reality to shrink. The innkeeper, terrified when the vast imperial carriage halted there, prostrated himself to the very ground. She asked who now served there; a trembling girl was led forward. Helena smiled, patted her cheek, and gave her a gold coin. The Empress entered the inn; she found at once the room that had belonged to Constantius Chlorus. She searched, and recognized on an oaken beam the letters *C* and *H* that he had carved there. It was a thousand years ago, and it was yesterday. She kissed the letters on the oak and then the ring, and offered her swift, long life to God.

On the way home she caught cold and made no attempt to resist approaching death. Constantine was summoned but could not come at once. So, since she liked her attendants to sit behind a curtain and keep the light veiled, she died, once more alone and in the dark, but in the company of the eternal Christ upon whose cross her hands were clasped.

4

A.D. 445

PILLAR POINT OF VIEW

SIMEON was the son of a Christian shepherd who lived in a village lost in the Cilician mountains. So he spent the days, and, as he grew older, often the nights, too, in solitude and silence. He grew satisfied with the presence of his sheep and of God who reigned above the stars. Therefore, when the sheep were safe asleep, he kept trying to reach nearer to God by climbing some high crag and singing hymns to Him, or, even better, keeping silence.

Still, he found that he took his body with him and also

his thoughts. In his extreme poverty he had never eaten much, but now he resolved to explain to his body that it must not interfere with him and must be punished if it did; so he ate nothing but a few roots and drank only water, not milk. As for his thoughts, they were more restless than any sheep; they would not stay where he put them nor come when he called them. Sometimes they were actually strangers and he did not know their names. But at other times they went to sleep, and he could think, without thinking, of God. At last, when his father died, he sold his flock, gave away the money, and entered the monastery of St. Eusebios at Teledas that he might be still more free.

Unable to read or write, he had learned by heart the gospels, the psalms, the liturgy, and parts of what St. Basil had written. Yet he was useless in the monastery because if he was filling the lamps he might remember the oil of gladness with which God had so plentifully anointed him and fall into a joyous wonder that might last for an hour. If sent to fish, he so delighted in these swift and silvery creatures that he always put them back. He could not even weave reed mats, because if the reeds made a cross his tears for the sufferings of his Saviour made work impossible. The monks, exasperated, and maybe shamed by his penances, expelled him.

He wandered around till 412, and then, being about twenty-three, he entered another monastery near Teleskhin and lived in a hut without a roof that he might be more like Him who had no roof but slept beneath the stars. But people bored holes in his door to look at him,

and even climbed up to peep down at him. Boys shouted
the names of wild beasts at him. At first he did not mind
this, for beasts are good creatures of God and live without sin; then he was sorry, because the boys meant it unkindly, which was not Christlike.

So he built a sort of platform, four feet high, and placed
his hut on that. But this was useless, so he built higher
and higher, and lived walled around in a space no more
than about four feet square. He could not lie down flat.
But why should he? When he was not standing to praise
or pray, or crouching head to stone in penance, it was
enough to sit, chin on knees, and sleep what was needful.
At last no one could reach him without a ladder; he was
invisible behind his parapet save to the birds, who flocked
there. He knew them all, even the vultures, who came
there at first because they thought he would die soon;
everyone else hated them, but he loved the birds and
stroked their naked necks.

His bishop, alarmed by so strange a life, ordered him to
come down. At once he prepared to do so; but, docility
being proved, the bishop revoked his order.

Pilgrims came in hundreds, hoping to see him. Theolo-
gians arrived to question him concerning the Trinity and
the Incarnation about which the world was quarreling.
To the first he would answer nothing but the prayer:
"Glory be to the Father, and to the Son, and to the Holy
Ghost. As it was in the beginning, so be it now and forever, Amen." To the second he would answer: "Let all
generations name blessed the Theotókos!" thus proclaiming his loyalty to the Council of Ephesus. Famous gen-

erals would ask his advice about war; but all he would answer was that God had permitted them the use of force for the protection of justice and the weak. The generals did not come again.

Simeon himself had never used force against his sheep; and even if he had to hurt wild dogs and jackals he apologized to them, and sometimes they would come back to be healed of the wounds he had dealt them. Only to the very rich he was severe, even to those who offered great alms. He asked if they suffered by giving what they gave, and said that to give of their superfluity to the necessitous was but a partial restitution and not charity at all; and that it was they who made the poor, and then, by their gifts, kept them alive indeed, but still poor, so that they themselves might continue to be rich and idle. "Weep for yourselves," he said, "and for your children."

The Empress Helena's jewels had been stored in the imperial treasury save for unimportant pieces that were given away. Among these was the gold ring, regarded as hopelessly old-fashioned, and it was offered to a lady who passed it on to her son. He, being a merchant, decided to sell it as a curiosity. Being near Teleskhin, he visited Simeon as still more of a curiosity, and by a sudden impulse embedded the ring in some bread that was going up in a basket, for the saint's edifice was now some sixty feet high. Simeon always refused gifts, but he felt that the ring had a destiny and shouted to the merchant to come nearer, which he did, much alarmed.

"May Christ be born in your soul!" called Simeon, his usual salutation. The proper answer was, "Christ dieth no more," but the merchant, not knowing this, merely replied, "Thank you very much, holy man," and waited.

"You are going," said the saint, "to a place called Gaul, farther off even than Constantinople. In a certain town there lives a consecrated virgin, Genovefa, a treasure house of mysteries. Give this ring to her from me, and say that as she is the end, so is she a beginning."

The merchant begged Simeon to repeat this, for he did not understand it.

"Neither," said Simeon, "do I. But soon I shall see my everlasting life; you, within your own years, will see the end of something you thought eternal, which it is not, while that which is invisibly imperishable shall endure. In golden Constantinople, that thinks herself the second Rome, little shall last. But in Gaul, what shall seem to perish, shall endure; and what is conceived, is not yet born. Of these, Genovefa is the daughter and must be the mother."

Simeon then threw the ring over his parapet. The merchant was far too bewildered to catch it, and it struck him in the middle of his forehead and made a cross-shaped mark.

"Men shall come from the East," said Simeon, "carrying gold." Thus the ring started on its way to Paris.

As for Simeon, a few years after this he felt he was dying. A sailor, driving iron pegs into the masonry, climbed up and let down a rope and thus a priest, a deacon, and a doctor were hauled up. The priest anointed Simeon and gave him holy Communion. Then he died, and the birds left the tower, lamenting.

5

A.D. 545

THE PALACE AND THE HUT

IT cannot be denied that Siugard, Queen Clotilda's chief serving maid, did not like the consecrated virgin, Geneviève. Siugard was a true Frank and despised the Romans except the saints Peter and Paul, of whom she was afraid; and she hated the Gauls, whom she thought quarrelsome, talkative, and restless.

Now Geneviève was both Roman and Gallic by origin; yet if you had said she scarcely ever spoke, and had lived in her cell for nearly fifty years, Siugard would have answered that she ought never to have gone into it but have remained to help her parents on the farm. Fancy that old Bishop Germanus saying she should be dedicated to God just because she had picked up a ring with a cross upon it! Then she would add that Geneviève did *not* stay in her cell, but that when Attila and his Huns threatened to invade the little Paris island, out came Geneviève and persuaded the people not to flee. No wonder the men were for stoning her as a witch; nothing prevented them but a message from that old Germanus, dying overseas.

Disgraceful that Geneviève should be talked of overseas and Clotilda not at all!

Of course Clotilda had been in those days only a small Burgundian princess, unheard of by Siugard herself. But it would have been useless to remind the jealous serving maid of that, so fierce was the devotion she had developed for her mistress. She would have continued breathlessly that when the great Clovis invaded these parts and ended Roman rule, it was a pity he didn't extinguish Geneviève, too. He certainly had intended to starve the Parisians out; but that scandalous woman — at her age! — constituted herself captain of *eleven* barges and slipped up the Seine and brought back fodder for these despicable mouths. But here she felt uncomfortable. For Clovis had married Clotilda, a Christian, and had allowed his first son to be brought up in her cult. Naturally he died. The second son, too, had seemed likely to die, but he got better — the older gods did not succeed in their vengeance that time. In fact, when Clovis seemed about to be beaten by the Alemans, he remembered his wife's God, invoked him, and won. He went straight off to the bishop Remigius, inquired about this religion, and was baptized.

Siugard remembered the magnificence of Rheims, decorated for the occasion — even Clovis asked if it was the Paradise of which the Christians spoke so much! Finally, Clovis and Clotilda had gone to live in that old, old palace built by a Roman king called Constantius Paleface. It was no distance across the river from Geneviève, and why a dirty old woman well over sixty should have such an influence over her queen, who at most was twenty-two,

Siugard could not understand, and objected very strongly.

However, she liked the gardens of that palace which sloped down to the camp, if only because when Clovis was away, drenching new fields with blood, she could have agreeable flirtations with the sergeants of the home guard. But she was angry when, one day, the Queen told her to arrange with the guild of ferrymen to row her across to Geneviève. There was a cathedral on the island of Paris dedicated to a hero Stephen, a mere servingman, Siugard understood, and Geneviève had chosen to lean her hut against this church, and the alleys that led to it stank foully.

The Queen entered the hut and sat down on a box. Geneviève sat on the earth; Siugard remained standing.

"I have come to tell you," said Clotilda, "that the King is going to build a basilica on our hill in honor of Sts. Peter and Paul."

"That is really thanks to you, my child," said the old woman. "But for you he would, of course, have become an Arian, in league with Constantinople, not Rome. The Arians build and build, but on sand. Peter and Paul are Rome, and Rome is Rock."

"But," said Clotilda anxiously, "he proposes to throw his battle-ax as far as he can, and that will be the length of his basilica. Thus when Thor threw his hammer of lightning on the earth, all that it struck belonged to him. I do not like these memories."

"Dear Clovis is a baby," said Geneviève. "Let him have his way. His ax may as well cleave the sweet earth as skulls. Now I want to say something. May Siugard wait outside?"

Siugard, always irritated when Geneviève called the Queen her child, and furious to hear Clovis called a baby, was even angrier when the noise of children playing, watermen shouting, and quarreling women emptying refuse from the roofs, prevented her from hearing anything through the latch hole.

"A holy man," said the saint to Clotilda, "who died some years ago toward the sunrise has sent me this ring. They say it belonged to the Empress Helena, but who knows? Anyhow, rings are not for me. You are a queen, and to you I lend it, for no thing is given to any mortal save in Christ. But I will tell you two things. When I touch this ring, I taste bitterness; and for you, dear child, there will be — ah! the bitterest of bitterness. Yet I breathe also the sweetness of incense, and your evening sacrifice will be sweet. As for gold, I do not love it; yet it was accepted by God's Mother for her Son, and in its own way it lasts. Longer than any ax. Longer than Clovis's basilica. Before you die, give this ring to St. Martin."

"But he died years and years ago," cried the Queen. "Certainly I mean to live in Tours when Clovis is killed. Well" — for Geneviève had smiled, though sadly — "of course he *will* be killed sooner or later. I suppose I could bequeath the ring to Martin's basilica?"

"No," said the recluse. "Give it to *him*. Not that he will always keep it. Now Siugard may come in."

"Siugard," said Geneviève when the serving maid was inside, "stop thinking the thoughts you are thinking. The ring — which I think you heard me mention — will not be yours. He who sent me the ring sent also a message. He said that I am an end, but also a beginning. How, I do not know. But doubtless Gaul, of which Clovis has made an end, will be named after you Franks. Will that name, too, disappear? I cannot tell, but the thing hidden within the ring will always be there, and, so long as it is necessary, I shall be there to guard it, and so will Bishop Martin. So no more of these ideas, Siugard! Be off home, and see that the Queen does not catch cold in the boat."

She kissed the Queen's hand and saluted Siugard with much courtesy, and was lost in prayer before the door had so much as closed.

Clovis hurled his ax: the crypt was built; an army of mosaic saints, grim and glittering, prayed round the walls and populated the vaults. Clovis offered to take Geneviève there to show her how grand it was. She laughed and looked into his eyes — ferociously blue, melting at times into dreams, crinkled round the lids by tortuous intriguing, but mostly wide and infantile, and swimming, just now, with tears.

"Good-by, my baby," she said, kissing him. "Your old mother will try to take care of you. Go off to your crypt, and you and I will see it together, if God so wills."

In fact he was killed soon after this, aged only forty-five, and was buried under those very vaults in an enormous stone sarcophagus covered with crosses. Five weeks later Geneviève, too, died, and was buried beside him, having lifted Gaul into being Catholic France at the head of half of Christian history. Clotilda, Clovis's widow, felt herself a ghost and went to Tours. She was fantastically rich and utterly desolate. Her sons Clodomir, Childebert, and Clotaire, and indeed Theodoric, a son of Clovis but not hers, held mock courts at Paris, Soissons, Rheims, and Orléans. Her only daughter was married to a fanatic Arian Visigoth, Amalaric; it was hoped that the marriage would wipe out his ancient hatred for the Franks. But soon enough Clotilda's sons were at fratricidal war.

Clodomir's was the first head to be carried on a pike, its yellow hair now scarlet. Clotilda took his three little sons into her care, but her love was their doom. What could her surviving sons suppose save that she meant to educate them to be the heirs of Clovis? They kidnaped the children and sent to Clotilda a sword and shears. Should they be shorn or slain? Now to be shorn meant to become a monk and renounce all hope of thrones. For a moment the old fire blazed up within her. "Better slain than shorn!" she cried.

The children ran from one uncle to the other; that did not help them. The two older ones were killed; the smallest, Clodoald, was hurried into a monastery where he became St. Cloud. Clotilda collected the poor little relics — her sons fled before her — and buried them beside Clovis and Geneviève. Finally her daughter, treated with appalling savagery by her husband, died on her way home to her mother. It was a sealed coffin that arrived, and that made the last coffin but one. Clotilda had drunk her myrrh to the dregs.

It was May, and up into the dying woman's room came the scent of hawthorn and of lilac. Yet there should be a sweeter fragrance still. Must she forgive her sons? She felt she could not. All night St. Michael battled for her,

· 27

and with the dawn she knew he was victorious. The good warmth drew up from the earth its thousand scents, but she felt sure that among them she could distinguish the incense burning before St. Martin's house hard by. And then her weary mind was not much astonished to see an old man standing in the shadows.

He nodded kindly. "You shall have better frankincense than that," he said. "Your sacrifice rises sweetly before God. But the ring — offer it to me now, though I will not take it yet."

"My sons," she whispered.

"Geneviève and I have seen to that," he said.

That evening they arrived. "Who sent for you?" she asked.

They were confused. Childebert thought that a bishop had come. . . . Clotaire said something about an old woman.

No matter. She forgave them; they could do nothing but sob.

On the night of June 2, 545, she was anointed and received holy Communion. At one next morning she made her act of faith in the Holy Trinity. One of the ecclesiastics standing by lifted her hand to help her make the sign of the cross. In doing so, he withdrew her ring, and she died. Instantly the room became flooded with perfume and so golden a light that, said they, "when the sun rose with all his strength he could seem no brighter."

Siugard watched the coffin being taken away to Paris where it was placed between those of the King, the little princes, and the peasant. She had agreed to stay at Tours to arrange the Queen's effects for distribution, determined that she would make sure of the ring for herself. She was stunned when she could not find it anywhere. "Of course," she found herself saying tearfully to St. Martin as she watched the funeral procession leave, "I would have given it to you before I died!"

"I told you," said an old woman standing near her in the crowd, "that *I* would take care of it!"

Meanwhile, in St. Martin's Church, two of the treasury guardians were puzzling over a ring with a strip of parchment attached to it.

"That," said one of them, "is undoubtedly the Queen's writing."

"Then it has become amazingly like St. Martin's," said the other. "What does it say?"

" *'To be kept for him who shall seek it in the name of what endures.'* What — what can that mean?"

"The blessed Martin," said his friend, "will have his own ideas about that. He will certainly keep it till the proper time. He is not an easy one to make fun of in his tomb — our saint!"

6

A.D. 545–750

THE RING ASLEEP

N<small>OBODY</small> came to claim the ring and it slept forgotten in the treasury of St. Martin's church till the story was ferreted out by the insatiable curiosity of the Italian George, now called Gregory, who had become bishop of Tours eighteen years after Clotilda's death.

"Clearly," he cried, "this ring is meant for Queen Radegundis! Who more exalted? Who more humble? To have watched her brother murdered by her husband — is she less of a martyr than Clotilda? To have fled, but in her very flight to have founded that mighty monastery at Poitiers; is she not greater even than Geneviève?"

Radegundis, though in love with relics, attached no value to the ring, the more so as she had been concentrating her efforts on obtaining part of the true cross from Constantinople. However, the bishop of Poitiers, who disliked powerful nuns, refused to allow the sacred wood to enter the town. She appealed to the king, who on his side disliked bishops and ordered the relic to advance. As the procession drew near, with the great casket shouldered by six deacons, a second procession came from the city gate to meet it. The whole population seemed to be chanting the hymn of welcome written by Venantius Fortunatus, who lived in the Poitiers monastery. *Vexilla regis prodeunt,* chanted the multitude, *Fulget crucis mysterium;* and its echoes floated wide over the land till you might have thought they would fall back from the skies that they struck, upon that land and all lands and rise up again, and yet again, till the centuries should finish.

However, when Gregory heard the hymn, he said that Fortunatus was flattering the royal nun and that he not only ate too much but made poems about his food and, worst of all, was writing a new Life of St. Martin about whom he could have no special information, whereas he, Bishop of Tours, had plenty. So he lost interest in Radegundis who, in fact, died in 587 without ever paying attention to the matter of the ring.

But in 590, Gregory of Tours began to pay heed to another Gregory — in Rome. At first he disapproved. "A monk on the apostolic throne?" he cried to a nun who saw visions. "Having abandoned sackcloth, does he return to silk?" (For indeed the Pope, before becoming a monk at St. Andrew's on the Caelian, had held the highest places in the city.)

The nun replied that even as papal legate in Constantinople the present Pope had lived like a monk, though in palaces.

"Perhaps," said Gregory. "But what manner of monk? He follows the customs of that Italian Benedict, and not the thorny traditions of Egypt to which our Martin was so loyal."

But in time the old man's optimism revived. "What a Pope!" he exclaimed. "Always sick, yet even we are in the hollow of his hand. He sweetens the chant; he ennobles the liturgy; he reforms monasteries. What did I always tell you? Shall not *he* inherit the ring?"

"He already wears a ring," said the nun. "I see no other ring for him."

Gregory of Tours died in 594, and at that time the eastern emperor, in his palace-shrine of intrigue and assassination, and in a panic of Persia, could not turn his eyes to the West, which he was told had long been a place of barbaric ruins where owls hooted from the towers and flitting bats blinded the eyes of men. So Gregory of Rome found himself forced — for there was no other — to act as king in Italy, nay, as crownless Emperor of the West. He must legislate for schooling and for prisons; must supervise weights and measures and coinage; must negotiate peace terms with the fierce Long-Beard invaders.

"*We* believe," said visitors to the aged ecstatic, "that the Pope is turning his back on the East, mother of heresies, worshiper of its Caesar. Is he looking to us Franks? Ours is the future!"

"I see further," she answered. "Over the sands of Arabia a black cloud is gathering, and in the cloud, a man, a man already grown, who shall march through both East and West proclaiming that he alone is God's Prophet and will drench the lands with blood."

"But you cannot deny," they rejoined, "that Gregory

looks not only westward but even to the north. Did he not send Augustine with monks into the mists of Kent to convert those wild-beast Anglo-Saxons? And whom did he find there if not Bertha, granddaughter of our blessed Clotilda, the queen of English Ethelbert? Yes, the future shall be Frankish!"

Yet it was Bathildis, the English slave girl, who became queen of Clovis II and mother of three kings and regent of the Frankish peoples for eight whole years. Like Helena, she never forgot her origin but toiled to put an end to slavery; like St. Radegundis, she became a nun and thus still more powerful; yet she felt herself but the shadow of Clotilda and the ghost of Geneviève. She died in 680, and the sons of Clovis continued to degenerate: nobles became brigands; bishoprics were bought; there were many prophets, but none were listened to, and the ring, forgotten by all, remained — no more disturbed — dark in its casket.

7

A.D. 750–795

A TOWER OF STONE

I

T<small>HE</small> boy Alcuin sat on a North England rock ridge staring at illimitable forests. Deep to his right the brook Meadda glinted beneath an ancient bridge. Rather higher, in a clearing, smoke rose from the house where he was staying with Ecgbert, archbishop of York, who, like Cuthbert of Lindisfarne not sixty years ago, visited every hamlet from east to western sea, taking his favorite scholar to serve him.

Alcuin, as young men are, was in love with the infinite and torn by incompatible desires. Just now he was sad about that house. When his father took him, a child of six, to school in York, they had stayed there. He recognized the trenches round it, the ramparts of earth and rock and thorn, and then the wooden house itself. Why, he had laughed to find, on the same shelf in the same room a little gospel of St. Mark that Cuthbert himself had left there. But how shrunken it all was, how primitive! No stone, no glass! Yet it was he who had changed: *he* had already grown out of a paradise, and he hugged what he hurried from.

Well, the house must be built anew up here! A stone tower for the cattle, in case of attack. It would be farther from the Meadda, no doubt; but then pure water poured, not five minutes off, inside the rock: you could see it through two lance-shaped orifices. A fairy had lived there. It had been hung with rags to propitiate her. A pipe could bring water thence to a well beneath the tower. Trees must be felled, to give no cover to enemies.

He jumped up, to measure levels and distances, and felt afraid. The water, tumbling secretly behind the rock, living a life of its own, would resent inspection. The lance-shaped windows had been meant for those who would worship water. Then, indignant, he asked what demon could hurt God's servant? He went back to his starting point, and returned, counting his steps.

Three hundred and fifty-seven honest strides. What should that mean? Three hundred — a mere hundredth of the men who built Solomon's temple. And Alcuin now meant to build not one house only for one family, but one thousand God's houses throughout the land. Well might he need 300,000 workmen before *that* was done! Well, 300. What next? Fifty. That would do for Pentecost — and the books of magic burned at Ephesus were worth 50,000 coins; and though this fairy well was small compared with the ancient evil city . . . ah! evil was never small! He recited the *Miserere*, forcing himself to stare at the rock windows out of which mournful and faded eyes were peering at him. . . . Then he recalled that if you divided the mysterious number forty into its perfect parts — a half, a quarter, a fifth, eighths, twentieth, a fortieth, and added them up, you got fifty! Heaven's reward on earth — four corners to the world; four winds and elements; if forty, then, stood for man and his world-work, fifty must be his heavenly wage "exceeding great." And seven was perfection, too. Thus he had reached 357!

Delighted, he climbed the rocks again, first, to a little cave where he rested on a flat stone with indistinguishable letters on it. Then he climbed farther, to a stone cross placed there by St. Paulinus. He sat down on its step, and his thoughts drifted in their favorite direction — the best — for all and for always! But ah, the past. Alas, the Britons! They refused Augustine's prayer that they should help convert the English; they cowered crablike into mountain shells, cut off from the Catholic world.

Happier that other island of monks and students, of saints who hung their cloaks on sunbeams and sailed enchanted seas. Colum Cille, whose ferocity grew so sweet that his sons did help in that apostolate, and, as he died, his old white horse laid his head upon his breast to say good-by. The lovely Irish tales of the good communion between birds and beasts and the men of God! But Alcuin's smile grew rueful as he thought of that other dove saint, Columbanus, dove with eagle's claws, who flared from Brittany to Burgundy where they still stuck their hair down with rancid butter and reeked of garlic. Columbanus railed at royalties, fled by way of Tours, was robbed of his luggage there, and returned to inform St. Martin, acidly, that not for *that* had he visited him. . . .

Well, his children's monasteries refreshed the whole world with their learning. Alcuin blushed, comparing his slow thoughts with that flashing genius, and that mere customs should separate these brilliant Irishmen from the worldwide charity of Peter's Law — Peter, on whose successor Columbanus himself fawned even while scarifying him.

Alcuin gazed at the vast view before him with sorrow and love. Forests; shadowy mountains skeined with waterfalls — oh, for stability, unity, throughout this dear land. Even now midnight gifts were made to the imprisoned fairy. Paulinus from Rome had baptized Northumbrian Edwin in the wooden church of St. Peter hastily built at York, but pagan Penda and still more savage Christian Ceadwalla had slaughtered his work. But then, mighty Oswald, invoking help from Columba's Iona, offered himself as catechist to the gentle Aidan. Alas, when Aidan died, they quarreled again over the date of Easter. True, men returned from Rome saying they had heard Romans, Greeks, Scythians, Egyptians singing Alleluia on the self-same day. And in 664 King Oswy had ruled that England should obey the holder of the everlasting keys, and the land became one within itself and with the world.

Theodore, a living symbol, born at Tarsus, educated in a Greek monastery in Rome, was told by the Pope to exchange those furnace heats for the mists and chill and, though already old, to become archbishop of Canterbury, so that England should no more be a distracted land of missions but one province of the universal Church. Theodore, gentle enough to lift the tired old bishop Chad on to his horse that he might still make his pastoral rounds, yet bold to resist the all-too-lordly Wilfrid. What names! And Benet Biscop who, five times a pilgrim to Rome, filled the land with books, paintings, choristers. Why, Benet Biscop practically kidnaped the precentor of St. Peter's basilica himself! Yes — York, Hexham, Ripon must rival those basilicas! Wearmouth, Jarrow, Malmesbury must repay their debt to Ireland. Now Alcuin saw clearly: he must *teach* — not only in York, but all the clergy, all the people, all the land.

In the year of Alcuin's birth the beloved scholar Bede had died. Every golden grain of ancient knowledge he had preserved, purified, and burnished, anxious to add no baser metal of his own; and his sweet and special spirit had animated every word. "Dear and venerated master," cried Alcuin, "you lived at the very hinge of time! Help me to learn, that I may teach." The taste of bitterness melted from his mouth; smoke rose sweet as incense from invisible homesteads; the sky was golden. He leaped down the rocks and persuaded Ecgbert to offer Mass next day above the secret water. He did so, chanting, "You shall draw waters with gladness from the fountains of the Saviour," and the place grew peaceful.

Next day they prepared the people for Communion. Alcuin, helped by penitentiaries from Ireland, taught the young men to make their confession. Appalled by some of the sins mentioned in the books, he was told by Ecgbert to say nothing about them — these simple folks would be horrified. "Abbot Bede," he said, "would have liked all to receive Communion daily. The land is full of both young and old fit to do so. But for lack of priests, yes, and our own ignorance and indolence, they do so but thrice a year."

That evening he distributed relics — grander ones should come when they had a stone church for them. Meanwhile, for daily use, here were chips from the post on which Aidan had leaned when dying; dust from the pit into which was emptied the water that had washed the dead Cuthbert, and a strip of calf's hide. For a certain Aethelwald had inherited Cuthbert's cell and had hung up a hide against the rain; the next anchorite, Felgeld, had put it to his swollen face which was soon cured, thanks to the merits, Ecgbert said, of one or the other saint and perhaps of Felgeld, too. For holy people sent forth holiness into all that touched them, and faithful prayer set stirring the loving power of God.

Next morning they all trooped up to Paulinus's cross for Mass. The chalice flashed golden in the sun; the incense mingled with the perfume of fir tree and of pine. The men's voices echoed back from the little cave as if the hills themselves were singing. On the way home Alcuin kept telling Ecgbert about his plans for England. "Yes," said the prelate, "but paganism goes not out save by prayer and fasting." And the faint taste of myrrh returned to Alcuin's tongue.

Aelbert, master of York School, expanded Alcuin's vision, telling him of Northumbrian Willibrord and his failure in Frisia; of Boniface from Devon, apostle in Westphalia, Thuringia, Bavaria, and his martyrdom. A

Frankish student told of the stupendous defeat of the Mohammedans at Poitiers by Charles the Hammer and the coronation of Charles's son Pepin by the first Pope to cross the Alps.

Thus vanished into the void the dynasty of Clovis and Clotilda, and Alcuin's heart turned over because of the impermanence of things. In 768 Pepin died, leaving his kingdom to his sons Carloman and Charles; but Carloman became a monk; Charles stood alone.

Aelbert took Alcuin to Rome to collect manuscripts; Charles sent for the learned Englishmen and implored Aelbert to return and be teacher of France. Alcuin was beginning to think that England was small; perhaps *he* would be called to France; and at Tours on the way home the thought returned. He prayed so long before St. Martin's shrine that the sacristan, who wanted to lock up, asked him what he was praying for.

"I am torn in half," said Alcuin. "From boyhood I have longed to work for England; but, after all, am I meant for France?"

"The English," said the priest, "are learned and we have degenerated. We rejoice if a priest knows the *Pater* and the *Credo.* Your Boniface helped us — he insisted that a priest should know how to baptize, that people must not pray alternately to Wotan and to Christ nor give Communion to corpses. Adelbert, who said he was a prophet, was imprisoned — he gave clippings from his hair and nails as relics. But where kings and saints have failed, what could you do?"

"Teaching might persuade when the sword could not enforce."

"Well, you start early tomorrow, and should go to bed. I will give you something to remember us by."

He opened an old iron chest and took out a ring. "I may have no right to give you this," said he, "but it is ugly and no use to St. Martin. They say it belonged to Queen Clotilda. But who knows? Can you read the letters on it?" Alcuin said they were the name of Christ in Greek, part of the cross of Constantine.

"If nothing else endures," Alcuin said, thinking of Constantine, of Clovis, "this will! Give it to me in the name of Eternity."

They had not noticed that an old priest had come in. He took the ring from the astonished sacristan and gave it to Alcuin.

"*I* give it to you, my son," he said. "Wear it, not on your finger, but against your heart, that Christ may be the center of your life, and that your life may embrace the world. Yes, under your tunic, lest you seem ostentatious, or tempt thieves."

He blessed them and departed. Alcuin asked who he was, but the sacristan was upset and hustled him off.

Alcuin became master of York; students flocked to him from France and Germany. He followed tradition, rising at dawn, teaching the students one by one till noon when he received Communion. After dinner he discussed what most interested his men. Life seemed fixed. But in 780 he was sent to Rome to fetch the pallium for his new archbishop and visited King Charles at Pavia. How he had changed! Charles was not tall, but stout. His heavy mustache seemed odd to the Englishman who was as bearded as any Lombard; his voice was shrill but could hallo to tremendous distances in the hunt; only his enormous eyes and a strange charm held men spellbound.

Back in England, Alcuin instantly petitioned to return to Charles.

II

He was given five abbeys and a lodging in the little town whose name was crumbling from Ad Aquas Grani to Aquisgranum into Aix. The small god Granus had presided over the healing waters there. The new town began as a simple palace farm on the gentle hills between the Rhine and the Meuse; but Charlemagne (as some began to call him) meant to make a new Rome there. The Seine ran no more across the midmost of the world; Cologne, Worms, Mainz were meaning more than Paris. The Rhine flowed through what must be an empire with one government and one faith. Charles needed a fixed center; it was bad for books and the treasury to travel. All great rulers had had such pivots for their rule.

Alcuin watched, fascinated, a new palace being built at Aix. It was on a hillside. From the ground floor, with five vast rooms, you mounted up stupendous stairs crowned by a bronze eagle to the audience hall, fifty yards long. In the largest of three apses to the west towered the throne. Pope Hadrian had sent marbles and mosaics; there were a golden table and three silver ones with maps of Rome, Constantinople, and the world. In a great piscina 100 men could bathe. A court, some 150 yards long, sloped down to the "chapel" where the *capella*, St. Martin's cope, was kept. In the midst rose a gilt statue of Theodoric on horseback, a huge bronze fir cone and a bronze she-bear spouting water. Cloisters, sacristies, and council rooms led to the chapel which pleased but puzzled Alcuin.

He had loved the simple arches of York, its thirty altars, and how, level by level, men climbed toward God. His friend Benedict of Aniane was to build a church with a high altar having three altars before it, homage to the Unity and Trinity. In fact, the triangular monastery of St. Riquier had a church at each corner, so that psalms, ceasing in the one, might begin in the next. But this chapel of Christ and his Mother was to be sixteen-sided, and within this an octagon rising nearly 100 feet, covered by a leaden cupola bearing a golden apple. Charles, from his throne high up, looked across the octagon to the choir with its two altars, sacred to Christ and the Mother of God, and, inside the cupola, the figure of Christ as King. Round the tribune ran an inscription in red, begging God to keep the place intact. All was gay with paintings, grilles, red, green, and turquoise columns recalling Ravenna, Constantinople, and even Armenia.

Well, the King clamored to be educated, he and his folk, all within a year. He studied even while he dressed. Alcuin said, "An overhealthy boy! Always running; wasteful, losing his breath!" Charles, his family, and the "boys of the palace," who had once formed a school of arms, now joined in making Aix a "second Athens." They sat on striped mattresses and discussed with Alcuin whatever subject came into the mercurial monarch's head. They all had nicknames: Charles was David; he called Alcuin "Flaccus," though the latter had far rather been the pure and visionary Vergil than the plump little favorite of Augustus.

Still, for the time, Alcuin was having altogether his own way, and was wise enough to begin at the beginning. "Read! write!" he cried, "but as *I* tell you!" (And indeed in 300 years his clear round script triumphed throughout Europe.) To get leather for binding books, even monks, he said, might hunt. Charlemagne could not deny that languages were in the melting pot — French, a stammered German. But the realm must be *one,* and one its language.

Alcuin agreed. "So long as Rome is Rome, Latin will be Latin, but let it be pure! Let them speak *properly,*" he cried. "Breathe properly, pronounce each syllable! *Understand your audience,* and don't get drunk!"

This northerner could not help being practical even in his arithmetic. "How many cows can *this* field pasture?" He hated the barren speculations of the East and distrusted the brilliant mysticism of Ireland. But he began to make enemies: the King kept displacing Italian scholars and telling nobles that their sons were not so clever as baseborn boys. This was put down to Alcuin.

Meanwhile, he was dragging the liturgy out of chaos; he purified the Gregorian missal and returned the sacramentary to Rome the richer for its sojourn in the West.

He prepared a daily missal; wrote books for private devotion and inserted the names of English saints, for in England he saw the "destined folk of God." Thanks to the unity of the realm, he became nearly the "spiritual father" of Europe as well as its "prefect of studies."

Charlemagne himself was constantly writing to England, chiefly to King Offa; intermarriages were discussed; the English clergy had already begged Charles to protect them. Alcuin was sent to interview the English king and discover the state and culture of monasteries. He welcomed this choice, since he wanted to ransack England for manuscripts as once he had ransacked the continent for England's sake. Yet he felt anxious. Who knew while he was gone what influences would be stealing their way into the monarch's gusty mind? He went to York, and visited the hamlet of Meadda, and could hardly believe his eyes when he found John, now lord of the place, still living in the shabby wooden house. And yes, St. Cuthbert's copy of St. Mark was still there on the very same shelf.

"My lord," he said, "surely the time is come for building the stone house that already Abbot Ecgbert spoke of?"

"I see," said John grimly, "that the thing must be done. My boy — named John like me, of course — has already begun to build. I confess it is uncomfortable for him and his family all to live in here. In fact, we have had to build outhouses for some of them, and some of his children have already married and it is not easy to keep the peace. I am too old for quarrels. He will show you tomorrow what he is up to."

The two men, therefore, went up the hill next day. Not

much more than foundations were visible. Alcuin, accustomed to monumental buildings abroad, said that this would do well for a secondary structure, but the great tower must be more massive and the foundations deeper. "It has to last," said he, with sudden youthful enthusiasm, "forever and ever!"

"The well," he insisted, "must be *in* the tower; the water must be brought from lower than the place where it falls behind the rock. Do not injure that!"

He climbed alone to the mysterious lance-shaped orifices, where no offerings now hung. In fact, they were getting overgrown. He cut some of the leafage away, and wondered how much that water had once frightened him. He went high, to the little cave, and tried to clean away some of the moss from the letters on the flat stone, but could not make them out. He then went to the top of the ridge and sat down on the step of St. Paulinus's cross. Here he had sat as a boy, and now his life could not last so very much longer.

He had dreamed of doing so much. Well, he had done many things; but many didn't mean much. And a strange anxiety clouded him. Suppose the whole edifice on which Charles sat came toppling down beneath him? The least weight, added to what was in reality so frail, might create the crash.

The very next day he was summoned back. The Spaniards were beginning a heresy. Charlemagne would not tolerate heresies, splitting the mind of his realm. Alcuin, not a bishop or even priest, was involved in councils where he was evidently meant to say what the King had

decided on. Charles was more and more the arbiter of
orthodoxy; was actually acclaimed by some as superior
to the Pope. Alcuin, old and tired, tried to escape by
carrying out the mere material of the royal orders: priests
were not to dress in silk nor hunt with falcons nor gamble
nor keep jugglers nor allow dogs in church. . . . Yet he
could not forget that his guiding star had been education; but even here Charles was being fascinated by vivid,
daring Irishmen.

"Learn to accept direction," he said sharply to the aged
scholar. "You don't know Greek!"

There was a reconciliation; but old faces were passing,
old hopes were fading.

III

The year 800 drew toward its close. Charlemagne suddenly said he was going to Rome. Alcuin, seizing the
opportunity, traveled to Chartres. He went by boat up
the Loire, by carriage over the vast plain. He was op-
pressed by the sense of terrible imminent things. He
sighed with relief when the basilica at long last showed
itself, humping its heavy curves over a huddle of huts.

The ancient church, half-buried in the earth, was already almost the crypt that one day it would become. A
tenuous light filtered from loophole windows or flickered
from tiny lamps. He went down into the Druidic cavern
where the earliest converts, little more than a century
after the death of Christ, had built a shrine. Then they
had been martyred and thrown into a well there and had

never won more personal a name than "the Strong Saints." But a church was built over that ruined shrine by the Paleface Constantius, and over the foundations of this had been piled the indomitable walls of the church which should serve as crypt for churches built and rebuilt above it. It contained the somber statue of "the Virgin who shall be Mother," and here Alcuin would sit and dream.

It was here that news was brought to him that Charlemagne had been crowned Emperor by Pope Leo III upon Christmas Day. Alcuin trembled and grew cold. Had this, he asked himself, been due, after all, to him? He had not counseled it; but with his passion for unity and permanence had he half-consciously inspired it? One Pope for the Church, one Emperor for the West — for the *world?* Had Charles foreseen this? The messenger said that Charles professed himself thunderstruck — he would never have gone to St. Peter's for mass at all had he foreseen a coronation. But then why did he go dressed as a Roman patrician? And if the Pope had not foreseen it, why was there a crown lying ready on the altar? How were the nobles and the people able to roar with one voice the traditional acclamations, so long disused? Was it, then, for the Pope to create emperors, or for the people to elect and impose emperors on themselves? Was, after all, Charlemagne the one who had intrigued till he could issue orders to Pope and world alike?

Alcuin shuddered. They had said of Byzantium, "This is the second Rome"; now they would say it of Aix. Already he heard the flatterers: "You, O Emperor, are the star, the rock; on you the Church reposes!" Charles was inspired; his

words were "sacred," so were his officials. "Armor of bishops! Hope of the laity! Through thee the hierarchy holds its
sacred rights!" Charlemagne spoke seriously when he said
that the Pope's business was to *pray* for the Church; in the
concrete, *he* would rule, even if by lavishing favors on the
Church he disguised that he was her master.

Alcuin bowed low. He had wanted the right things —
unity and permanence — but had he mispictured them?
A new house was growing up above the Meadda; the old
one would soon enough be firewood. Was that not right?
He had left York for Aix. Well, he had not been wrong to
educate, nor was it wrong that others should supersede him.

In the glow of sunset the ancient statue was just visible.
That was what lasted. . . .

"O Lady," he sighed, "O more than any empress, you
who held within your breast what the whole world con-
tains not, who dost hold Him in your arms whose own
arms clasp all that is or ever will be . . . " And almost
without his knowing it, his hands groped beneath his tunic
and took hold of the ring that had sanctioned his leaving
England. For the first time its strong chain snapped.
Snapped? No — parted like a mist.

"Take it," he said. "I abdicate it — abdicate my work,
my self. To you, together with this ring, I transfer it all."

The sunset faded. In the quivering lamplight the statue
seemed to lean forward. The stern features grew mild. A
hand was stretched forth.

"Keep it," he whispered, "for him whose it shall be."
Then he went home. Afterward a few worshipers noticed
the ring and felt vaguely disconcerted. But it had rusted

deep into the stone and was immovable. Clearly it must always have been there, unobserved.

Five years before Alcuin had been given the abbacy of Tours. In 801 he got leave to live there altogether. He prepared for death, not neglecting his abbey lands; but it was Martin, really, who ruled them from his reliquary.

A final tempest struck Alcuin. A fugitive from the bishop of Orleans sought sanctuary at Tours; to exclude him would injure the rights of Martin; to admit him would infuriate the Emperor whose man the bishop was. Alcuin welcomed the trembling suppliant. Soldiers were sent who rioted in the very church. Charlemagne wrote accusing Alcuin of every imaginable crime and sent an envoy to scourge anyone he could lay hold of. Alcuin protested to the Emperor, but Charlemagne had ended in a daze, being, like most aging autocrats, not quite able to distinguish reality from hallucination.

Alcuin, trusting no more to the spirit of man, wished to die on the feast of Pentecost. He selected his grave, near St. Martin's. Each night he visited it and prayed, "O Key of David, O Scepter of the House of Israel — who openest and no man shutteth, and shuttest and no man openeth — lead forth the chained and the captive from his prison, those who crouch in the dark and the shadow of death!"

On the Feast of the Ascension, 804, he fell really sick. He could see nothing but the stream of the Holy Spirit falling in rainbow loveliness down God's mountain. The mountain was one city: the city was one house. The house was being built in England amid the fells skeined with waterfalls: a firm house, an enduring house, a castle as he had dreamed of it. The water streamed continuously, though at times you but glimpsed or guessed it through small rock windows veiled with fern. Then his mind slipped back again. What house was other than a prison, that man rebuilt for himself whenever it fell into ruins? No perfect circle . . . it kept being broken into arcs that had no meaning. But suddenly he saw the circle — not a line enclosing a point, but a point triumphantly radiating in all directions equally. A house that should embrace all men and last forever. But the center? The center? Ah, Martin of Tours, Mary of Chartres, Peter of Rome, you are all at the center! And he died, very happy, on the feast of Pentecost when the Holy Spirit came, and on that day many a pilgrim to Chartres saw the ring on the statue's finger glow for a little, and then die into dark again.

8

A.D. 860–1090

AGAIN ASLEEP

CHARLEMAGNE died in 814, and his towering ghost looked down upon descendants known as the Fat, the Bald, the Stammerer, the Simple. St. Martin was much concerned about the next claimant for the ring, and was pleased when over fifty years after Charlemagne's death a certain nobleman of Le Mans came and asked him to obtain for him the grace of having a son.

Martin was delighted to obtain this favor for his suppliant, especially as no sooner was the boy born than his father brought and offered him to that pearl of pontiffs, Martin. But alas, the young Odo grew up careless and went to court and then fell sick and seemed likely to die. His father said, "Blessed Martin, I gave the boy to you, and now you are indeed taking him. You are rather a hard saint, but he is in your hands." St. Martin cured the youth, who came to his right mind, and cried: "Oh, Martin, I belong to you. I knew it in my heart, and now I know it properly. Here I am, if you will take me back."

And he did in fact hand himself over to the basilica of Tours. But the canons there seemed to him to fall short of religious perfection; they fought with their fists while singing choir, and in fact a poor man, who was a guest there, saw Martin in a dream, who said, "These brothers are a great nuisance. They gave me no peace. I shall go away and live at Tulle."

The basilica was soon enough burned down, but after a while it was rebuilt, only Odo could not feel Martin's presence there any more. So in 909 he and his friend Adhegrin, Count of Anjou, decided to go to Baume, a monastery governed by St. Berno, and later took over from him the control of that of Cluny, which Berno had founded. And at once St. Martin manifested himself again.

To begin with, Adhegrin fell a victim to melancholy. "So many years have I served the Lord," he lamented, "without the least consolation. Does He reject me?"

St. Martin forthwith appeared to him. "I have come from Rome," he said, "but have turned aside to visit you and my son Odo. How is he?"

"Will you not rest in my cell?" said Adhegrin. "Then I can tell you, and take you to him."

"They are consecrating the King today," said the saint, "and if I am to be punctually in France I have no time to waste."

But he allowed himself to be persuaded and explained to Adhegrin that he must rouse himself, because his work in life was to help Odo, whose destiny was a high one. Martin, after courteous exchanges, blessed and was blessed by Adhegrin, and his cloud of tedious monotony faded away, especially as Martin said he would return.

This he did, while the great church of Cluny was being built, but he was not recognized despite his alb and cope.

"But you are celebrating my octave," he said with a certain severity.

Odo was sent for, and after due homage told the saint that they had not enough money to finish building.

"Courage," said St. Martin. "I am going back to Tours after all, and shall pass through Aquitaine and Gothland and find plenty of funds." So the church rose in splendor, and in it Odo instituted the solemnity of All Souls, to be observed on the second day of November.

But after this he visited Rome and fell sick. Martin asked that Odo should not die till he revisited him at Tours. He arrived there in time for the saint's feast, November 11, 942.

He wrote: "Oh, Martin, giver of peace to souls, lord above the stars, obtain for us the mercies of the Lord and offer him these verses which Odo wrote departing from this life!"

And he died on St. Martin's octave day.

All this time the ring continued to sleep at Chartres on the finger of the Virgin over whom fierce men kept destroying her churches, till in 1020 St. Fulbert built a cathedral that should outlast the next Inheritor.

As for Rome, it was sacked and resacked by men from over the Alps and Saracens from overseas. Brambles filled what had been open spaces round the fortress towers of brutal lords; yet somehow the basilicas survived. Ceaselessly pilgrims, streaming Romeward, would fall on their knees when first they caught sight of those campaniles. They still would chant their *O Roma nobilis, orbis et Domina,* their immemorial hymns in honor of Peter's keys and the sword of Paul; and Hildebert of Mans was singing with Vergil's voice his *Par tibi, Roma, nihil, cum sis prope tota ruina,* and extolling the triumph of the two princely saints over the long line of Caesars, of Rome alive above the series of her dead and buried selves.

What could this mean save that through the ruins and the entangled thorns the Holy Spirit was stealing, like a secret water — like the water ceaselessly pouring behind the rock in the far north of England? This Spirit sent John of Medby — as after the Danish invasions the lord of that region was called — forth from his tower into Palestine. For in 1009 the Caliph Hakim had sacked the holy places, and John was amid the many thousands who pilgrimaged thither to rebeautify them with gifts. And now, too, those Magyars who so long had swept westward only to vanish like eddies of dust and mist felt the baptismal water falling on their foreheads, and found at last stability when tower and spire rose side by side upon the cliff of Buda, and St. Stephen of Hungary merited an apostolic crown.

9

A.D. 1090–1179

ABBOT AND ABBESS

I

THE Lord and Lady of Fontaine, near Dijon, had seven children. The third child, born in 1090, was called Bernard. Handsome beyond the ordinary, and horrified by the sting of temptation, he buried himself at twenty-one in the austerity of Citeaux, where the Englishman Stephen Harding was abbot. In 1115 Bernard was sent to begin a new Cistercian house at Clairvaux, and added so severely to his penances that nobody expected him to live.

Now eight years after Bernard came into the world, Hildegard was born to the lord of Boeckelheim and his lady, whose castle lay near Mainz. Since she was a tenth child, she was offered as a "tithe" to God, and entrusted to a relative, Julitta, an anchoress in an ancient monastery. How should these two, Bernard and Hildegard, both dwellers, as it would seem, in tombs, come to meet? Yet Bernard was to find the whole twelfth century upon his shoulders; Hildegard became a prophetess for that world, and, like him, admonished popes and emperors. Their orbits went on curving till they crossed.

One day two Cistercians, Roger and Guy, met in a wood to talk. This broke their rule, but they were too thrilled to keep silence, since they had been told they must accompany Bernard to the council convoked by King Louis at Etampes. It was to decide which of two claimants to the papal throne was legitimate. Roger said that the prospect terrified him.

"But who," asked Guy, "is likely to hurt you?"

"Many! You know what councils are. But it's Bernard! I'd as soon travel with an earthquake — a volcano. What is this force within him? Look at him! A skeleton! Too weak to keep his eyes open; even his red beard has gone parchment color. And yet a tornado! His proper place is in his cell, and yet here he is, called by kings to settle who should be pope!"

"Yes," said Guy more slowly. "From the start he sweeps brothers, even uncles, into the cloister. A mere boy, he arrives at Citeaux with thirty noblemen, and makes them monks. *I* say it is God's Spirit; others say the devil. What are men, when one man can thus influence a hundred? Bernard *might* have been the world's worst egoist. . . . "

"That doesn't console *me*," said Roger. "He has always been wrestling with lesser men, and has won. Will he be afraid when he deals with kings and popes? Look when he quarreled with the abbot of Cluny! He said that the abbot's escort was enough for any two bishops. Sixty horses, golden candelabra, chests full of bedding! No wonder those Black Benedictines regard us Whites as enemies!"

Guy said he exaggerated. That was only one abbot, and he was deposed by the Pope. The Blessed Odo would recognize the Clunyites for his sons.

"Maybe," Roger admitted. "Maybe it is Bernard who exaggerates. He says that at Cluny they can cook eggs in a dozen ways, and sniff at wines till they find what suits them, and finger cloth to see if it's soft enough for cowls. How does he know? He's never been there!"

"Ah, but his imagination whirls him away! He doesn't need to *see*. What does he see save God and souls? Does he see hills, or lakes? How many windows a room has? When he hears of the splendors of Cluny, he thinks they are meant to be looked at; but if one looks, prayer suffers. I *have* been there, and *I* wasn't distracted!"

Roger tartly remarked that Guy hardly aimed at a prayer like Bernard's. Guy smiled; he knew that; but he was reseeing the Cluny church with its nave of more than 400 feet with four aisles flanking it. It had two transepts with two towers ending the larger one, and a tower of lamps over the midmost altar. Three hundred windows gleamed faint in the forest of columns; eight pillars of African and Greek marble supported the ciborium before which was the gold and copper candelabrum, gift of Maud, wife of Henry of England, and its seven lamps set ablaze the gold, the crystals, the beryls.

Bernard heard with horror of the mosaic pavement figuring man's history. "Here you tread on the face of a saint; there, you spit upon an angel!" Had not monks vowed to renounce the senses? Hence he would have none but blank walls in his monastery; rough-hewn stone — no marble — wood for the crosses. And as for grinning gargoyles? Fantasy in the House of Wisdom? Never!

"Ah, he is too intelligent," thought Guy. "Cluny's church is the school and library of the poor!"

But to Roger he said, "His ferocity is tenderness disguised. It was torture to him to think of rich churches when peasants starved in pigsties. He forgot that Cluny is a world — its monks work for the peasants and teach *them* to work. With its farms, tanneries, bakeries, forges they can marry and make families. Would Bernard turn all the world into one monastery? No, nor all monks into Benedictines. He is happy with the Carthusians in their snows. Norbert in Westphalia is already called a second Bernard. They are brothers!"

Roger sighed. Brothers were very apt to quarrel. And did not Bernard *create* dissensions? His rebukes to bishops — about their very dress! At home in Clairvaux the young monks had seen nothing and guessed but little of Bernard's work among the laity: how he preached to the nobles, first justice, then charity; a second Joseph, he opened vast granaries for the famine-struck. True, his invective made him many enemies, especially among great ladies whose dress he — he who saw nothing! — derided in such detail. To the adoring peasantry he showed how to wash the vegetables that he planted for them till they could grow them for themselves. They must give homage to those green and humble things, since God made them, God preserved them. Yes, he who saw nothing knew the flowers, as he knew the stars, each by its name.

The travelers to the council kept meeting knights — sometimes hostile, always nervous, for in 1128 Bernard had been asked to make a Rule for the Knights Templar. Knights had policed the pilgrim routes to the new Kingdom of Jerusalem. They became warrior-monks, taking vows. Bernard had the Church's horror of wars with their attendants — cruelty, plunder, lust, disease — but was entranced by the idea of the Christian knight, fighting only to protect the weak. The world was full of soldiers, and of monks. . . . The monk-soldier must be born! He wrote a whole treatise on this new army. What though scoundrels poured into it? These wolves, he sincerely thought, would become lambs, though their fleece was made of mail. But this very thought made him mock the knight of fashion, with long hair in his eyes; vast embroidered shirts entangling arms and legs; helmets topped with balls of colored glass; their scurrilous songs and bloody tournaments. . . . So the monks met with a mixed welcome from knights as they advanced.

But the nearer Bernard drew to Etampes, the darker grew the storm clouds. His enemies asked who was this monk, who claimed to rule the Church of France and insulted the King by name. Even his friend Cardinal Haimeric, chancellor of the Roman Church, was told to write and bid him mind his own affairs. Bernard plaintively replied that God's affairs *were* his affairs. Haimeric asked what a monk had to do with courts and councils? Let not cloisters croak and annoy the Holy See! Bernard said that he, poor frog, would remain in his marsh till obedience called him forth, but that his silence would not stop the growlings of those to whom Rome did not do justice. . . .

Well, arguments clashed to and fro between the lawyers, till Bernard brushed them equally aside and recalled how the antipope, Pierleoni, had been called "Precursor of Antichrist" from youth up; Innocent, true to his name, was the rightful Pope. King Louis paid him homage. Bernard visited Henry of England who had hesitated but now pilgrimaged to Chartres and laid sword and scepter at the feet of Innocent.

As always after success, depression clouded down on Bernard. He made his way, exhausted, to the crypt of the cathedral, down steps worn by two more centuries of pilgrimage since Alcuin. Blacker than ever the stern statue brooded over the altar. Bernard knelt and bowed till his forehead touched the pavement. His brain rocked on the waves of memory: kings, barons, prelates, lawyers, banners, armor, traveling, noise — all that he had not foreseen! What had become of his silence and his peace? Words had kept welling up in his head, words often of violence, even when they were little but quotations from that Bible which he knew almost too well. A fire had been shut up within his bones, and how could he *not* have spoken? He sank into the sense of his intimate nothing-ness, and forthwith remembered the fathomless self-humbling of the Word of God, who had come all the way down — to *save!* But if he was nothing at all, how could grace save a nothingness? Ah, there was in him that terrible fact, free will. May grace save *that!* "O Jesus, save *me!*"

He could see Mary better now. The austere face was gentler; in that majesty was a humbleness sweeter than his humiliation; humility and virginity mounted like in-cense to God in His repose. An aureole of tender heavenly blue circled round the statue. Bernard began to sing; the whole cathedral sang. . . .

"Let *him,* O Blessed Virgin," he cried out, "keep ever silence about thy mercy who can remember that in his need he cried to thee and was left unanswered."

The tender vaporous brilliancy grew rosy and golden

at its heart, and he could see the Child distinctly. It laughed without sound, twisted its little feet, took hold of its Mother's fingers one by one, pulled off a golden ring and held it toward Bernard. Bernard stood, reached out his own hand, and Christ slipped the ring on to the saint's own finger. He knelt, and looking up, saw that the Child was now grave. Mary held him out above the altar; he spread his arms wide; it was a Child-crucifix. Sacrifice? Yes, but his head bent down, his arms outspread — all of him breathed love. Bernard accepted a future of love and sacrifice, work and failure, glory and annihilation. The light faded.

Bernard was swept off in the company of the Pope, and king and Innocent visited Clairvaux. The monks, headed by a wooden cross, met the gay retinue without looking at it. In the refectory a great fish, found with difficulty, was put before the Pope; all the others ate coarse bread and cabbages and a few herbs for dainties and drank water in which raisins had been soaked. A sacred joy was experienced by all, at any rate by the monks. The guests departed; Bernard might have fancied himself back in peace had not the ring, sewn into his cowl, struck from time to time against his breast. This was in 1131.

There was now no question of suppressing him. At the elbow of warring potentates he had to reconcile city with city, state with state; cope with the anarchic heretics of southern France and the disruptive intellectualists of the North. Emperors had to uplift the frail monk in their brawny arms to save him from the worshiping crowds. Acclaimed "father of the fatherland," he constantly refused bishoprics and when one of his Cistercians was made Pope as Eugenius III he was delighted, but lamented that they would now be saying that *he* was Pope.

He was not; but when the imperiled Latins of the East appealed to Rome and France for protection, Louis VII announced a crusade and Eugenius blessed it in a bull. Bernard inevitably became its official preacher. He was whirled from France to Flanders and Germany; he was writing to England, Spain, Bohemia, Moravia, Denmark. Meanwhile, Archbishop Adalberon of Trèves, who had caused Conrad to be elected emperor, aspired to the greatest glories. The Pope should visit him escorted by innumerable prelates and a score of cardinals; three months of celebration should mark his taking possession of his see with helmet and sword; he would outrival the Caesars. Hither, too, came Bernard, in his dingy white, with no ornament save the ring which clasped him, body, brain, and soul.

II

The Abbess Hildegard was sitting on St. Rupert's Rock near Bingen, thinking out a drainage system, for she proposed to leave her house at the Disibod — to the indignation of monks and populace, because her visions attracted profitable crowds — and to build a new house at St. Rupert's.

She was not clear how to get water up from the Rhine below and how to make one system of pipes serve efficiently for the sewage, for the kitchen, and for sluicing the floors. Then she remembered she had not even got leave to build the monastery at all. . . .

"Trèves," she said to herself, "is not far off. I will write to the Pope and to Bernard, and settle about St. Rupert's and my visions at the same time."

Indeed, she had already written to Bernard, regretting that she could not express herself well in German nor her visions in any language; but still . . . Bernard replied, asking her to forgive brevity; he was very overworked. He had heard it said that she probed into heavenly secrets. Well, what advice could *he* give to one possessed of such interior light? She must not believe all that foolish people said of him, and would she please pray for him.

Hildegard felt that this was very inadequate. If there was probing, it was done by God into her soul; if she disregarded Him, she fell sick; in fact, while she had tried to resist the idea of going to St. Rupert's she had become blind, and recovered her sight only when she yielded.

So she wrote a determined letter to Pope Eugenius, asking for her visions to be examined. He appointed a commission. It visited her, and returned with the first part of her book *Scivias,* a name into which she had packed the syllables of *Si scires vias (Domini),* and over which she had spent ten years.

It was read aloud; Eugenius read some of it himself. Bernard now cried that such a light should not be hid. The Pope wrote that the abbess might go to St. Rupert's but must remain obedient. She replied with a torrent of parables; she begged the Pope not to plunge his flock into hell because of the worldliness of his cardinals, and added meekly that she had anticipated his permission and was already at St. Rupert's.

Bernard, enchanted to find a prophetess as fearless as he was, went to see her. He found her, with voluminous skirts tucked up, planning a medical garden, though there was as yet no earth or water there.

"I am always adding," she said, "to two books that God has shown me: *The Book of the Subtilities of the Various Creatures,* and *The Book of Medicine Simple and Compound.*"

Bernard looked doubtful. "I tolerate the use of herbs," he said, "but to run after doctors is for worldlings. Our ancestors built their monasteries in damp valleys, so that, being constantly exposed to illnesses, they might always have death before their eyes."

Hildegard paid no attention.

"In all things," she continued, "is to be seen the living power of God. I give my herbs to those who ask, and observe what happens. Thus I learn; and thus the herbs, if they heal, praise God by doing what they ought. By healing, an herb fulfils its end and thus is much improved."

Bernard smiled. "Yes, a thing is better for fulfilling its function. That is philosophical and even scriptural! All Nature groans and strains toward its perfection. But what of functions rightly unfulfilled? Thus neither you nor I can marry. And a Christian may not marry many, though he could."

"God preserve him," said the abbess; "but whether we

choose to marry or choose not to, we are fulfilling our function of choosing. And in either case it is God's will that we should *choose*." And she discoursed on marriage in such terms as to startle even Bernard.

"Your mind pounces and probes," he said. "The smooth current of your writings bursts into little bubbles. Twice in a page you cry: 'Why is this?' 'How so?' Is there here risk of curiosity? Do you wish to know, so as to possess? To have power? Ah, you must not! Then, they tell me, you write little plays, and tunes based on the Gregorian chant. I, too, tell my disciples to rediscover the true chant, which should be neither harsh nor honeyed. But my monks do not like it when I sing, and tell me that my verses are very bad. That may be, because I attend to the sense and not the scansion. But is it true that you have invented a new language that you talk only among yourselves — full of the letter Z? May they not think you guilty of magic and invoking the demon Zabulo?"

"The divine wisdom," said Hildegard serenely, "plays in its manifold creation, and my nuns must have their games! In all that exists, a harmony must be restored. Things exist first in the mind of God. How should that *not* be all music in a single sound? A tree is a *tree*," she said, nodding wisely, "but trees exist much better when we take them into our minds and make a melody of them. But they exist, too, in a way that is proper to faith. Is not the true earth the Church, with trees fruitful in good works? See the stars. The sun is fixed in the center of the world and controls the other orbs in their movement, till they reach that Sabbath rest when their effort will cease yet their strength in no way be diminished. Yes!" cried Hildegard, standing up, "that giant Man, the divine exemplar, toward whom all things move since in Him alone they truly have their being, stands with His feet in the abyss and His head in the heavens. He turns, east, now west, uttering a rhythmic trumpet call, and from His impulse the whole dance of created things takes its origin, even our dear Rhine swirling down there, up to the saints and angels who weave their way through innumerable flowers."

"You," sighed Bernard, "seek to trace God's ways. *My* ways are a labyrinth, or a cord on which I must walk between a precipice and a marsh. I go to Rome, hoping . . . But now, when I would say a man is bad, I must say, 'He is a Roman!' I turn to the north, and not for six years could I finish with that simoniac wretch they wanted to enthrone at York. But there is much in England that I love; and even some noblemen are good, like my dear earl, John of Medby."

"Such things," said Hildegard, "are not for a weak woman like me."

"My dear Abbess," he said, laughing, "your letters go everywhere, and a hundred of them for one of mine, or of the Pope. Kings and cardinals come to you, or, when they are frightened of you, say the roads are too bad or brigands too dangerous. Though where your old coach can go, could not imperial carriages? And I do not know the brigand who would face you!"

And indeed Frederick Barbarossa called Hildegard to Engelheim, and agreed that all she prophesied came true, though she told him to beware lest the King of Kings should strike him in his blindness. And when Pope Anastasius IV, nearly a hundred years old, asked her to write to him as she had to four of his predecessors, she was to reply: "Oh, man, you who care nothing for that king's daughter, Justice, you leave that princess prostrate on the earth, stripped of crown and dress by the brutality of your officers!" And to Henry of England, still young, she was to write that he possessed gifts able to win heaven, but behold, a black bird comes from the north and says: "You can act as you please! If you trouble about Justice and her laws, you are a slave, not a king!"

"Yes," said Bernard, "you write and I preach, and kings will be overwhelmed by your oracles and my sermons, but the moment passion besets them they will trample on you like a scorpion and forget you. Alas, Mother Abbess, your science shall crumble and your imagery become meaningless; my many words will seem absurdity to another generation. But at the heart of this multiplicity is the Truth himself, and in God alone is stability."

"Man's soul," she proceeded, hardly aware of him, "is a harp on which exquisite melodies should be played. Sin has broken the sweet instrument; in man, only a vague knowledge of powers, dormant within him, remains like the quick-fading memory of dreams. The soul must be restored, so that God may again play upon it his lovely music. But woe," she suddenly exclaimed, "to those at Mainz who close churches with an interdict! They shall not merit to hear the songs of angels!"

"Did I not say," cried Bernard, irritated, "that your

mind loiters and then leaps from peak to peak, down to the valleys, up to the clouds! Souls, harps, then interdicts!"

"How can I help it? I see in so many ways. I see with my eyes, as you do, but often not with my eyes. When I was five, I was walking with my governess and saw a cow" — Bernard stared — "I said: 'Look what a pretty little calf — white, with marks on its forehead and its feet and its back are all colored.' And in a day or two it was born, just like that. But not so is what God shows me, nor what I see when I ask, 'Why? how so?' From childhood," she said gravely, "a light has been lit in my mind which I call the 'shadow of the Living Light.' On to this the Living Light itself casts images of things. Compared with that Light, they are shadows; compared with the things, they are light. I see all this, not with my eyes, nor with my thoughts, nor am I paralyzed with ecstasy. There is the Living Light: it lights up its own light in me; and in *that* light I see what I do see. Nor must you mind if I describe things in such imagery as the Scriptures or else my memory supply to me — clouds, castles, mountains! What else could I do? And it is God who supplies me also with these."

"I on my side," said Bernard, after a pause, "will give you something." He drew off his ring.

"This was given me by Our Lady of Chartres. It has bound me close to my vocation. But it is no more for me. I have learned that I must work as I am working, though with less self-will. Ah, one's will, that keeps curving back toward self! I always knew that I must love all men, yet not for my sake, nor only for their sake. I know clearly how I must love — not even my own salvation just for my own sake, but because, being saved, I am pleasing to God whom I must wholly love. *Then* I can return to loving men, because *He* loves us, and with a love infinitely greater than any human love. As for the ring, God will show you what to do with it. But I, I must start upon my greatest purgatory."

They separated. Bernard was whirled away into the disasters of the Second Crusade. The wrath of the nations poured upon him, its preacher. His very vocation was disbelieved in. But after no long while the will to continue a crusade revived, and again he was ordered to preach it. Thus he met the son of his old friend the lord of Medby, who told him that this house had stood firm amid all troubles, though the old wooden house, of course, had perished long ago. Bernard thought of the City of Jerusalem on its undying rock, of the Church, firm upon Peter, and of the Heavenly City. The years went by, and Bernard died in 1153, and Hildegard, very old, in 1179, both having carried so much of men's lives upon their shoulders.

10

GOLD AND GRAY

It was always the enchanting habit of nuns to preserve things, for fear of waste, of course, and for piety's sake. So St. Hildegard's long life bequeathed an immense number of holy objects to St. Rupert's. But at last a serious-minded chaplain so alarmed the prioress by allusions to moths, rust, and treasures upon earth that she sold all that she could to a peddler, including the ring, for, after all, the convent had to be kept in repair.

The peddler in due course crossed the Alps and came to Cremona, where he offered the unsellable ring to a shopman called — so his fellow townsmen said — Omo-buono. This good man's soul was thrilled when he heard that the ring had belonged to the Teutonic prophetess. So he bought it, but did not tell his wife, who thought he was far too charitable in so perverse a world, and, for a tradesman, far too honest and very much too pious. But one day she found him kneeling before the ring which was on his table.

"What are you doing?" she exclaimed. "Are you having ecstasies?"

His good face wrinkled itself into laughter. "Am I one to have ecstasies?" he asked. "Am I not a businessman? Do I not grind and grab? But this ring . . . don't you see it . . . *shine?*"

"I certainly do not," she said. "Get up! Rings? Have I not enough with my wedding ring? When have you ever knelt to that?"

"Always, my dear," he said gently. "Always."

And he thought humbly of great saints such as the blissful martyr Thomas of Canterbury, given by a king to God while St. Bernard was still alive, and he hoped there would be many such, and did not know that St. Dominic and St. Francis were already born, and certainly not that only twenty years after St. Hildegard's death, and only two years after his own, he would himself be canonized by popular demand and that his statue outside the Cremona cathedral would outlive the centuries. As for the ring, it passed from hand to hand till it came to Rome.

The Lady Jacopa di Settesoli was sitting in her private garden on the Esquiline Hill. A trellis of vines shielded her from the sun and the air was sweet with the scent of creamy and crimson roses. She had been married for a year to Graziano Frangipani and was still young enough to be pleased with so brilliant a match as well as with so adorable a husband. Though she regarded her Norman-Sicilian family almost as good as his, she felt she could not quite catch up with a man whose ancestors won their name as long ago as 717, and who even claimed descent from those distant Roman Anicii.

Even up here the secret waters of Rome came through immemorial channels to leap in little jets and keep the garden cool. "My son," she thought as she watched them, "will have blood flowing in his veins from farther off than even these old Roman fountains!" So she was taking care of herself and preferred the Esquiline palace to their low-lying house across the Tiber where there were evil mists and turbulent people. Besides, she could see, over the garden hedges, the ruins of Septimius Severus's Septizonium, and liked to think that her husband drew his second lordship from that very place and so was called Settesoli.

A servant approached and said that a peddler of antiquities implored an audience. She liked ancient jewelry, and felt he must not have had his climb in the hot sun for nothing. He was admitted, and, bowing low, he showed her some Egyptian scarabs. She agreed that the blue-green enamel was pretty, but she disliked beetles. Still not wishing to disappoint him, she picked up a ring.

"What is this?" she said.

"Oh, noble lady," said the man, "I would not have dared to offer you that. It is so old and ugly! Still, they say the marks on it are oriental. It belonged to St. Omobuono of Cremona who died almost thirty years ago, and *he* said it had been St. Hildegard's. No doubt prioresses have rings . . . ?"

Jacopa was interested and bought it, then sat turning it over in her hands. "I believe," she thought, "I am losing my taste for rings. Except my marriage ring!" She kissed it. "Frangipani!" she whispered. "That old ancestor of his broke bread for the populace. I am very behindhand with my charities. But I will keep this for my boy. It *must* be a boy! He shall have it when he is betrothed."

The boy was duly born and was called Giovanni. Jacopa said: "He must be the one who leans upon the heart of his Lord!" But her husband said he would be content if he should act as herald, like the Baptist, for one greater even than himself.

Time passed, and in 1212 a very poor man, Francis, already known as "of Assisi," came for the third time to Rome and was brought by a cardinal to see Jacopa, for, thought he, this Umbrian has the talent for extracting alms, and God knows the city needs them.

But Francis stayed only a few minutes and said nothing about alms, though he saw in her a vigorous character, and she, in him, something that would be more than a herald, though what she could not guess.

Alas, in five years' time she was a widow. Soon after her husband's death another boy was born, whom she named Graziano after so dear a memory. In 1223 she heard that Francis was again in Rome and asked him to stay in her palace, which he did, for he could make a cell for his soul in a palace no less well than in a hut. To her surprise, she found herself not only his disciple but a friend. Her touch of northern brusquerie was pleasant to him; and his vivacity and utter inability to imagine that total renunciation for Christ's sake could interfere with forthrightness and joyousness delighted her. He sang French songs to her and the lauds of Lady Poverty; and on her side, she felt that she must strip herself of all that she could for the poor. But he refused her jewels, and especially the ugly old ring.

"You must keep this," he said, "for your boy, as you intended. Did not Mary accept the Magi's gift for her own Son?" And he fell into an ecstasy, remembering the holy Childhood.

But when he was about to leave Rome, he gave himself no peace till he had found a lamb. He loved lambs, because they reminded him of Jesus on His way to Calvary. If he met them going to the slaughter, he bought them, and they followed him about and came to Mass with him and bleated just when they should. He gave the latest lamb to Jacopa. It loved her small boys and butted her gently with its head if she overslept and risked being late for the Holy Sacrifice. In the end, she wove a tunic from its wool to give to Francis. "But," thought she, "will he ever wear what I weave for him?" For by then the wiry little man looked like a skeleton. Yet they had no self-pity; each enjoyed the other's company. Francis called her Brother Jacopa, and on her part she confectioned for him a marvelous cream of almonds which he relished highly.

Three years later it became known that Francis was dying. Jacopa hurried to Assisi, arriving just as he was causing her to be sent for. She felt abashed that she should be admitted, while Clare must remain within her adamantine cloister. Yet Clare did not need to see with her eyes the man who had transformed her life and was for her the incarnate imitation of her Lord. Jacopa brought the woolen tunic and they laid it over Francis. He had often asked for her almond paste. Poor lady, she had made some and carried it to his hut together with incense and candles for the burial now so near. Francis, not to distress her, tasted the cream, gave the rest to his brothers, and not long afterward, on October 4, 1226, he died, and a chorus of larks, triumphant in the sunset, sang him toward his glory.

Jacopa was the first to visit him after his death. She kissed the hard nails on his hands and feet, and knew that she could now live nowhere save in Assisi. She left Rome, where her boys had the whole Frangipani clan to look after them. Francis, after all, had told her to keep the ring till her death — it was the ring of her espousals to Christ, so far had she traveled since the old days on the Esquiline.

She built a house near Assisi and it became a rallying point for the poor and for the disconsolate disciples of St. Francis. Four years later his body was transported amid great tumult to the basilica that Brother Elias had caused to be built upon the hilltop. Could she attend that ceremony? Would not the contrast between the mighty church and the hut where the saint had died have proved too sorrowful? Well, not for that reason did she stay at home, but because she felt she must be as poor as Francis — poor, therefore, *of* Francis; and though she had a portrait of him painted upon wood, she saw him almost wholly in her soul and in the poor who flocked to her.

But after all, when she died, very old, she was buried in

the basilica which she had never entered while alive. Her son took the ring but did not care for it. He bequeathed it, with the rest of his equipment, to a friend of his, a noble near Cortona to whom a girl of the neighborhood called Margaret had fallen victim. This man had kept promising to marry her, but never did, though he let her wear the ring. He was murdered, and she was turned adrift but never lost the ring, and little by little she, too, was espoused by it to the Lord who lovingly said to her that he would make her a mirror for poor sinners. She died in 1297 and the ring was put in the treasury of her shrine at Cortona.

11

A.D. 1370–1380

A WOOD NEAR SIENA

HUGH, third son of the powerful Earl of Medby, seemed a changeling in his family, so dreamy was he yet so restless. He would sit long in front of a hillside near his father's castle, watching, through two lancet-shaped openings in the rock face, an imprisoned water falling.

The water ran off underground, of course, to join the little river once called the Meadda, but that name had now lapsed and it was alluded to simply as the "Beck." However, the secret stream seemed to Hugh to be falling into unfathomed depths and its voices seemed to summon him to visit a horizon beyond all seas.

So he told his father that he wanted to make some pilgrimages and to study, perhaps, at an Italian university. The old earl thought that his son had better be a priest; then he would certainly become a bishop and perhaps a cardinal and might induce the Pope to modify some of his taxations. The Pope was then at Avignon, so he told Hugh to go there, and gave him letters of introduction to allied families and more money than the young man had expected.

Hugh went first to Chartres and was almost overcome by the beauty of the cathedral seen from afar, a shadow on the floating greens and gold and lilacs of the enormous plain. Thrice struck by lightning, it had been rebuilt in 1220 with a vault like a tortoise shell, fearing nothing but the crack of doom; but the ancient statue still kept its vigil deep in a crypt; and Our Lady's veil, given by the Empress Irene to Charlemagne and brought from Aix by Charles the Bald to Chartres, seemed to enfold the young man's mind and to pull him away from Avignon. In fact, he never went there.

When, however, he reached Siena in Italy, he caught cold which turned into pneumonia, and he was often half-delirious. During his dreams a lady in a white dress and a black cloak put her hands upon his head and cooled him and then went away. But what dream, he had begun sadly to ask himself, did not vanish?

As he recovered, he liked to sit staring at the mountainous church of St. Dominic, over valleys full of walnut trees or the silvery mist of olives pierced by bronze-black cypresses. Never had he seen such loveliness. As he grew stronger, he went for solitary walks, disinclined for this city of savage quarrels, and finding himself healed by the peace of nature. Once he went quite far, to a place called the Wood by the Lake, three miles to the northeast of Siena. He sat down to rest, wondering if he could climb to the little monastery on the hill. But just then he heard a woman's voice singing — high, very pure, and gay. The notes trembled in the air like petals thrown about by a sunlit fountain. At last he saw her, but not distinctly; she was like a shining shadow against the sun. He asked himself how so transparent a woman could even walk, let alone sing. She turned to him and smiled; it was the lady who had visited him when he was ill. He stood up and bowed.

"Can it be," he said, "that it was you who were so kind to me when I was sick?"

"I was visiting my sweet Christ," she answered. "But you must not think of climbing to the monastery. Lean on my arm, and I will show you where to find a friend."

Hugh thought he might as well have been asked to lean upon a sunbeam; but when she put her long fingers on his arm he felt that she was strong enough to carry the whole world.

"Dare I ask your name?" he said.

"Do I need a better name," she replied, "than Christian? But in this poor world they call me Catherine." Then she showed him a small path. "Go by that," she said, "and in a moment you will meet the friend I spoke of, though I consider him an obstinate, bad child. Good-by for a time, and may sweet Jesus guide you."

And she disappeared in the dazzle of the sunlight. Hugh, his own mind rather in a dazzle, turned a corner and saw, seated in a little cave, a middle-aged man in a monkish dress with books and a writing form beside him. Hugh saluted him in his far-from-perfect Italian.

"Are you by any chance an Englishman?" asked the hermit.

"My name is Hugh Medd, of Medby," said he.

"And I," said the man, "am William Flete. I remember someone of your name at Cambridge. A relative?"

"You must mean my father's younger brother, my uncle Roger. My father is Earl of Medby."

Flete bowed and said, "I am a simple bachelor of Cambridge. I became an Augustinian friar and traveled to Italy for study; but university towns are so noisy! Even our friary up there is too full. I never speak to anyone save by necessity."

"I apologize," said Hugh, rather taken aback. "But a friend of yours, who visited me when I was ill, has just met me and told me to come to you. She is called Catherine. She mentioned no other name."

"There are many Catherines in Siena," said Flete. "Unless you prefer to think there is only one. What was this Catherine like?"

"Not tall, incredibly thin, with long, transparent hands; the sun dazzled me rather, but I *thought* she had a ring on her marriage finger. Her hands looked . . . Ah! Master Flete, I have been ill and this walk has overtired me. Getting better is worse than being sick!" He added that she wore a big black cloak over a white dress.

"It sounds like her," muttered the hermit, "but it can't possibly be. *Our* Catherine is in Avignon persuading the Pope to return to Rome. Let us be sensible. If it had been she, she would have come up here and given me a terrible talking to."

Hugh remarked that she *had* observed he was an obstinate, bad child but had said it with a sweetly malicious smile.

"She is often very angry with me," said Flete nervously. "She says that I ought to stay longer in my cell, and yet that the only true cell is self-knowledge, which we never need leave." He sighed. "But I am *not* melancholy. I don't think too much about myself. Well, perhaps I do . . . " And he broke off helplessly.

Hugh did not like William Flete very much; still, he did not see that a lady had the right to scold him.

Flete said that Hugh was obviously not a Caterinato.

"Do please understand," said the irritated youth, "that I have no idea what you are talking about. What *is* a Caterinato? And why should I be one?"

Flete said that Hugh must come to see him again; it was too late to begin to discuss such mysteries that night.

When Hugh returned, Flete started at once: "First, she eats nothing; she cannot swallow even a lettuce leaf or the juice of a cherry without being sick. Then she is as strong as a mule — as two mules. She does all the heavy work of her house down there at Fontebranda when she is at home. Then in her prayer she is always in ecstasy. Her mother Lapa tried to pull her out of one, but was afraid she'd break her bones. I've just heard that the court ladies at Avignon found it funny to examine her after Communion and even stuck a needle right through her foot. She didn't feel it then, but afterward she couldn't walk for a fortnight."

Hugh said he would be terrified to meet her.

"No," said William, "she frightens only the wicked. But she is mad on cleanliness. How can she stand our town, where the pigs of Sant' Antonio are the only scavengers? But it is spiritual foulness that she hates. She reconciles one half of Siena with the other. She goes from town to town — she rebukes the Visconti."

"But then," said Hugh, still irritated, "why aren't you down there helping her? You're a Caterinato, aren't you?"

Flete sighed. "I am, but I'm also my poor self. I am not made for moving about. Yet I could write her letters for her. She dictates to three or four persons at once, and often when she's in ecstasy. They get terribly muddled, but in the end they find their sentences all fit together quite well."

Hugh was appalled. "To whom does she send all those letters? I *can* write, but it takes me a whole day to concoct a single page."

"She writes to everyone," said Flete. "Even popes. If

we'd not had Birgitta of Sweden here, no one could have imagined such things being said to popes. But it is really the cardinals that she scourges, and the nobles who devour the Church. She is determined not only to bring the Pope back to Rome, but to start a new crusade."

Hugh doubted whether Christians were united enough for a crusade, and knew that many a pope had lived and died outside Rome. He said nothing, however, just then, but returned in two days to announce that he was homesick and anyhow had hardly any money left.

"Who," said William, "has not heard of your home? Perhaps you were planted there before even the Romans came!"

"I don't know how long," Hugh said. "We lived in the old Saxon house before the stone house was built. But men are changing; the house is changing. It was at first a fortress, to keep safe in; now it is becoming a home, a nest! Still" — he smiled — "even when Alcuin came there we had an ancient gospel written by St. Cuthbert, and there it always is. Even Alcuin was five hundred years ago. Can the world last another five hundred? Will Medby last? Can anything human clasp the world and be eternal?"

"I will give you a ring to remember me by," said the hermit. "An English pilgrim gave it to me. His father saw it at Cortona in the sacristy of the glorious penitent St. Margaret, and since they had too many things there already the guardian gave it to him, and he to his son. But the young man seemed rather frightened of it and gave it to me. But what have solitaries to do with rings? If it does not clasp the world, at least it has neither beginning nor end and may suggest to you eternity!"

Hugh went down into the gold dusk of the Tuscan evening, and shortly returned into the keen-scented northland air. But somehow it had grown bitter to him, though he knew and loved every stone of Medby. Besides, his father was building yet another tower, higher than the keep, and it made the poor original tower look squat and thrust aside. He grew restless, and in the autumn of 1379 went back to Siena and found Flete shivering in his cell.

"The crusade did not happen," said Flete. "But the Pope is back and Catherine is also in Rome. She is angry with me because I stay here; she says it is time for me to come out of my woods and bushes saying paternosters and that God is found not only in the woods but even in the city."

Hugh suddenly felt that he must go to Rome and meet Catherine.

"Rome will bewilder you," said Flete. "A reforming Pope may be very terrible. Catherine sends him oranges that she has gilded, but the schism between the French and the universal Pope remains. Have you kept the ring?"

Hugh said he had, and next day he left for Rome.

One day in the vestibule of St. Peter's he saw a tiny woman prostrate before Giotto's mosaic of the storm-tossed ship, and knew instinctively that it was Catherine, and that on her support depended more than the bulging walls of the basilica and its threatening roof. He followed her back to her house near the Minerva. She whispered only, "All, all! Eternity!"

He wondered how this woman, less than a skeleton leaf, than a gossamer spider's web, could be alive at all. Barduccio Caninagni said that in her veins only the Blood of Christ could run. "Blood? What else has she been seeing all these years? The human blood that has soaked her dress has faded, but she lives by the Blood of Christ."

Finally she said, "Thou callest, and I come. Not through my merits, but through Thy mercy alone which I ask in virtue of Thy Blood." And she died at noon, April 29, 1380, aged thirty-three.

Hugh was present, and had never yet seen anyone die. This ecstatic passing into eternity shook his own bodily life to its foundations. He wrote to his father that he would not return to England. The earl shrugged his shoulders — he had other sons. The stream of life ran strong in the arteries of Medby; the tradition was unalterable; even the ring, which Hugh bequeathed to his eldest brother, became an heirloom never to be said good-by to. And the ancient water continued to pour within its rock face under the cave where a half-buried stone paid homage to the Sole Unconquered.

c. A.D. 1360–1430

PORTUGUESE SACRIFICE

WHEN the Earl of Medby heard that John, King of Portugal, was asking to marry one of the Duke of Lancaster's daughters, his mind leaped into the future and he told his daughter Anne to come for a walk. They climbed up to the weather-beaten cross of St. Paulinus and sat down.

"My dear," he said, "this marriage will certainly take place, because Portugal likes to be friends with England, and there are other reasons. And *I* think that he will ask for the elder daughter, Philippa, though she is already twenty-six."

Anne opened her mouth to speak, but the earl hurried on. "My reason is that Lancaster's second wife was the daughter of Pedro of Castille and he would like to be king there in his wife's name. So if he gave *her* daughter Catherine to the King of Portugal there would be war all round. No; it will be Philippa."

He said all this because, though he didn't like John of Gaunt, Philippa had made close friends with Anne, despite the fact she was only seventeen. He had not objected to this, because Philippa was as sensible as she was kind. *But* if she became Queen of Portugal . . .

This time Anne did interrupt, but though she saw what her father was leading up to, she hung back, and said it would be a real sorrow to say good-by to Philippa.

He steeled himself and replied, "There need be no good-by. Philippa will need companions, and whom should she take but you?"

Once a thing is said there is relief as well as doom. Anne looked down over the vast view. Much forest had been cleared away, but as for the castle, nothing had been demolished save that the spaces between the ramparts were now grass and flowers instead of paving stones, and much had been built. From here the castle looked almost like a village, with its new high-pitched roofs and slender chapel spire. The old tower still stood at the corner but was now the special playground of the children whose noisy games replaced the yells of raiders, the shouts of men-at-arms, the wailing women, and the groans of prisoners. She had known that she must leave it someday, but she had grown into it, and it into her.

But the earl could be serious as well as shrewd. "Look, my dear," he said, "at our old bridge down there. The Romans built it, but how often *we* have strengthened it. You can see three happy villages where once there was nothing. If you are to help to build a bridge between two peoples and to establish the future, you will be true to the spirit of your ancestors and of Holy Church herself. Come down to your cave."

For just below was a little cave that Anne had cleared

out and made into a shrine. The men had unearthed a great stone with letters on it which no one could read, but also a cross, which fitted it for an altar. A figure of Our Lady sat over this. Anne knelt in inarticulate prayer, and then went still lower, to where water poured, visible through two orifices in the rock. Here, too, Our Lady sat. Much rough greenery had been removed and the place was called the Virgin's Bower. They tried to keep her flowers blossoming there all the year round, from the snowdrop, "the fair maid of February," and Our Lady's milkwort for the Purification and Annunciation; then, tended by Anne, flowers became uncountable — Our Lady's mantle, her lace, her slipper, her comb, and of course "the deep violet of the valley of humility." The water poured underground into the Beck and thence to the sea. So, she prayed, might her life go forward, always consecrated, into its hidden lands.

"I shall lend you," said her father, "that old ring which has belonged so long to this house and must always return to it. It is pure gold, and will bring purity wherever you go. If part of your life is to be bitter, the ring will wed you to Our Lord and the bitterness will turn sweet."

Anne had never heard him speak like that before; she was sure it was a prophecy. And indeed next year the alliance was ratified, and soon enough Anne sailed with Philippa for Portugal.

Heaven favored them. The seas, usually rough, were kingfisher blue and burnished gold. Anne, who had never even seen the sea before, could not believe her eyes. Whichever way she looked there was nothing but this blue and golden water, and then the delicate line where the sky leaped upward toward God. She realized, as never before, the presence of the Creator and the flooding of the Holy Spirit. One day their chaplain actually said Mass upon the deck; the ship became the House of Nazareth, and the Blessed Trinity was complete.

Philippa had crossed the sea before, and she was perhaps less sensitive than Anne. But she had learned the psalter according to the Sarum rite and said it daily. Anne found that she had never prayed so easily, and learned to love the Scriptures better still, though Philippa wouldn't let her share her fasts. However, she liked playing ball with the other ladies, though on these tiny decks the balls kept flying off into the sea till Philippa caused nets to be put up all around. Her two Portuguese ladies approved of the misty England having sent so practical a queen. Three ships formed this little retinue, and Anne asked who an old man in the second ship — who seemed to be always drawing on large boards — might be.

"Ah," said Philippa, "when the King marries *me* he will have to keep his promises! When he defeated the Moors at Aljubarrota he vowed he would build a church to Our Lady's honor. Well, he did rebuild an old abbey, but rebuilding isn't building. And I am bringing one of our own architects and a clever assistant to succeed him, and they will add some of our English loveliness to what John builds. They say half the Portuguese churches are as massive as fortresses — like the oldest part of your Medby!"

They arrived. John with his nobles came down from the cliff of Porto to welcome them. He was twenty-nine, dark, with very determined features. Philippa whispered to Anne that despite his nose and his chin he wasn't going to be master altogether.

At first it seemed that he would be. There was war in Spain; John of Gaunt himself was there. The marriage kept being put off, and when at last it took place in the grim cathedral on February 2, 1387, the groom went off at once for more fighting. But in the summer the English duke fell sick; he tied the situation up by marrying his Catherine to the King of Castile and went home. So did the Portuguese John, and found that the whole people and the very court not only reverenced but loved his queen, and he began to do so, too, and henceforward gave her his whole fidelity. He already had two children; Philippa put their mother into a convent where she soon became prioress. The children were educated at court. Alfonso, the boy, assuredly became a nuisance afterward; the girl, Beatriz, was married off, very young, to Thomas, Earl Fitzalan, and lived quietly till she died, and had her tomb in the chapel of the castle at Arundel.

Finally, in 1388, the votive priory began to be built. Philippa tactfully did not dispute that the main plan should be credited to the Portuguese Alfonso Dominguez who died but a few years later. The work was then carried on by her own importation, Hughete. The honey-colored stone rose into a towering nave and the aisles were roofed by terraces along which crowds could march under mighty buttresses curving overhead, carrying down the thrust of the great vault.

"My dear John must learn to like this," said the Queen

to Anne, "and we will call it Batalha for his sake and his great battle. I know he would like simply another Alcobaça — to see every bone of the building. And so he shall! But my Englishmen shall enrich these bare surfaces with delicate upright lines, delicate as harp strings; and as for those flat roofs — I suppose we daren't put gables, but at least the stone shall froth like frozen surf, and every pinnacle shall blossom into rosebuds."

But suddenly poor Anne of Medby was swept by a longing for her northland home and its harebells and tiny pansies and yellow ragwort and the silvery birch trees by the Beck, and she began to cry. Philippa was distressed and suggested a little holiday — two or three months in England. But now Anne felt that it was better never to go back. She clung to Philippa and begged her not to send her. So the Queen decided that the child must be married, and in 1390 she became the wife of Luiz, Lord of Penacova, whom the King kept near him. So two little families began to grow up together.

Philippa had two children who died as babies; but then came three brothers, Duarte (for, after all, the boy had the blood of two English Edwards in his veins!), Pedro, and Henriques. The two elder boys grew up tall and fair like their mother; but Henriques, tall, too, was dark, with somber eyes that could dream but also flash. The three were inseparable, stalwart and spirited, but tremendous readers, peering into a world beyond even Philippa's and far beyond King John's. Then came a daughter, Isabel; then a son John, in 1400; finally, some two years later, Fernando. His birth was difficult; he grew up delicate

among books and praying like an angel in his chapel
where Philippa had installed the Sarum rite. Deferential,
morally austere, the brothers were helped by the Do-
minican friars now at Batalha to delve into philosophy;
but Henriques read especially history and travel; he felt
the ring that had enclosed his ancestral world was melting — its circumference was ever receding — a horizon
was not a limit, but a summons to pass beyond it.

When Duarte was twenty, it was agreed that the brothers should win their spurs. But how? A mere tournament,
however grand, seemed to them ignoble. There must be
a war. But with whom? At last the Moorish Ceuta, opposite Spain, was suggested. Capture that nest of Moham-
medan pirates, that hell for Christian slaves! The King
began by laughing — difficulties were unsurmountable.
But the whole plan of Ceuta, ingeniously modeled in sand,
was mapped out; prophecies were quoted; the Queen herself preferred that her sons face hardship rather than
mere games.

Nunalvarez Pereira, the "holy constable," victor at Aljubarrota and John's closest friend and counselor, approved when the King said he might thus cleanse his
hands from Christian blood. Did he mean that long ago
he had killed the lover of his brother's wife? Anyhow, the
lot was cast. To Henriques was entrusted the equipping
of a fleet. In order that masses of meat might be salted
for this, the citizens of Porto ate nothing but tripe. Men
from France, Picardy, Normandy, and Germany sent re-
cruits; a London merchant, Mundy, equipped four ships.
A splendid fleet sailed down to the Tagus and anchored

off Belém. Until, later on, the expedition started for Africa, no one save the tiny royal circle had the least idea whither it was bound.

The Queen, who wished her sons to sail, and even her husband, bled in her very soul when she said good-by without even seeing the young men knighted, on which she had set her heart. Perhaps weakened by much fasting and daylong prayer, she fell sick, but remained so cheerful that a family feast went on gaily. She caused three swords to be made, long and strong; she gave them to her sons. With these must they be knighted. Serene, even happy, she would not allow her lady Anne so much as to cry. "It does not help at all! Let us play *our* part, pray unwearyingly and do good works that God may hear us." Her mind remained clear. "You must sail! You must sail! I must not delay you. The wind is good for you; you will sail within the week. But I shall not see you go." And on July 18, 1415, she died, still smiling. In fact it was by her wish that the expedition set forth, gaily decked, on July 25, feast of St. James.

The siege was savagely resisted; the carnage was horrible; the valor of the princes was reckless; they all were knighted. In fact, the King, unable to make Duarte more than his firstborn and heir, made Pedro Duke of Coimbra, and Henriques, Duke of Viseu. So far there had been no dukes in Portugal. And at last the brothers diverged. Duarte, who had organized the war, now shared with his father in organizing the realm. Pedro, suddenly restless, went off to Hungary and other lands. Henriques increasingly wished to be alone; he built an all-but hermitage on distant Cape St. Vincent, and here, on the heathy, dusty cliffs, he studied and meditated, till suddenly one day he was done with dreams, and he resolved to hunt unceasingly for new realities. So ship after ship went south; island after island was discovered and colonized; in 1433 that almost mythical Cape Bojador was passed.

By 1460, when Henriques died, the west coast of Africa had been mapped out down to Sierra Leone. After his death what was directly due to his life was accomplished: in 1488 the Cape itself was rounded and ten years later Vasco da Gama reached India. Two years later Cabral found Brazil and the first mass was offered in South America. One third of non-European land now belonged to Portugal. Henriques, the more determined because so often disillusioned, had changed the proportions of the globe.

Lavishly generous, paralyzing in his icy angers, chaste and austere as any friar, yet a whirlwind fighter when need arose, he would have been an enigma had not the men of his time seen that he was dominated by his faith, and that, for him, the empire of Portugal meant the extension of Christ's kingdom.

Meanwhile the lady Anne, who before the Queen's death had always traveled around with Philippa who would not let go of her and made the Count her husband come too, had developed a taste for travel. This was very useful to King John, who was growing tired and had great faith in her reports. She always took her daughter Isabel with her, for she perceived that the girl had fallen in love with the Infante Fernando; and though the child's blood was quite as good as his, she had an instinct that the wonderfully other-worldly youth would never marry anyone. The King would have welcomed the alliance, because he could not feel that the political marriages of Don Duarte and Don Pedro boded any good.

King John died at Lisbon on August 15, 1433, and was taken by slow stages to Batalha and was placed to rest in the Founder's chapel; there, in the great starry-roofed octagon, his effigy lay showing him clasping in his hand that of his queen, Philippa, to whom indeed his hand and heart had ever been devoted.

Anne, after a while, decided to revisit this tomb, having first pilgrimaged to Tomar, headquarters of that Order of Christ of which Henriques was Master. Thence they traveled to Ourém and then lost their way and found themselves in a desolate hamlet called Fatima.

Here Isabel said, "Mother, Our Lady is in this place, and she is asking from me a sacrifice. What can that be save *not* to marry the Infante? May I become a Poor Clare, as my namesake did, the peacemaker Queen Isabel of Portugal, and as did her aunt, Elizabeth of Hungary?"

Anne sighed, for Isabel was her only daughter, but she thought that this vocation was a real one. In 1437 Henriques and Fernando sailed against Tangier, and the Moors overwhelmingly defeated them, and Fernando was handed over as hostage, and died in ignominious and treacherous chains, after suffering which made the Holy Infante still more sanctified.

Therefore Anne and Isabel were sure that their sacrifice had been accepted. Isabel, who had been espoused to

· 95

Christ as a Poor Clare with the ring that her mother had lent her, now gave it back.

"Mother," she said, "now that Fernando has died, it is time for me to go to heaven, where it will be explained to me how I was espoused both to Our Lord and to him. I have had much sorrow in my life and could have had so much gold! I can but hope that my years may have risen as incense before the Lord. Fernando will no doubt be brought back to Batalha; but I do not wish to go there. He never thought of me, but he will discover that my prayers — my loving prayers — were his support during those horrible years at Fez."

And indeed Fernando's heart was brought back and buried in a lovely recess in line with his brothers'. As for Anne, she never returned to England, and the ring was kept, after her death, in her private reliquary, till the state of his country caused the Earl of Medby to send his great-grandson Odo Medd to fetch it back. It was, he felt, in some way the guardian of his house, and must come home again. Odo therefore brought it back in 1534.

13

NOT TO BE BROKEN

The ring was hurried home from Portugal by Odo of Medby because by 1534 even the old Earl of Medby was becoming agitated. He was well over eighty by now, so there were four generations at Medby: the earl, his son and grandson, and his great-grandson Odo, who was twenty-four. The old earl had lived as long as he could, convinced that the world would not and certainly should not change; but he had to give over the management of Medby to his eldest son, Lord of Avondale, though he demanded to be told of any alterations that were made, and grumbled about all of them.

As he sat, muffled in furs, in the great hall, he resented the daily change of rushes on the stone floor and still more the saffron and lavender that his granddaughter Gwendolen caused to be sprinkled there.

"In countries of culture," said Odo, who, having traveled, felt he knew the world, "the servitors themselves lie, not on rushes, but mats."

The old chaplain, who himself had been to Italy, said

· 97

that of course mats were needed there because marble would be too cold to lie upon. "But," he added, "I am inclined to think that even servitors should lie in beds."

This so evidently annoyed the earl that Odo refrained from saying that the King himself had half-a-dozen noblemen to prepare his bed, to ruffle the mattress and bolster lest a dagger should be hidden there, and to insure His Highness of having blankets of the right color over him. For he knew that the earl not only hated Henry Tudor but despised him even more.

"I resent," said the earl, who read Odo's thoughts, "my last days being confounded by this Tyddr. Do not tell me he has Plantagenet blood in him. That makes him all the more shameful. Happily London is far off and at least I need not see his bloated carcase, for I am told he is already half-decayed."

The others tried to divert the talk by exclaiming that those "last days" were still far off.

But the priest, divided between his care for charity and a conviction that the end was drawing near for very much more than the earl, said, "The changes began before you were born, my Lord. It was the Great Death that murdered half our land. Innumerable priests died. They say that nine out of ten monks perished, so that monasteries cannot till their land. In fact, who that once freely earned a wage can do so now? Work is far more necessary and the produce far smaller; and so men ask for wages ever more great. They cannot be granted. Hence the land has become full of valiant beggars."

"My land," said the earl severely, "was too well guarded

to be struck by the Great Death. My harvests never rotted. My cattle never wandered loose. *I* never appealed to Parliament about wages."

"You say 'my,' my Lord," urged the priest, "and you are right: your forefathers were as you are, and *you are they!* But when was it that the really great change came — the change that so few see? Hardly two years ago did the King proclaim himself an emperor and his realm an empire; and he declared that to him the body politic, divided into the spirituality and temporality, is bound under God to render humble obedience. And this very year the act was passed declaring the King's Highness to be Supreme Head of the Church of England; it is to be he who shall correct errors and heresies, and anyone who speaks against this is a traitor."

"Parliament?" cried the earl. "Acts? Parliament hardly ever meets unless the King tells it to, to vote him more money. What if he does call himself an emperor? *I* don't. I don't and won't so much as use his newfangled title 'majesty.' The majestic Tyddr! Ha!"

"But, my Lord," said Odo's father Cosmo, "what the reverend priest means is, I think, this — tyrants come and go, and our present ruler is sure to go, especially as he is so ill, or so we hear. But what he has done is to hand over the making of right and wrong to a Parliament which is certain to go on in some shape or other. He does not see that he has cut his own throat."

"But parliaments, too, come and go," said the earl irritably.

"Yes, but Parliament won't. What you don't see, Grandfather, is that Parliament, which is the voice of the people, will remain. What have been our troubles so far? Lollardism? It died soon enough after Wycliffe. Translations of the Scriptures?"

"Who," asked the earl, "that can read at all, wants to read translations? There is our good Gospel according to St. Mark, given us by St. Cuthbert, which has stood on the same shelf hundreds of years before me!"

The priest thought, "Possibly. But who takes it down and reads it?"

"What did go on, sir," continued Lord Cosmo, "was the terrific taxation due to the Pope's filling our bishoprics with Italians who never set foot in their sees but drew their revenues. And that is only one thing. It is true that many of the King's subjects held posts abroad and drew *those* revenues. But who does not notice how many such positions are now being given to laymen who are not so much as ordained? Our country has been growling against that for a very long time."

"It is always one of two things," said the priest, "lust for money or for power."

"But money is not bad," said the earl testily. "I have power and not a little wealth; but I use them as I should. *Why* does this Tyddr need money? For his insane extravagances. We are far from London; but I suppose we can believe about half of what we hear."

"You can believe it all, and then double it," said Avondale. "And you can add his need of bribing his new friends. Why," said he, smiling at his aunt Gwendolen, who sat saying nothing but doing tapestry, "why have we the pleasure of our dear Lady Gwendolen's company tonight?"

Lady Gwendolen had been a nun for long years in one of those smaller monasteries that Cromwell had been suppressing all over the country so as to have lands and revenues for the upstarts, and indeed not a few of the older nobles were willing to replenish their coffers from the loot. Gwendolen had not wished to be drafted off into some vast monastery where she would know no one and which would in no long time be itself suppressed, as anyone could see. So she had returned to live at home. After all, Medby was large enough to house several generations; there were several oratories in it as well as the great chapel, so she could spend all the time she wished in solitude and prayer. All the same, she could not but feel a heartache at the thought of her convent. Her eyes filled with tears; then she felt ungrateful to all these dear people who surrounded her with love. She rose and said good night.

But after only a few minutes she came hurrying back, white-faced and holding a rather clumsy reliquary. "The ring!" she cried, sobbing. "The ring!"

She put the reliquary down on a table and they clustered round it. It was evident that the ring was broken — not fallen into two parts, but snapped near the top. They looked at it with blanched faces. Not one of them could have said what the history of the ring really was, but they all felt that it was in some way the guardian of their family and of their imperishable house.

It was Lord Avondale who first recovered himself.

"We must ask ourselves two things," he said quietly. "First, whether we can mend it, or ought to try. Possibly it could be fixed inside a larger and stronger ring. And then, *why* this has happened."

The earl exploded into indignation.

"Why it has happened? The wonder is that every marriage ring within this realm is not broken! For years that Welshman has been trying to force the Pope to proclaim his marriage with the most noble, gracious, and virtuous Katherine null, and last year — you were away, Odo, but you certainly heard of it — the base chaplain of Anne Boleyn was enthroned as archbishop of Canterbury and did proclaim it null, and rushed the scandal through and crowned her queen. Believe me," he cried, rising to prophetic heights, "though Queen Katherine must die, and may that be soon for her own sake, not Anne nor Cranmer nor Cromwell shall wear their heads for long. What ghosts will follow the King when his turn comes!"

But Lady Gwendolen had picked up the reliquary and had rushed to the castle chapel and put it on the altar. She took off her own ring and slipped it on to the finger of Our Lady of Medby, a larger version of the statue they had placed over what used to be the fairy well where the water continued to pour behind the rock face. Quite a considerable cult had grown up around this place; people trooped to it as to a shrine. An incredible accumulation of reliquaries, statues, rosaries of different sorts, marvelously woven stuffs had ended by heaping themselves up in that chapel.

Gwendolen felt suffocated and decided to go to pray

in her own oratory. She lit several candles on a hearse, and one very large one, the sort that was meant to burn all day or night. Then she set an upright wheel revolving, with little bells upon it. She meant that the candles should remind Our Lord of the flame of love within her heart and that the tinkle of the little bells should mean her own prayers flitting off to heaven, and hoped they would go on making their tiny music till she woke up next day.

But as she knelt before her own little altar she felt she could not begin to pray properly. So she said, as preparation, certain lines of Chaucer's that she cherished:

> *My knowledge is so weak, O blissful Queen,*
> *To tell abroad thy right worthiness*
> *That I the weight of it may not sustain.*
> *But, as a child of eight months old or less*
> *That laboureth his language to express,*
> *Even so fare I, and therefore I thee pray*
> *Guide thou my song that I of thee shall say!*

Her heart felt a little lighter; and then the little door that was over her statue of Our Lady swung open of itself. (She knew it could do this; the latch was weak, but usually some slight shock was needed to make it open thus.) Within the breast of the Holy Mother was a very small crucifix, delicately wrought. Light poured in upon Lady Gwendolen, and she knew that never for a moment must she forget Christ and Him crucified. She knelt and let the great dark light flood through her; she must be ready to be crucified with Christ, who in His Church was being so cruelly treated. Toward dawn she lay down and slept — longer than was usual for her.

When she woke she heard an unexpected agitation in the house.

"Chattering before mass?" she said to herself. "Impossible!" She went down. Everyone was crowded before the chapel altar. She heard confused voices. "It *was* broken." "It can't have been." "I tell you I could have slipped a knife between the two ends." "And if it wasn't, why did Aunt Gwendolen come rushing down?" "Ah, here's Gwendolen!" "Gwendolen, did you or did you not tell us the ring was broken?"

"Dear Grandfather, dear Father," she said, "you all saw that it was broken. It still was when I carried it back. Yet I could not believe" — she became confused — "I could not believe that the great work of Christ should be broken. Rather than that, I asked" — she hung her head — "that I myself might be yet further broken. And now look! You can see the line where it was broken and now is mended!"

They looked carefully and could see the mending, and as they stared, they saw that the ring had seemingly many times been broken but had always rewelded itself into one. They recollected themselves before the altar, and the world-embracing Sacrifice was offered.

Very soon, as anything does which is sudden and quite outside experience, the event faded from their awareness. But they began to talk much more about the Pope. The old earl, who died not long afterward, had always taken a pope for granted and paid no great attention if younger men, that is, anyone under sixty, argued about him. The Lord of Avondale, a somewhat harder man, perceived the pope chiefly as an Italian prince who collected taxes and deposited foreign prelates in England who were not wanted. But his son, Odo's father, had begun to have theories. Of course the Church, like the empire, had to have a head, and he would not admit that the Pope should be at the mercy of Italian nobles or French cardinals. The proper thing was a council!

The Apostles, he announced, appointed Peter as their head because they themselves were a council. Everything, he said, was an affair of common sense and understanding one another. He felt sure that men such as Fisher and More and those Carthusians need never have been executed if only they had seen that there were two ways of looking at everything.

At this point Odo, who had been under the spell of the ring ever since he brought it back from Portugal, took his courage in both hands and said that few in England — or perhaps anywhere, perhaps not even the Pope himself — understood what being pope really meant, and that More, with his hard-working head, including the loss of it, should have taught England what the successor of St. Peter really was.

Avondale said angrily that Odo had better go to Rome and teach the Pope his business. Odo said he would be delighted to go. On his way home he had done homage at Compostella, and to Our Lady at Le Puy-en-Velay and at Chartres and Paris and Boulogne, and now he wished to go to Siena and Assisi but above all to Rome, and to stay there for good. His grandfather said that if Odo felt like that, he had better clear out at once before his head followed so many others.

"Very likely your own will," said Odo's father, equally to his own father and his son, "for whatever your ideas are about the Pope, you are never going to admit that a king is supreme also over spiritualities."

The Medds had red hair and lived up to it. They loved one another tenaciously and quarreled fiercely. But Odo at the moment was for peace. He said that he had four brothers, and that even if he did settle in Rome the succession would be secure — if anything could be now. Who knew how long Medby itself would last, with all these confiscations? And in Rome he might be able to explain to the authorities what Englishmen really felt like.

The priest said that neither he nor anyone else would be able to explain what the English felt like just now. "Do you suppose the Spaniards understand the English? Certainly the English would never understand the Spaniards. Neither side even wants to."

Lady Gwendolen suddenly sat upright. She said, "Go to Rome, Odo. Go now. The dregs, the scum, the good wine, all of them flow to Rome. The world is going to be a different world. My knowledge is weak" — she smiled to herself — "but I am sure the ring was never really broken and never will be. But this means, my dear Odo, that we must have many wise men such as, please God, you will become; and many holy men and women such as I would like to be and, God knows, am not, who will offer themselves as victims for those who are doing their best to break it."

She rose, made her beautiful curtsey to all of them, with her detached yet loving smile, and a look that made them all feel she saw something that they did not.

"She must have suffered much," said Odo unexpectedly. They looked at him with surprise, but did not try to prevent his going to Rome.

14

A.D. 1560

THE CHASUBLE IS RED

DURING the last horrible years of Henry's reign the ring seemed to clasp Medby round about — an island of peace. But to the south and east especially the brutality of Thomas Cromwell and the King was unrestrained. England became a land of loot; monastery after monastery, shrine after shrine were plundered; upstart nobles pocketed what the King did not. Wool replaced wheat; common lands were enclosed; whole villages vanished; a population of the destitute was created, and when these could find no help they crept into the woods and lived, or died, as savages. Over half of England lay the "blanket of the dark."

True, in 1540 occurred the hideous comedy of Cromwell's fall. He had selected Anne of Cleves for the King to marry. Henry did not like the look of her and turned in a rage on Cromwell and on June 10 had him arrested actually at the council table. The Garter was torn from him, and he was accused of fantastic crimes and hustled to the Tower. The very judges whom he had installed forbade him to defend himself, and July 28 was fixed for his execution. He uttered ignoble cries. If he could once more kiss the King's hand, its very scent would waft him up to God. And yet on the very scaffold, who knows what happened in his soul? He stood erect, and declared that he died loyal, after all, to the ancient Faith.

As for Henry, he lived on for another seven years, a prey to his lifelong terror of death. Thousands of masses must be said for him; ten thousand candles burn. He who had said, "I will not that any man shall command me," knew that his soul must crawl toward the poorest of his subjects who would pray for him. As for his body, the coffin in which it was shut burst open; a dog darted between the feet of the attendants and licked the pavement. He had destroyed more beauty and more precious things than in all the past history of his land; he had engineered more unhappiness for their day and for the future than ever before.

Odo married in 1536 and his first son, John, was born the next year. His family held aloof from public affairs but continued to develop Medby Castle till it contained a hospital, a school, almshouses, and rooms where trades were taught. Outlying members of the clan no doubt took the oath of supremacy, "so far as the law of God allows it," thinking it nonsense anyhow. Some took Communion after the new fashion and, later, in the ancestral way, but they did not feel that they handed themselves over to heresy, since they were sure that the Pope would come back into his own some day. They observed that during the reign of the sickly little Edward, England was misgoverned worse than any other country by the baseborn or by nobles whom they thought quite inferior to their earl.

In 1533 the return to the Faith, which they in their simplicity had taken for granted, apparently occurred. Mary was acclaimed with wild enthusiasm by London itself, for which these northerners had a due disdain. Still, Odo, by now Lord Avondale, went there to offer the Queen his homage, and obtained for John a post under an important official in the Tower.

So it was that one very early morning in 1555 John climbed to the roof of the White Tower and even to the flat top of one corner turret after another. As most of the Medds intermittently were, he was afflicted by his imagination. Still, he was not troubling about the tremendous history of this place — almost 500 years of it — nor about the Conqueror, or Becket, or those who had built tower beyond tower, wall beyond wall, till the White Tower, though so huge, became but the center of a little city.

The early July dawn was beautifully clear. John could

see to the rich farmlands beyond West Minster and trace all the Whitehall buildings along the river, and look away to the calm Surrey Hills, and opposite, over the Finsbury Fields, to other hills, topped, like Harrow, with spires.

Slowly the town woke up. Smoke rose from the huddled wooden houses; bells began to ring. Soon Mass would begin in St. Paul's. John was glad of that, and would soon himself be going down to Mass in St. John's chapel. The Queen was visiting the Tower — perhaps she was already praying — she prayed a lot. But around and below her were her soldiers. She needs them most, thought he, against her friends! Which of these great nobles can be trusted? Which ambassador? Her husband? He dishonors her.

John went to his father. "We live," said the austere youth to Odo, "in a world peopled by the sons of him who was a liar and a murderer from the beginning. As I see it, the only hope is in Rome. If I were not your eldest son, I would ask to go there."

"You certainly shall not!" interjected Avondale.

"And," John proceeded, "my brother Richard ought to stay at home in case either you or I got our heads cut off, which may be happening to anyone quite soon — the Queen is really sick, and there is not an ounce of sincerity in that Elizabeth. But young Bobbie might be smuggled off when he is fifteen or so."

But Robert was considered too adventurous a lad to be trusted far away, till, when he was twenty-five and really wanted to go — for despite his antics he hoped to be a priest — John sent him off to Italy. He stayed a long time at Mantua, much longer than he meant to, because he caught malaria from the Mantuan lakes. Anyhow, his father wanted him to be on good terms with the duke there, since the Medds had helped the Gonzagas to send some of their superb strain of horses to Henry VIII, and he was wondering whether he could not sell some of his North of England shorthorns to Duke Vincent. But Robert soon saw that nothing could have interested that potentate less.

Not till 1565 did he reach Rome, remembering that John had said to him, as he left: "*Defecit sanctus, et diminutae sunt veritates a filiis hominum.*" That half the world was wandering after lies seemed to him obvious; but he hoped that he would learn that there were still some saints.

He was, of course, presented to Pius V, but though his impertinence had not died out, he rather shrank from explaining to that pontiff that he was not dealing wisely with Elizabeth, and he hugged to his own heart the fact that the Queen was already nearly bald and wore a reddish wig — "not *proper* red, like ours," he reflected, "but Gloriana might as well be golden. Of course she can't help her teeth being black, yet she exults when her flatterers call them pearls."

He lodged with a Florentine, Philip Neri, too near the Tiber, so that he fell sick again and time dragged on. But he liked Philip, who was amusing and kept losing his spectacles and was fond of music, as was Robert himself.

"If you are to be a priest," said Philip, "you must study at the Roman College which was begun by my old friend

Inigo de Loyola. He died some years ago. I fear I annoyed him badly because, as you see, I can't help taking hold of the dress of the person I'm talking to. He said I ended by pulling all the buttons off his chest. He didn't like that; he had a most orderly mind. And yet, how angry he could get! Still, his eyes were all crinkled up as if he cried a lot — he probably did. You must stand on the balcony from which he used to look up at the stars. Yes, ours is a *poor* world. But then you must meet my *great* friend Camillus, who has a much worse temper than any of us. *I* may be huffy, but I don't explode as he does. He is about eight feet tall and one leg is in a sort of iron frame and he has at least five mortal diseases, but he consecrates himself entirely to the sick. Our opinions have differed much; but if only I could be as good as he is! Ah, my boy," said Philip, his eyes flooding with tears, "meet as many such men as you can. There are plenty here."

"I am glad to have met *you*," said Robert, "and, forgive me, Father, but here are your spectacles on the floor. And *please* let me give you a dinner glass so that you may remember England" — for Philip hated not having his own glass to drink out of — "and this very small offering which you must spend entirely on your cat." Philip had a cat to which he was very devoted and liked it to have first-rate food.

Time passed, and Robert was ordained. In 1586 he watched the astounding upheaval of Caligula's obelisk, deeply embedded near St. Peter's, which no one had dared to touch till this new pontiff, Sixtus V, crashed his way through impossibilities. At last the obelisk was raised from the ground on which it had rested for a thousand and half a thousand years. It was crowned with the Cross and was part of the Christianization of Rome. Every architect, every workman, had received holy Communion before transporting it to where it now stood firm in the space before St. Peter's. Also, just before Robert left Rome, St. Peter's heavenly cupola had all its vaults completed, which all, save Sixtus, had despaired of ever accomplishing.

He left because his directors told him to go — there was too much fever in Rome, and, "England needs some more martyrs." While he was making his tour of good-bys he was approached by a young Jesuit, Aluigi Gonzaga, courteous, grave, and clearly a man of God.

"You will, I think," said Aluigi, "pass through Mantua again. Will you give my respects to my cousin Vincent? And if it is not too much out of your way, it would give my mother great happiness if you called at Castiglione and said how I never forget her. She is the very best of mothers."

Robert gazed at this tranquil haggard youth, the abdication of whose marquisate had upset half the empire, but he could find no adequate words.

Aluigi said, "You must forgive me. I have much to do in the hospitals," and he returned to the wards where the stench, the sores, the obscenities, and the blasphemies made him turn white and sick.

Robert returned to England dressed as the servant of a Welsh Catholic farmer and called himself Brough. It was decided that he should travel north; his mother would want to see him and his native air might strengthen him. Thus he reached Medby and remained hiding there ten days.

He said Mass in a smaller chapel, but one day asked to offer it in the cave, which he loved. The lettering on the ancient stone seemed clearer than before; in Rome he had learned about antiquities and saw that it had been pagan. "But it has been Christed," he said, "and that is why it has survived. Not all the Elizabeths of the world can make an end of the sole-unconquered Christ."

After Mass he climbed up to the wind-worn cross of St. Paulinus and sat down upon its steps. He wondered how many, through the generations, had sat there before him.

"Can the world last as long as it *has* lasted?" he asked himself. "How long can our own house last?" If, he meditated, he were his family's first martyr, his blood might fortify those walls. He felt very happy. The sunrise encircled all the land in a ring of gold and drew up the scents of the pines and the wild thyme. He, too, looked at the little north-country flowers with affection, the tiny pansies, the tall ragwort, the blue wild geraniums. "God has taken all the bitterness away," he said. "O death, where is thy sting? *Vexilla regis . . .*" and he repeated the words that would soon be one thousand years old and felt he must be the One King's standard-bearer.

Going down, he knelt before the rock and the maiden-hair fern that veiled the falling water, and commended himself to Our Lady in all the most consecrated prayers, and asked that Medby might not go the way of Walsingham.

When the time came for him to go he embraced his family with happy tears. "In you," said his father, "we are wedded to Christ."

"We have been that," said Robert, "since very long ago."

At that moment a pure, grave, and joyous music seemed to well down from the recess where the ring was now hidden, but it was so unearthly that they none of them said anything.

So Robert left, and very soon was arrested and was executed at York. Just before he died he said: "The ring of my espousals." But no one knew what he meant, and perhaps he himself did not altogether know.

15

c. A.D. 1675–1682

THE TWO HEARTS

I

THE Earl of Medby was patrolling his topmost terrace, and on it he had planted eight yew trees which should later on be clipped into fantastic forms and also used for bows, because he did not admit that gunpowder would quite abolish bows and arrows. He himself would add, but not destroy. Thus he had forbidden anyone to cross what people called the Rovers' Bridge, though the old priest who lived in the castle said it should be "Roman," as the architecture showed, but he had built another bridge higher up the Beck. The castle, with its honeycomb of walled courts, now climbed right up the hill behind it to what was certainly a Roman road. Lower down, the spaces between the ramparts had been further softened into terraces; and still lower, when the sun shone level, you could see the outline of the old wooden Saxon house.

"All I ask," he said to his eldest son, "is that you should build nothing in that new Italian style — nothing that came in under those Tudors. If you must, build a wing or something behind the stables for guests who don't matter."

True, the chapel had been a good deal changed under Mary Tudor, but that was because she was a Catholic and might have been a saint had she not been infatuated with that Philip. No doubt Philip, too, was a Catholic, but a Spaniard, and the earl resented Spain and even France. Rome he admitted because of the Pope who, after all, had to live somewhere.

Just then the earl saw his second son Ferdinand walking moodily below him. Ferdinand, a restless youth, found a Catholic's life under Charles II very dull up here, though not dangerous.

His father shouted to him, "Come up here. I've got an idea."

The earl's ideas were apt to make people nervous; but Ferdinand duly came.

"Your aunt Sybel," said his father, "must be getting quite old and ought to be visited. She has had to go to the Holy Marys at Dijon. I think I will send you there. And if you get as far as that you had better see your sister Gwendoline who is with the Ursulines at Paray, wherever that is. They would tell you at Dijon. I cannot let Avondale leave Medby at present. But I do beg of you, my boy, keep yourself in hand. Frenchmen will often infuriate you, but remember they are far better swordsmen than you, and dueling is, I believe, forbidden under pain of death; anyhow, it was."

"And," said Ferdinand demurely, "it is against the law of God."

"Yes, yes," said the earl, "remember that, too." And he gave him some more advice.

Ferdinand paid no great attention to this, but was so excited by this "idea" that his very hair seemed to get redder.

"I do not see," said his father, "that you need attend upon King Charles; but you should see our ambassador in Paris. He may show you Versailles, but do not get mixed up with that court. Look what the gardens are like and tell me, so that I can do the opposite."

So Ferdinand went off with a friend whom his father considered reliable and only two servants. They must find coaches in France. They were bored by the flat drive to

Paris, but they behaved extremely well. They were taken to Versailles, but felt too hopelessly ill-dressed to be presented to the King amid the throngs of little marquises pirouetting on silken legs and the voluminous satins of the ladies who, enviously curtseying to one another, tried to catch even a single ray of the royal sunshine. But he liked to see the fountains rushing upward and was delighted when a sudden breeze sent the spray from the great jet of the Basin of Apollo spattering those fluttered ribbons.

Fluttering enough was done by Ferdinand's aunt at Dijon, where he arrived depressed because of the appalling poverty of the land following so soon after the insane extravagance of Versailles. He was shown the green velvet mask worn by the Visitation foundress, the Baronne Frémyot de Chantal, which she wore when riding, her book of Psalms propped up on her saddle. They also gave him a copy of a manuscript by the late Bishop of Geneva, "their true founder," they said with no little candor. He read it during the tedious journey to Paray and his companion began to think him rather dull.

He found his sister was quite happy at the Ursulines, but she said he must at once visit the new rector of the Jesuit church there; he would probably tell him something about the special graces given to a Visitation nun hard by. Ferdinand said, rather sulkily, that he knew nothing about special graces.

The young rector, Father La Colombière, began by irritating him, so correct was he, and yet so kind that Ferdinand felt himself rather an oaf. But soon the

Frenchman fascinated him. They went together to the Visitation convent and looked into a garden planted with nut trees and through a grille to an altar where, said the priest, Our Lord had granted those special graces. Ferdinand still held back.

"Possibly," said La Colombière, "you have had too little heart in you so far. You may not know how Jesus Christ speaks to hearts and wishes to speak through them to this frozen world. Your own land, if it but guessed it, is longing to come back to the Heart of Christ."

Ferdinand thought how little this good provincial knew of England, yet he could not detach his thought from him. The highly proper La Colombière had said that the whole world was clasped, as by a marriage ring, by the golden love of God. Ferdinand at once thought of the ancestral Medby ring and became so preoccupied that after a day or two his English companion left him in search of amusement, and Ferdinand returned home alone.

His mother, a direct-minded woman, saw at once that something had happened to him, and asked him if he had fallen in love.

"Perhaps," he said. "My father wouldn't understand and I don't myself. Well, at Paray-le-Monial I was introduced to the rector of a little college there, a man of the provincial nobility, on quite a small scale, of course, but very respectable and with a real dignity and simplicity and far more cultured than we are."

"I see you are learning some sense," said the countess.

"Or else plain lunacy," said he. "This rector followed one who was very vivacious but rather rustic. This one is much criticized; his very kindness, his polite mannerisms, seem dictated by rule. The provincials prefer something rougher. And then he has got mixed up with a Visitation nun who sees visions."

"Oh, my dear boy," cried his mother, "I cannot suppose that *you* are going to get mixed up with visions!"

"But I *am*," said he miserably. "And these visions have to do with the love of Christ for us and ours for Him. Well, I haven't had much heart for anything, except perhaps this house, and of course you, darling" — and he kissed her — "but as for — well — our Faith . . ."

"Yes, yes," she interrupted him, "but you are a red-headed, obstinate, contradictory son of your father, and if," said the uncompromising countess, "this lady has somehow altered you, she is indeed miraculous."

"Of course I've never seen her," he went on, "and the Paray people think her crazy and so do many of her Sisters, and her superiors treat her very severely."

"That's the best thing I've heard so far," said she. "If they had encouraged her, I should have thought them very rash women, if not frauds; and if she didn't have trouble at home, it wouldn't matter where else it came from."

She looked at him sideways, smiling, and he laughed and kissed her again, and said that he was a very bad lad, but she the very best of mothers.

That night he said he wished to ask his father a favor. "I want to beg you to put two or three heart-shaped windows into the new bit you're building. This isn't a fad! The Bishop of Geneva who founded my aunt's order gave the Hearts of Jesus and Mary to be their crest. Then there's been a Father John Eudes who preached a regular crusade on the subject, and when I came to Paray I found that a mass in honor of Our Lady's Heart was celebrated there before ever the nun — oh, I haven't told you about her yet — came there, and I think a mass in honor of Our Lord's Heart, too. And this isn't a new thing. St. Augustine and St. Gertrude — "

"Never heard of her," growled the earl.

"Well, after all, I had a great-aunt Gertrude."

"So you did," said the earl, somewhat mollified.

"And the Jesuits are trying to make her better known again. Do, Father, make those windows. I've never asked you for that sort of thing before!"

"You certainly haven't," said the earl. "But have it your own way. Tell the masons what to do. After all, we've had the devotion to the Five Wounds here for quite some time, and the wound in the Heart can be seen in many of the escutcheons of this house." And he discoursed on heraldry.

II

Soon after this Ferdinand, who had been appointed to some inferior position at Whitehall, wrote to his father that Father La Colombière had been named chaplain to the Duchess of York, Mary of Modena.

"You know the poor man," replied his father. "Get leave to go and fetch him. Meeting him at Dover would not be enough. You seem to say he is half an innocent;

the ambassadors will regard him as their proper prey. You will also strengthen your position, especially with the Duke of York. But be careful; the less you talk, or are talked about, the better."

Ferdinand thought he had better see the King first. He did not try to accost him in the long stone gallery where Charles had hung all the portraits he could rescue; it was too full of surging petitioners. When the King walked through it, he could do no more than scatter God bless you's to right and left, though such was his charm that they all felt quite satisfied. So Ferdinand went behind the tennis court and the cockpit into St. James's Park where fifteen years ago disbanded soldiers had dug a canal; among the trees the deer paraded, and antelopes and Arabian sheep among the flitting of fantastic fowls. Here Charles walked among the crowds, timing himself by his watch, and could just hear of Ferdinand's intended travel. He viewed it, unexpectedly, as important.

"Come," he said, "and watch me dine. I shall leave early; do you slip out, too. A gentleman will be at your gallery and escort you to my private room. The matter will concern my brother and even England."

The King dined, served by kneeling lords, while music — Byrd, the young Purcell, Lawes, but especially violins and light French melodies — made all Whitehall tuneful. From the gallery people could look down at the royal repast, the draped crimson and gold, the gigantic coat of arms behind the throne. Ferdinand preferred the gaunt austerity of Medby with its armor, hunting trophies, and dim tapestries. When the King rose, Ferdinand easily passed behind the staring crowds. The gentleman was waiting, bowed silently, and escorted him through a maze of passages to a small flight of stairs at the end of the stone gallery. The King appeared and said stiffly, "Come, sir," lest Ferdinand be thought a new favorite and create rumors.

"There are only two keys to this room," said the King, "my own, and my man has the other." Ferdinand gasped. Here were the King's Titians, his Raphaels, his Holbeins; his maps four yards long; his models of ships; his innumerable clocks all ticking anxiously.

Charles smiled wryly. "Of course they can't all keep time," he said. "Nothing does. Time itself, Master William might have said, is out of joint." Quick melancholy descended upon his mobile face. "I am forty-six," he said, "and many would like to have another Charles's head."

"God save Your Grace," said Ferdinand, sincerely shocked.

"I am glad," said the King, "that a Frenchman has been selected for my sister-in-law's chaplain. Everyone will be suspected of plots; but your man sounds harmless and Paris is the fashion now. It sends us our nice chairs and our toothbrushes. I have to get my gold sealing wax, even, through my sister. They tell me that as many as four thousand mirrors reach us from Paris in a single summer. Alas, we are still barbarians."

"But," said Ferdinand politely, "there is Chatelin's new cook house at Covent Garden. I have supped there and am still wondering how to pay my bill."

"Your friend," said Charles, "will hardly want to go

there! Send him out to get a morning mess of cream at the World's End, out beyond Knightsbridge. But bills, money! Our seamen —— But brother James must see to that. And meanwhile, those Dutchmen! To say nothing," he added ruefully, "of my duchesses!"

He talked a good deal about finance and then reverted to the priest. "If he is a man of tact, he can do a lot for me with King Louis. Oh, without knowing he is doing it, but he can tell Père de la Chaize how Catholic I am at heart. Did you know I was baptized in this house? The puritan Archbishop of Canterbury should have done it, but he had shot a keeper by mistake for a buck a day or two before, so Bishop Laud of London did it and prayed: 'Double his father's graces upon him, O Lord, if it be possible.' The last words were rather ambiguous, don't you think? But he certainly meant to baptize me, and did. Well, I don't expect Louis to lend me money *because* he is religious; but if he is in a good mood about me from the religious end, he might be in other ways, too."

Ferdinand said, "The Father is very simple, though I'm told he preaches brilliant sermons."

Charles laughed. "Only the other day," he said, "I wrote to Minette, my sister, that we have the same disease of sermons that she complains of, but that I hoped she had the same art as the rest of the family of sleeping most of the time, which is a great comfort to those who are bound to go to them."

Ferdinand risked saying that he had heard that one preacher called out to Lord Lauderdale that if he snored so loud he would wake the King.

Charles said it was quite true, and he had heard it, because that day he *was* awake. "I can't risk coming to hear your holy man," he said, "but he had better be presented in my little garden where I pick herbs for the cordials I brew. No Frenchman, not even a Jesuit, would refuse a tiny glass of liqueur. Then I can have him carried to Wren's rooms in Gresham College and meet him there and impress him with our serious studies — our calculating machine, our methods of weighing air and extinguishing fires, and a new gun to shoot one charge after another without trouble — very pretty. Still, he might disapprove of the gun! But would he be upset to see that a spider *can* walk out of a unicorn's horn? Anyhow, we meet once a week and would choose our experiments so as not to shock him."

So Ferdinand met the priest at Paris, and as they lumbered their way to the coast he tried to cheer him up. Father Claude changed into lay dress only just before reaching the ship. Happily for him the day was calm and it was still light when he sighted the chalk cliffs of Dover and recalled that he lived always, after all, in the Heart of Jesus. This was October 13, 1676.

"England," said Ferdinand, "is much rougher than France, I expect. The butchers are always fighting the weavers, and so on, and even in Oxford the professors come to blows. But all learned men are quarrelsome. You need not see any of that. You will always be at court."

"I must surely visit the poor," said Claude, "and Catholics who cannot come to court, and my fellow priests when I can find them."

"You must be careful. On certain days the populace goes mad and parades the streets with effigies of the Pope and cardinals and devils stuffed with live cats so that when the effigies are burned the cats may scream like hell. But you would be warned of such days."

"I must not be frightened," said the priest, "but I am totally unfit for this position. I was a simple country gentleman and know nothing of courts. At Charolles I founded a confraternity in which gentlemen and working-men shared as equals. I was very happy there. As for powerful men, Our Lord had nothing but contempt and death from them, so I mustn't mind if that befalls me, too."

"After all," said Ferdinand, "you will be chiefly at St. James's which is little more than a big farm. Whitehall is a regular town, and the populace presses on the King indoors and out."

"I cannot understand this world," said Father Claude. "Our King kneels before the crucifix and prostrates himself before the Blessed Sacrament when It passes him in a corridor on its way to a sick servant. Yet is not all his life a war for the glory of France? When kings attack, they try to ruin the surroundings of the enemy towns, to cut off all water, to destroy the crops. That is but natural. But when they retreat, they devastate their own country, they burn villages, they block up wells, they cut down trees so that the enemy shall have no supplies. Well, I just *translate* that and destroy the very outposts of the enemy who wants to occupy the citadel of my heart. What is self-love but the shadow of Satan's own self-worship?"

Ferdinand could not properly answer this, but was conscious that the priest was working a change in him and that he had in fact been changing ever since he had been at Paray.

They would have had to cross the Thames by London Bridge, for there was no other bridge for fear of the Wapping watermen, the King's nursery of seamen, whose trade would be hurt by bridges. No heads were on that bridge just then, but Ferdinand could point to the Tower which in this light looked as though built of powdered oystershells, like so many of the new churches springing up since the Fire. He decided that they should row the short distance upstream to St. James's, to spare the Father the sight of the squalid streets on his first day. Thus they passed the whole of Whitehall — half a mile of chapels, banqueting halls, Bedford House, York House, of every style but all most gracious to see. The river here was still limpid, for all to the west was countryside. They soon reached the palace, hidden in its trees. On taking his leave Ferdinand said:

"My father wished me to lend you this ring while you are here. It is said to have belonged to many saints, so you mustn't wear it even if they make you a bishop. It will bring you a blessing; but be sure to return it. It has been in our family for hundreds of years, and is holier gold than most that you will see."

Claude treated his small rooms as a cell. He liked making additional vows, and now vowed to give his salary to the poor and say nothing that could turn to his credit. King Charles, to whom he was duly presented, found him so irresponsive even about architecture or astronomy that he became irascible and invited the poor priest to join him at his daily tennis, or to come swimming with him and his brother James at Putney, and to visit the lunatics at Bedlam, a recognized entertainment on Sunday afternoons.

The priest saw he was being laughed at, smiled, and retained his dignity, whereupon Charles recovered his own. Nor did Claude make headway with the Duke of York who talked of nothing but the navy and Catholicism and was dourly annoyed when Claude begged him not to court disaster by favoring Catholics too much.

But he preached weekly before the duchess, pious and very lonely in her exile; she meditated daily for half an hour and received Communion more than once a week. Claude, then, preaching on November 11 about All Saints (for such was the English horror of papistry that they had refused to reform their calendar), said that he knew she had commanded him to mount the pulpit simply to sanctify his hearers.

"But," he continued, "however good be Your Royal Highness's intentions and however hard I try to be loyal to them, I should expect but scant fruit from my labors did I not know they would be supported by your example. Bad Christians may resist arguments that should convince them, but how should they resist the example of a princess who, in the flower of youth, of a rank in which most men imagine that all is permitted to them, of one who has all the graces of body and mind which usually inspire a love for this world, proclaims herself loudly on the side of piety and practices all holy exercises with such accuracy and fervor?"

Speaking, then, before so irreproachable a person, he would not fear to rebuke even the worst vices; nay, they would appear but the more shameful owing to the contrast provided by her virtues. Foreign listeners found this style simple and noble, sober and rather colorless, duly rhetorical yet apostolic.

He was, however, kept busy. He taught devotion to the Sacred Heart to the little duchess, who actually petitioned the Holy See for a feast in its honor. He created a veritable crusade of prayers in France, for England. He revised his first view, that England contained many Catholics but few of value; had they the religious facilities of France, their virtues, he thought, would soon flower into sanctity. But his sedentary life, his resolve to study, and the pall of London smoke began to affect his chest.

Sometimes he wrote to Ferdinand, now back at Medby, asking him to salute his venerable father. The earl had never been called this before, but felt it came well from a Frenchman. Claude said that the ring consoled him much, but he did not add that every time he touched it the bitterness melted from his soul; he felt he was offering sweet perfumes to the Lord; his love expanded till Love took the whole world to its heart.

He wrote more frequently to Sister Margaret Mary at Paray. She answered briefly and with insight. He kept saying that he tried to please men, so as to be "considered." She wrote: "Dear Father, none of that has its *house* in you." But she added that not even all persons consecrated to God would like his sermons, but that the grace of God would correspond exactly with the trust he placed in Him.

He began to feel much more free; he abdicated all sense of self-distrust, and asked, indeed, to be taught the perfect *forgetfulness* of self. But though he began to spit blood and there was talk of his return to France, the nun told him that he had still "some time" to remain in England. There were still troubles awaiting him.

There were indeed. The infamous Titus Oates proclaimed the Popish plot. The Pope was to seize the crown. . . . England should run red with Protestant blood. . . . The Jesuits, the Yorks, the Queen herself were implicated. "What," Lord Shaftesbury was asked, "do you propose to do about this plot that none but an idiot would believe in? How make the sane men, let alone Parliament, believe it?"

"The more absurd the better," answered the cynical statesman. "If we cannot make them swallow worse absurdities, we shall have no success with them."

England, in fact, became delirious; the prisons overflowed; judges were panic-stricken or corrupt and dared give only one verdict. And in November 1678 Claude was arrested in his rooms at St. James's. He was accused of advising apostates to return; of helping some anonymous London nuns and sending missionaries to America; of saying that the King was at heart a Catholic; of being in-

timate with Mr. Coleman, secretary to the Duchess of
York.

Here was a tragic irony. Charles himself had begged
his brother to dismiss this busybody; Claude had strongly
deprecated Coleman's fluttering around the French ambassador, Barillon, who was always intriguing with Louis
at Charles's expense; and in Coleman's papers was found
the draft of a letter to Père de la Chaize begging him to
get from Louis a sum of £29,000 "for a purpose useful
equally to France and to the Church." In the end, he
expiated all his imprudences by being executed.

As for Claude, he was imprisoned in the King's Bench
and remained there for three weeks, expecting to leave it
only for the scaffold. Life indeed seemed suddenly over.
In his solitude he saw once more the poplars round his
home at St. Symphorien and the old walnut furniture and
the tapestries of a house proper to the sober provincial
nobility of France. He recalled the college of La Trinité
at Lyons; the tall walls surrounding the playing yard
where the gray Rhone water poured round the roots of
the plane trees. Out of the studious years that followed
he remembered best the long retreat of his tertianship,
but above all Sister Margaret Mary and her astounding
declaration that he was to be the apostle of Christ's love
for men. Apparently it was over, that apostolate.

So it came as a shock to Claude to hear that Versailles
was furious at his arrest; that even the Jansenists, even
Calvinists, were laughing at the absurd charges laid
against him. He was, then, to be freed, and shipped back
to France. But his hemorrhages began again and his

departure was postponed for ten days, during which Ferdinand of Medby came to recover the ring.

"You must forgive me, Father," he said, "but we cannot do without it. Medby is not the same when it is not there. Some say it shines in the night; I have not seen that, but the room where we keep it always smells strangely sweet. And don't forget that I got my father to put in those heart-shaped windows *before* you came to St. James's! So you are not the first apostle of your dear devotion in this barbaric land!"

"You now look out at the world through the mind of Christ," said the priest, smiling. "Save for the promises of that divine Heart I could never have imagined that I would be the apostle of anything. You, evidently, are my Baptist, though it is now you who must increase and I diminish."

And indeed Claude Colombière died four years later, at Paray, aged forty-one, surrounded by the incense of Sister Margaret Mary's prayers.

16

FRENCH AND SPANISH FOUNTAINS

Lord Medby was talking seriously to Father Bernard Blake who had just returned from the English College at Valladolid.

"You will agree with me," he said — and who was poor Blake to argue? — "that my old sister Isabel must be brought back at once from Toledo. Even though we are not just now at war with Spain, we are sure to be soon, and anyone can see that France will be a hell brew. Nun or not, she must come back. England is bad enough, but she should be safe in Medby — it is half a monastery already. I am, in fact, sending my son Avondale to fetch her. And what I wish, sir, is that you who speak Spanish should accompany him. A couple of months won't make any difference to your work here."

"Charles III," said the priest, "makes a good king for Spain and things are prospering."

"He turned out the Jesuits," growled the earl.

"But that was due to the Minister Aranda," urged poor Blake, "who has no more power."

"But," said Lord Medby, "the Bourbons exist, and there are plenty of Jansenists left and people who flatter kings and treat them as gods on earth, and you know as well as I that it was really because the Jesuits never believed in the divine right of kings or absolute monarchs that they everywhere got turned out."

"Still," the priest insisted, "Charles is such a good king — his new roads, his canals, his glassworks, his zeal for studies! And so well living. Awakened every day at six, and then he admits his doctors and hears Mass. Then he sees his children, and again at eleven, and before supper! From eight to eleven he works at state papers in his study; and as for his supper, practically nothing: soup, veal, an egg, salad, and a glass of Canary wine. And his dogs eat half of that. Then his long prayers and the official disrobing."

"Very edifying," said the earl, "but off the point. Charles cannot live very long and Aranda was steeped in Voltairianism and will have infected many even in Spain. As you go through France you will hear more than you could in your college. Just beyond Tours you must visit my kinsman, the Marquis de Sablon de Maronnay de Festugières." The priest gasped. "Oh, you needn't remember all that; but I wish my son to meet his daughter Marie-Geneviève who is, I am told, an excellent and virtuous young person and not without charm. The journey is, in fact, arranged," said the earl placidly, "with your superiors." So they set out.

They went by way of Chartres. Avondale had never seen a *living* cathedral where Mass was openly and nat-

urally offered. The centuries weighed on him. He recalled that Alcuin had been actually at Medby, and also
here. And St. Bernard.

They went on to Tours, where everything was St. Martin. Then came Festugières, simple, not too huge, but with
a noble sweep of steps up to the great door. A dignified
personage, with servants eclipsed behind him, observed
that his lordship would doubtless wish to sponge his face
and execute a change of dress; he would then be escorted
to M. le Marquis. He and the priest were duly taken to a
vast room at the far end of which stood the marquis and
his wife. They advanced timorously over yards of ice-
smooth parquet and made their bows. When salutations
and inquiries had been accomplished, they were invited
into a small round parlor where wine and little cakes
were set out around a *bouquet de cérémonie*.

"Ah, Madame," exclaimed the priest, clasping his hands,
for he knew the rules, *"quel goût exquis: on dirait un véri-
table arc-en-ciel! Vous permettez?"* And he bent to sniff
the lovely blossoms pressed into the solidity of a cauli-
flower.

The marquise said that her daughter had arranged it,
and called: "Marie-Geneviève!" The girl had been waiting
for this. She drew aside the tapestry and made the due
curtseys. The refreshments were then dealt with.

"You are perhaps fatigued, my lord?" asked the marquis. "No? Then since M. l'Abbé will doubtless wish to
recite his breviary, this dear Marie-Geneviève will show
him to the chapel and take you to the gardens. We meet
at dinner."

Father Blake had finished his breviary but did not dare to say so. Avondale thought the marquis was losing no time and was faintly amused; but Marie-Geneviève certainly had charm.

Two wings were built out at the back of the house; the one on the left ended in the chapel; on the right was an orangery with tall, round-topped windows. Between lay the formal garden with a central fountain where dolphins spouted water around a *jet d'eau*. The chapel was white and gold with a few statues of chilly marble; the altar was baroque; but the lamp was lit before the tabernacle. Above this was an enormous picture of St. Louis in a blue mantle *semé* with fleurs de lys. The abbé was duly deposited, and Marie-Geneviève said: "There is really nothing to see but woods and the Royal Canal where Louis XIV made us build a Grotto of the Nymphs. But you know that sort of thing by heart, I expect. I will show you my private retreat where I sit when it is warm enough."

It was a wide circular lawn of most velvety grass entirely surrounded by a tall hedge of clipped box. In the middle was a round basin whence rose a slender jet of water, straight and pure in this golden windless evening.

"It is the hour," she said, "when Christ was taken down from the cross."

Avondale was too surprised to answer. He just thanked her for the privilege of seeing the place.

"You will return," she said.

They stayed there three days. The marquis admitted that Avondale was of a real distinction, serious, and of most untainted blood. The young Englishman accompanied Marie-Geneviève and her *gouvernante* on her errands of mercy, and the peasants for their part agreed that she was an angel from heaven. The *curé* said so, too.

In the candlelit evenings the marquis foreboded ill for France, to say nothing of the taxes. He remitted most of what he could collect, and was regarded with stupefaction by his neighbors. He deplored the recognition of the American republic only seven years ago. "Not that I think," he added, "that your own country, my lord, has behaved with dignity to its possessions, but I fear that the foundations of authority are perilously weakened. But by whom above all?" he cried with bitterness. "That scoundrel Arouet who calls himself Voltaire — *de* Voltaire, *je vous en prie* — and that Diderot with his absurd Encyclopedia that even Arouet mocks at, and the pitiable Rousseau. They all of them execrate one another. Be sure to visit us on your return."

The moment they turned the west tip of the Pyrenees Avondale gasped and said: "But this is a new world!"

"It is Spain," said Father Blake, "but it will be still more different. Alas, that we cannot visit Pampluna! Its ramparts! Remember, Spain is a *fortress*, spiritually, too. You could have seen the gun emplacements, the recoil rings, where St. Ignatius had his leg shattered. They still have bullfights in the streets there. And Compostella! It is a sin to be in Spain and not visit Santiago. Just to see that silver censer that six men can hardly lift, swinging from the roof . . . You hear," said the priest, off into fragrant memories, "its tiny creaking above the very chanting of the Office and the cries of the multitudes. But we must turn our backs to the Pyrenees and not look toward the Atlantic."

They came to Burgos. The cathedral, wedged into the hillside, lifted twin spires that looked like heavy lacework.

"I prefer Lichfield," said Avondale.

"Though this is Spain," said Father Blake, "the stonework decoration is German. But let us go in."

Avondale was already stunned by the tremendous gateway through which they entered the city. One severe archway; but above, what a superstructure! How massive, yet how rich with rows of saints! Yes, half a fortress, half a church. But on entering the cathedral he was thunderstruck by the towering golden reredos and its crucifix athwart a dazzling sun. And then the ironwork of the grilles: rigid upward lines flowering suddenly into grace and topped by — an angel? A saint? Threatening? Welcoming? He could not trouble to make sure.

He was engulfed by Spain. He saw the golden staircase sweeping into the cathedral from the hill. He could not but think: "We have nothing like this at Medby, nor shall have, nor could have." The windows at Medby were rich with coats of arms, but who would dare compare them with these vast escutcheons, triumphant over altars, upon tombs, above the gates?

The priest was longing for his friends at Valladolid, so thither they hastened. Here, too, was a cathedral — grand, granite, but Italianate? Avondale felt himself so

ignorant, uncultured. But he felt it was not altogether
Spain. He heard that Columbus had died there, brought
home from his third voyage in chains. He saw Cervantes's
house where, having lost a hand fighting and having been
refused a clerkship, he thereupon wrote *Don Quixote*.
Avondale hadn't read it; he knew nothing of the Cid.
Well, he clung, as it were, to the ring at Medby; he knew
he must learn, learn much — but never let go of the ring!

But at all costs they were to visit Avila. They reached
it in the evening. The plain was a field of gold. Avila rose
like a citadel of bronze and silver. It was protected by no
less than eighty-six towers, great round towers so close
together as to make the walls between them seem un-
necessary. Storks stood on the towers, sentinels immovable
though the Moors were no more there. One of these
towers was the very apse of the cathedral.

Next day the priest said they must go to the house of
St. Teresa. "It is now a church," he said, "but very simple.
So are her two convents, but you must see her guitar and
the little silver bells she made her nuns dance to."

Avondale found the heat tiring, and when the priest
decided to sleep after dinner, he went and sat down by a
fountain in a small empty square. Everything felt unreal
to him. After a while a friar came and sat down near him.
They saluted each other.

"My name is John," said the Englishman, and added,
"of Avondale."

"Mine is John, too," said the friar, "of the Cross."

Avondale said he was seeing too many things. "I can't
remember; I can't even think."

"It isn't necessary to think a lot. To see much, yes; to see many things, no."

"I am in the dark," continued Avondale. "I have begun to wonder if I had better be a monk."

"There is no harm," the friar said, "in being in the dark. But a monk? You? No, since you are to marry."

"But what makes you think that?" asked the astonished Englishman.

The friar seemed gently amused. "Go back," he said; "you are expected." And he stood up.

"Go with God," said Avondale.

"Rest in his love," said the other John, and went away.

Father Blake appeared. "I was looking for you everywhere," he said. "You don't know how easily one catches cold here."

"You don't happen to know who the friar was I was talking to?"

"You weren't talking to anyone; and I'm sure that no friar here talks English."

"Well, he was in brown with a white cloak."

"That sounds like a Carmelite, but I think they wear their cloak only in choir. My dear lord, you've been asleep." They looked at an old sundial; the hour was invisible, but the lettering said: *Ultima multis forsan tibi.* "It can't be *my* last hour," said John, "if I'm to marry."

"Oh, yes," said the priest, "you've been dreaming — of Festugières." He added the last to himself.

Avondale relished these austere Castilian uplands and tiny churches, rough as the rock outside, so golden within. But never had he met a land so alive yet so aware of death. Here you would not have thought that the hour had struck for Christ to be taken down from His cross. Everywhere haggard crucifixes black with blood. The Mother of God, pale under her ponderous crowns and pyramidal robes — almost more embroidery than velvet. Her Child, pale, too, peering out from His smothering dress. He began to understand this land of fierce sunlight and jagged black shadows. "A land without compromise," he thought. "*One* thing, and no mercy to the other."

But once they lost their way. A ragged shepherd, bowed on his long stick, saluted them. They asked their way, and he went three miles to show them. Avondale fumbled for a coin.

"Sir," said the man, "we poor people have nothing but favors to offer!" He bowed, kissed the priest's hand, and was lost almost at once in the sierra.

"In Italy," said the priest, "there is pride, too, but a different one. My brother told me once that he had spoken in polite terms to a beggar. His guide, who was very poor himself, said, 'You did right, sir, to use those forms of speech. The poor have nothing but respect to offer to one another; but, human nature having its weaknesses, respect requires the forms in order to maintain itself.' That was the Italian — an artist! Our shepherd was enselfed. But his self was Spain!"

They reached Toledo, white against a thundercloud.

"Ah!" cried Blake, "how else did El Greco see it? See the cathedral spires! See that tremendous Alcazar! *That* is Spain! Heaven and earth in one. You *must* see the 'Burial of Count Orgaz.' His shroud is his armor. But saints, just as real and solid as the nobles, put him in his tomb. And above, the Host of Heaven soars into light. Pain, death, holiness, Paradise — all that is *real* to the Spaniard even when he mocks. Enough! We go to the Cardinal for the mandate bidding your aunt to return."

While the final arrangements were being made, Avondale wandered through the craggy town round which the Tagus swirled. It had considered itself the center not only of Spain but of Europe itself. But its treasures, Avondale thought, must wait. "I have had not only much, but too many things."

His aunt, an alert and sympathetic lady, bought him a Toledo rapier that he wrapped round his finger like a ring. But no; he had had enough. He was ready to go homeward.

17

A.D. 1780–1830

THE FOUNTAINS DRIED

WHEN Lord Avondale and his aunt reached Festugières she became ill, and they remained there a whole month.

On the second evening the marquis said to John, "My dear lord, it is clear to you that we have much hoped that you would marry our daughter Marie-Geneviève, and your father would be glad to consolidate the alliance between our two families. Nor do I think that either of you is indifferent to the other. And I take so serious a view of the future that I would like you to carry her out of France as soon as possible. I, of course, must stay with my people, and I fear that my marquise will insist on staying, too. May God guard us! But my two young sons, whom you now know, would benefit much by the air of northern England, and your father has graciously agreed to accept them. He himself will arrive in some fifteen days, but your venerable mother — no! The journey would exhaust her. The marriage will take place in our village church and give joy to our people whom you have seen. God bless you. You will find Marie-Geneviève in her private parterre."

Half-angry, half-amused, but altogether happy, Avondale went and found Marie-Geneviève in her garden. She was wearing her usual white muslin with the demure fichu round her neck and a big straw hat. She was saying her Hours while the fountain sang gently to her; the top of its jet was gold in the evening sun. As he stepped through the boxwood hedge, he felt as awkward as a schoolboy; but he saw that her lips were tremulous with smiles, and he began to laugh and so did she, and all they could do was to go on laughing and kiss each other's hands. They proceeded to kneel before the marquis and marquise, and the marquis gave his blessing to their *fiançailles* and explained why the marriage must be hastened.

And it duly took place. After it Lord Medby remarked to his hosts on the evident good will and respectfulness of the peasants, their adoration of Marie-Geneviève, and their polite yet genial acceptance of his son. The marquis agreed, and said that not even the misery of parts of France would be what started an *émeute*.

"My reading," said he, "has convinced me that it is always a few men, theorists, unscrupulous or naïve, who are able to inflame passions if they know how to talk or to scribble popular flying sheets. France, not only Paris, is full of such men, and it is they who will be capable of driving my people mad. If the worst happens, my sons and daughter will be safe with you. If it does not, my boys will have profited by their stay in England, and my Marie-Geneviève will have a good husband. My wife is as content as she can be; her faith is deep, and so, please God, is mine. True, I should be sorry for my château if — if . . . " He broke off.

Lord Medby was deeply moved. The journey home was uneventful.

But things did go from worse to worse. Marie — the Geneviève was usually dropped in England, and even Marie became Mary — had to hear, in her exile's home, that Festugières had been burned down, that her father had been guillotined, and her mother had died in prison. Someone managed to let her know that in her parterre, now unkempt, the fountain jet still played a few poor inches. This seemed to her quite dreadful and she broke down altogether. But after a month of tears her essential heroism was conqueror, though at times she would go and cry in the little chapel-cave above the water that seemed to stream more strongly behind its rock face than before.

"*Oh, Saint-Esprit,*" she prayed, "pour down on my dear France!" The petals had fallen from the roses; the lilies had wilted and withered. "But O Mary, dew of souls, make our deserts to blossom once more!"

One day, to her surprise, she found a priest just beginning mass there. She could not hear his words; his long red chasuble drooped from his shoulders in a way new to her; but at his Communion she prayed: "O Lord, starve what is 'me' in me; nourish what is You! Blood of Christ, wash me white and intoxicate my insensitiveness!" She went home refreshed. That evening, after prayers, she noticed a dark portrait under the gallery and stopped short.

"That is our martyr," said Avondale, "Father Robert Medd. I told you about him when you came here first. But, well, you must have forgotten. We are very proud of him."

She tried to speak, but felt suffocated, and never mentioned that day in the cave even to her husband. Nor, when she went back there, did she again see that or any other priest saying Mass.

Meanwhile the Earl of Medby was growing old and, in the eyes of his neighbors, eccentric. He had always, of course, been shocked by the savagery of the revolution in France and considered that the people of England had been shocked not nearly enough. He remembered that the notorious Wilkes, an atheist, had been very rightly imprisoned on his return, in 1768, from his enthusiastic welcome overseas; but also that the mob had tried to pull down the jail in which he was, and only five years later he was chosen Lord Mayor of London and died in 1797 in his house in Grosvenor Square.

But the years became brief to the earl's aging memory, and it seemed only the other day that George III and Queen Charlotte had gone in terror of their lives and that a model guillotine had been put up in the Haymarket. All the same, what he had heard of taxation in France, when he went there for his son's marriage, caused him to be terrified of the mounting taxation in England, too. Bread, he remembered, had been 4d. a loaf in the country and now was 9½, and one-and-six in London, so no wonder that in England, too, the cry had been heard: "Give us bread!"

So he was one of the first to observe that hair powder was really made from wheat flour, and his own servants, to say nothing of the army and navy, had to use it. His chaplain, who had a mind for such things, calculated that 12,500 tons of flour were wasted thus each year upon people's heads, which meant nine and a half million loaves, which would have fed 150,000 persons, at any rate on bread. Therefore the earl gave orders that his household should cease to powder their hair and even left off his wig, so that the great families in the north thought he had turned revolutionary or gone mad — much the same thing. He did not care, but died loving his northland as much as his own Medby loved and venerated him, and convinced that the rest of England, by which he meant London, was sinking into an abyss not only of vice, but of vulgarity which he sometimes thought was worse.

John Avondale, now Lord Medby, had of course harbored his two young brothers-in-law till they were ready to be sent to a school in Twickenham kept by two French *abbés* who had fled during the Terror; John did not intend the boys to become English citizens and they themselves were determined to return to France as soon as they could. But, looking ahead, we can say that they remained in Twickenham, inherited the school, and made it into a very elegant academy for young English and French gentlemen alike. There was a whole colony of French *émigrés* in that neighborhood; the French, at least, wanted to be bilingual, even if few of the English, save the "quality," desired to learn French. However, manners were taught there, which was more than could be said for Eton or Harrow. In their old age the two brothers were able to return to France and buy back a fraction of Festugières where their families continued to live in a small way.

As for John and Marie-Geneviève, their oldest son, Peter, was born in 1787; then came a daughter, and then, in 1792, that appalling year for France, was born a son Cecil. A fourth child, a daughter, became a nun at Cluny. Their parents had lived through sufficiently tragic times not to wish to stir from their home, especially as John, always a serious man, became convinced that the quieter

Catholics remained the better. His son Peter grew up in much the same spirit and duly married a girl belonging to an old Catholic family. She made an admirable wife, knew all the Medby linen by heart, saw to the making of preserves, and had recipes for all sorts of things, such as the removal of corns. You melted a number of snails in the sun, made a deep incision in the corn, and rubbed the snails in. This proved an infallible cure.

However, initiative displayed itself in Cecil, the second son, who, impressed by the part of Medby that had become a hospital and sure that Peter would take no active interest in it, decided to become a doctor and went to complete his medical training in London. He saw the proper sights: the Tower in which many of his forebears had been imprisoned and where lions still roared; but he had no taste for the blowsy entertainments of Vauxhall, and heartily disliked seeing so many of the aristocracy laid out drunk on the pavement and incommoding pedestrians. Pleasantly enough, while visiting the Sablon uncles' school at Twickenham he met a Mademoiselle Ghislaine de Mirnay with whom he fell in love and whom he married in 1815. So that the French strain perpetuated itself in the history of the Medds.

Cecil Medd and his wife took a small but charming house at Richmond, sufficiently close to Twickenham to make visits agreeable but not too frequent. Since Ghislaine brought some lovely furniture as part of her dowry, most of her family being vehemently royalists, there was some difficulty in keeping the house harmonious, for one of her uncles was no less strong a Napoleonist and had given her two great gilt eagles which straddled and spread their wings in unexpected corners.

Cecil had brought some charming English furniture and a few hideous portraits from Medby, but he kept these in his own two rooms. But the surprise and delight of this eighteenth-century house was its oval dining room, where the table, too, was oval. This allowed Ghislaine to enable everyone to talk to everyone else, instead of being shut off from their *vis-à-vis* as in most English houses by a wall of silver tankards and massive flowers. But their entertainments were small; Catholics were still looked at askance, though Cecil, being a younger son and an Honorable, could not be quite ignored. Ghislaine, being French, was doubtless not respectable, especially as she was so lovely; but she had no difficulty in charming, and dispersing, the battalions of young men who fell desperately in love with her.

Cecil did not take his profession very seriously, though he paid his regulation visits in a small black carriage, and, with his wife, their more ceremonial calls in a bright yellow cabriolet with a large coat of arms on the panels. They went to Mass in the chapel built as long ago as 1793 (it would be hideously refashioned in 1824), but, strangely enough, Cecil never felt the spiritual world so near him as when he looked at an old picture of St. Luke he had brought from Medby. It seemed to change according as the light fell on it. The saint was holding a little casket in one hand, containing no doubt his simple medicines; the other was raised in blessing, and at times you could see a ring upon one finger. At other times this faded out, and a gold pendant was visible, hanging round his neck. But this again would vanish, leaving at least the old physician's kindly smile unaltered. Cecil felt he needed that blessing and that smile; he was in reality homesick for the north, the short turf, the heather, the rocks, and tinkling becks.

18

A.D. 1830–1877

A SHADOW UPON MEDBY

CECIL MEDD's nostalgia for Medby may have dwindled because of his wife's attitude toward the place. Ghislaine fully approved of its ancestral grandeur, but her French temperament made her feel tired in these enormous walls; she lost herself in the labyrinth of passages and kept falling up or down confusing little staircases, and found the vast canopy over her bed quite suffocating, and even in the smaller living rooms felt bound to sit upright. Even her mother-in-law, Marie-Geneviève, had developed a graciousness that Ghislaine felt rather uncalled for and she was glad to get back from her visits to her own light house where the garden sank so gracefully down to the placid Thames.

But Cecil found the very politeness of this view disturbing. He knew that even before his birth machinery was being developed and that in 1769 a steam engine was patented. Factory life was beginning to elbow home life out. It was with dismay that he saw, for the first time, from the Medby fells, a smudge of smoke on the horizon. He knew that towns, over the tilt of the world, were growing up, and towns needed food. His father, like his grandfather, would never have dreamed of enclosing common land and gaining profit from what might be made to grow there; but John certainly tried experiments in growing vegetables on land that none of his tenants used; and his own men sold these at a reasonable price to the host of desperately ill-paid workers in those towns. Moreover, he observed that London could not but expand, and he did not see that he could be wrong if he allowed his property outside of it to be gradually built with healthy villas from which, indeed, he was drawing an enormous revenue when he died.

None of this satisfied Cecil. He could give no shape to the shadows looming up, but he determined to take his own profession more seriously, and above all to make sure that his sons, too, should be able to earn an honorable living. So after long consideration he sent his eldest son Paul to Peter, now Lord Medby, to learn to be an agent, especially since Peter's only son was displaying no more interest in his home or in national affairs than his father was. Cecil, however, was determined that Paul should

· *151*

know personally also those new towns, and above all that new sort of population of whom a very few were immensely rich and the others in an ever-more-grinding poverty. As for his second son, Simon, he made a lawyer of him; his third son, Luke, born in 1819, he meant to have trained as a doctor and daily invoked the Beloved Physician for his welfare.

Unfortunately Luke developed a childish dislike for the picture of his Patron and would not look at it. He was taken a few times to Medby but was bored by the life there, and as he grew older he regarded it as unhygienic and talked a lot about economics, especially when the Reform Bill was passed in 1832. He said that this meant the end of the great landowners and he agreed with his father that a totally new race of men was springing up; and when the London-to-Birmingham Railway was opened in 1838 he proclaimed the fantastic theory that speed was going to alter the whole human outlook and the brain itself. Still, he could not quite extinguish in his soul its immemorial instincts, and he married a north-country girl of the Dacre clan, a Catholic, and she exercised a steadying influence upon him. They had two children, Clare and Charles, born in 1844.

These two children, then, were thought old enough to be taken to the opening of the Prince Consort's Great Exhibition in Hyde Park in 1851. Lord Medby held that the whole enterprise was pretentious and a speculation and firmly refused to come south for it. But Luke Medd thought that the children really ought to see it: it would be a historical event and a landmark of progress, and his uncle's influence obtained good places for all of them.

Certainly to the children, still young, Paxton's glassy house appeared enormous and the Queen so tiny that they could hardly find her at all. Victoria herself was overwhelmed. Even the Home Secretary was in tears. She told everyone that she had felt filled with emotion, more so than by any church service she had attended; and after seeing two acts of the *Huguenots* at Covent Garden she exclaimed that God was indeed our kind and merciful Father. This was Albert's Festival of Peace — all the industries of all the nations of the earth were united here; prosperity could but increase forever, and health, and wealth.

So in two or three years the Crimean War broke out and soon was followed by the Indian Mutiny. Luke found himself the guest of Miss Florence Nightingale, who told him in detail about the horrible conditions in which the ordinary soldier was left to fall literally into decay. While he felt a certain pride in her having not only accepted the presence of nuns in the Crimea but actually put herself into a convent for training, this in no way eclipsed the horror of her recital. It was reinforced by long letters from his brother Paul about the hideous conditions of much of the new northern midland towns. This engendered in him a cynical outlook and a real skepticism about the apparent prosperity of England; and when he began to hear among his confreres of the work of Darwin and the great book in preparation, the whole fabric of his world seemed to grow weak and doubtful.

The north-country Medds continued to feel that Catholics got on well enough among themselves. Catholic emancipation seemed to reinflame old passions rather than confer new privileges. Even Cecil had seen no point in the "restoration of the hierarchy." Hadn't the vicars apostolic been bishops? Well, what more did anyone want? As for the Established Church, they saw it as part of the state, but as a part in which they took no interest. They heard of the Tractarians, the Puseyites, the Ritualists, who were said to be introducing Italian customs into England. They heard, in 1845, that an important man among them, Newman, had actually become a Catholic and only hoped that he would now keep quiet: Catholics didn't need suggestions.

Meanwhile Charles, Luke's son, was growing up very unlike his parents. He was restive and impressionable — a throwback, his father thought, to his French grandmother, to say nothing of *her* mother. He was among the first of the generation of young boys who decided to be engine drivers. Then he resolved to run away to sea. Then he thought it would be best to be a soldier, especially in America, where, said he, all sorts of things were bound to happen. And run away he did, and was said to be living with a friend in London and leading as gay a life as he could on his meager allowance.

At last he wrote to his father:

I'm sorry, but it's better to say that I've broken out of the circle in which you brought me up. I could not honestly call myself a Roman Catholic or even a Christian — don't ask me why. It's just faded out. This is not be-

cause of books. I seldom read any. Nor because I am very badly behaved, anyway not worse than plenty of Catholics I know. But I simply can't be cramped and confined within the kind of ring fence of ideas that you — rather tepidly, you must confess — expect me to be loyal to. Do not ask me to worry about Medby; I hate the thought of it, and my uncles ought to have plenty of children to keep it going in its old dusty way. I don't intend to have any. There are quite enough Medds as it is. You know I am fond of you, but even fathers can't be dictators.

The shock to Luke was far greater than he had expected, though his silent but watchful wife had seen the crisis coming. She went on trusting, even when Charles somehow became a rather smart officer and married, apparently out of pure contradictoriness, yet another Frenchwoman, a Mademoiselle de Saint-Seds des Fenestrelles — than which what could be more traditional! But he overpersuaded her and they were married in a Protestant church. Their only son Rupert was born in December, 1877.

Meanwhile Luke had gone back to Medby and stayed some time. He had not realized his shock — he had never contemplated apostasy. He found Medby very shabby, extremely uncomfortable, but it had *lasted!* He saw, of course, that part of it was a hospital, part was a school; very few other big houses were used like that, and certainly none of them grew vegetables for the big towns they were content to deplore and avoid. But, traveling north, he had been unable to disregard a whole part of England that was turning black. Grotesque silhouettes

of winding wheels, smoking piles of slag, offended the
eye. From the towers of Medby he could now see not only
smoke but tall factory chimneys. Was *that* what was going
to last? If Medby didn't last, what could become of it?

He found himself slipping back into his ancestral atmosphere, though with a sort of wistfulness, as if it were
only half his own. He was pleased to find the little St.
Cuthbert's "Mark" in just the same place, but he reflected
that he hadn't read Mark or indeed any other evangelist.
He remembered how exciting it had been to paddle in
the Beck, but now nothing excited or thrilled him any
more — he neither liked nor disliked anything very much.

He climbed up into the old tower where children had
played. It was now empty, and the rafters were festooned
with cobwebs and bats flew about in it. He even sat for
hours in the great tribune overlooking the central chapel,
now the parish church, and was startled by the accumulation of reliquaries, vestments, medieval and baroque
statues that had piled themselves up there during whole
centuries. He suddenly resolved to ask for a selection of
these and to present them to the many unmoneyed Catholic churches that seemed to be springing up in England.
This act of faith somehow braced his will. He had always
felt there was something in Medby that he wanted to
revisit and now felt sure it was in his aunt's own oratory. He asked her permission to go there. He knelt down
before a very old reliquary and forthwith felt himself
gathered back into an embrace of which he had forgotten
the sweetness.

Nonetheless he knew he must say good-by to Medby

forever. The earl refused point-blank to allow Charles or his wife to come there, and Luke felt it would be tactless if he himself returned and would only widen the breach between himself and Charles. But Charles was killed in the Zulu war when his son was hardly two. Luke thought that his widow now at least would recover her faith and resume her Catholic practice; but she, too, was obstinate. She had worshiped her husband, and refused to be disloyal, as she felt it would be, to his memory. But she could not stop herself from saying a nightly Hail Mary for herself and her little son.

PART TWO

19

IN A LONDON SQUARE

Robert Brent and Rupert Medd lived exactly opposite
one another in a London square, and there seemed no
reason why they should ever meet. The square was destined to degenerate, but it was still secluded and self-
satisfied; each house lived its own life, and it did not
follow that anyone in the square knew anyone else.

Robert's Victorian childhood was compact of austerity
and little pleasures, fears, and affection, and lit by pictures in fairy tales and in the Gospels that were so unlike
the strange Old Testament read by his grandfather, in a
special voice, at daily morning prayers. His mother had
died in his infancy; his father was in India; he regarded
his grandfather as much the same as Abraham and super-
latively good — the evangelical doctrine that the human
heart was corrupt exceedingly seemed to be suspended
in favor of his own family. His grandmother, too, was very
good indeed, though, of course, slightly less so; she was,
moreover, consistently loving, and he could sit on her
knee and smell her delicious silks and laces and wonder

at her rings, and on Sundays she played hymns which made him cry, out of what his French nurse called *un cher attendrissement*.

There was also an eldest aunt, whose task as his guardian it was to see that he was always very good — at least as far as a little boy could be — and not catch cold. He said his prayers nightly beside her; he had to tell God just how he had been naughty during the day. The excuse that he "couldn't remember anything" was never accepted. "Think again, dear; you *must* have been." This enabled him, however, to ask God for what he wanted — tactfully, not too often. It was an early lesson in diplomacy, for that was what he was destined for. He was not allowed to ask anyone for anything during the day — he would be given what was good for him. There were other aunts and uncles who appeared at times and of whom he was very shy; their goodness was on a declining scale in proportion as they were further from his grandfather, but equally, of course, they were far, far more good than he.

All this was due to the Brents being in a state of reaction against their gambling Regency forebears who had practically ruined them, and their house was full of incongruous relics. The long dining room had curtains of black rep woven with red and yellow flowers; the black marble mantelpiece supported a marble clock and bronze figures of gentlemen struggling with stags or horses; the pictures showed rather surly ancestors with backgrounds of a curtain, a Corinthian column, and a thundercloud. Robert was still admitted here only for prayers and breakfast and tea on Sundays, when he was expected to answer questions but not ask any.

But in the drawing room above, though the curtains were still rep — red, with green and yellow flowers, upheld by silk ropes with enormous tassels — there were big looking glasses, delicate furniture — some of it too fragile to be sat upon — portraits of exquisite ladies and gentlemen with peach-bloom complexions and powdered hair, and cabinets full of mysterious Venetian glass, phials of amber scent, and above all a kaleidoscope. Ah, into what magical patterns those chips of colored glass would fall as he rotated it! But these were "Sunday toys"; nor did Robert come there save on Sunday evenings when his grandmother played those hymns, or when he was to be exhibited to visitors after "Their" tea.

His own small room was "between floors"; its fireplace was in a corner so that every angle of shadow was unexpected. China, little mirrors, old prints unwanted elsewhere, had gravitated thither and became "his." On the window looking out upon the grimy laurels and privets of the garden hung a stained-glass plaque showing a knight in armor riding out of some Nuremburg into the hills; and somehow the greens and blues and even grays had become half-golden, so that the world outside, too, must surely be flushed with gold, a mellow gold. In his nursery the curtains of his cot were yellow silk and the blinds were yellow, so that he always woke up into a sunlit day. But just as good were the times when he lay awake after some anxious little illness and the fire through the wire guard made criss-cross patterns on the ceiling and the lamp dreamed behind a great dark screen. The suffocations of nightmare were over; the pictures and wallpapers no more made grimaces at him; he no more needed to be *nursed* out of ache and bewilderment. It was a gentle, quiet world, seen through translucent gold.

Later, he was allowed to play in the square garden, provided he spoke to no child whose home, and no doubt goodness, had not been strictly vetted. Once, indeed, he overshot the mark. Some children whom he did not know asked him to join in hide-and-seek.

"Thank you," he answered politely, he was sure, but firmly. "I was sent out here to amuse myself and not to play with you."

Back home, he informed Them of this.

"Oh, darling," said They, "we didn't mean it quite like that."

"Well," he began to feel, "I don't suppose They *ever* understand."

One day, when he was staring, entranced by form and color, at the tulips and hyacinths, another boy, rather older than he, came and stood beside him but said nothing. They walked round the garden together till they came to the gate opposite Robert's house, but on the farther side. Robert saw a lady in black just behind it. She looked at him and smiled. She was so lovely that tears filled his eyes. The boy crossed the street with her and went straight toward a house; and immediately Robert saw the lady on the drawing-room balcony looking down at the boy. He wondered how she had got there so fast;

and she had put on a little white cap with a white veil hanging down behind it.

But his nurse took Robert home at once, to report, as always, to his aunt about his behavior.

"He has been *bien sage,* Mademoiselle," she said, unable to keep to English for long at a time, "save that at the end he was talking to a young boy we don't know."

"Oh, Mimi," cried Robert, "we didn't say a word. We just looked at the flowers till the lady in black came and took him home."

"But, Master Robert, *que dites-vous donc là?* True, the boy went away quietly into Number 17 where he lives, but all by himself!"

"But there *was* a lady — a wonderful lady! I think she was a princess."

"Robert, dear," said his aunt, "you mustn't imagine things. Who lives at Number 17, Nurse?"

"A Mrs. Medd, Mademoiselle; a widow, it appears, and French. She cannot be rich, though she keeps a butler — oh, quite elderly *et bien dans son cadre,*" she hastened to add. "It is said that she does her own kitchen work and a girl comes in to sew."

"Medd?" said Colonel Brent, who had just come in. "That might be a very good name. Perhaps she is in the Red Book."

She was indeed, though not a "close connection." Still, Robert was told he might play with the boy if they met again.

Robert soon saw him and, being a direct-minded child though shy, went up to him and said, "How do you do?

I may play with you if you like. My name is Robert Julian Brent."

"Mine," said the boy, "is Rupert Charles Jehan de Festugières de Mirnay Medd. I can't imagine what we could play at. Shall we look at the flowers again?"

Robert, as always, felt a lump in his throat at the sight of such colors, and couldn't speak.

"I like them," Rupert said, "because they are so delicate and upright and so strong. They are all lords and ladies from the court. But of course they will all be guillotined."

Robert hadn't heard that word before, but said, "What I like is to look down a long street of nothing but hard, flat houses except in *one* place where there's an almond tree in flower, or lilac, or laburnum, *full* of sunlight — like a pink or golden fire, only better."

"Flowers are *persons*," said Rupert. "The only thing that matters is *persons*. *Maman* says so, too. Houses can be persons, but bad persons, or dead persons with something else inside them hating you and waiting to pounce. They have windows without eyelids, like snakes."

He had turned quite white. Then he said in a perfectly ordinary voice that his mother was going to call on Robert's family, or leave cards or whatever people did, and invite Robert to tea. "But," he added, "there's nothing wicked in *our* house — at least not yet; because *I* might become very wicked, mightn't I? *You* couldn't."

Robert was rather bewildered by all this, but the social ritual was duly performed. Mrs. Medd fascinated the whole Brent family and was quite evidently *not* a Roman

Catholic though French, and though not attending their own church of St. Matthew which they considered sound. She enchantingly eluded anything that might imply any interest in where she *did* go, and was gracefully touched by their having Robert taught French so early. He had been produced after tea and without being prompted had said *Bonjour-bonsoir, Madame,* quite cleverly.

So one day Robert went off to tea. Rupert himself opened the door. They went straight into the dining room and Robert was surprised how few things it had in it. The walls were paneled with light wood, and he had just time to see that the curtains were of a dull rose-pink and that there was a drawing of some castle over the mantelpiece when Mrs. Medd came in. She wore a dress of filmy black and the small white cap, pointed in front, and a white veil that fell in mist round her shoulders. Robert instantly remembered the lady on the balcony and then the lady by the gate who had been all in black. They *couldn't* be the same! But Mrs. Medd gave him no time to feel puzzled or awkward when she sent Rupert off to fetch the cakes.

"You must be sure to like them," she said. "I cooked them all myself."

Robert was slightly shocked. Surely a real cook should have done that!

Mrs. Medd instantly saw what he was thinking and laughed deliciously. "And I have put out my prettiest china for you," she said.

Robert said that all the room was *very* pretty. Mrs. Medd said she feared she had made it rather too French for London. "But I *am* French," she said, perhaps a little sadly.

"And is that castle in France?" Robert asked, looking at a painting.

She hesitated, and then said that behind him were portraits of her great-grandparents. They were pastels, and Robert was proud to say that they, too, had some like that upstairs. Just then Rupert arrived with a trayful of marvelous pastries and Robert forgot the castle.

After tea Robert found himself telling Mrs. Medd that he liked French fairy tales much better than English ones. He was never allowed to talk English between breakfast and his dinner. She asked him to tell her one. He said he liked the one where the Bad Fairy who had been so grand turned into a toad and her castle — "*le château s'écrrrroula dans un fracas épouvantable.*"

"I don't like that one," she said, almost sharply.

He began to tell her about the poor organist who had been forgiven by a kind bishop: "*Insensiblement, une musique vague se répandit par la cathédrale . . .*"

"*Assez!*" she said, standing up.

Rupert looked at her quickly and said he wanted to show Robert his model theater.

"*Petit malheureux,*" she said, herself again, and pulling his ear gently, "*il n'a déjà que trop le goût du théâtre! Et toi qui es tellement nerveux!*"

On the way up they looked in at the drawing room. Here the panels were filled with a soft brocade of a faded blue and the curtains also were gray blue. "Alas, I spent too much over my *boiseries,*" she said ruefully. "But the silks, they belonged to — well, *enfin*, they came with me."

She left Rupert to take Robert to the top of the house. The theater was indeed superb, much grander than Robert's little one. Rupert drew the blinds down and lit some candles, so that when the stage curtain went up you looked into a cavern of light; by an ingenious system of gauzes Rupert had made the effect of mists, and yes there at the back the castle of the picture floated in a pearly dawn. Robert could not but ask where it was.

"In the north," said Rupert curtly. "It belonged to my father's family. He's dead, you know."

The back scene was really a transparency, so by gradually shifting the candles behind it and setting them to shine through a screen of blood-red gelatine the castle was now made to stand out, a black, threatening silhouette against an angry sunset.

"Someone called it 'The Everlasting House,'" said Rupert, "but it can't be. It *can't* be, even though it's older than the whole of English history." And he rearranged the lights and the colorings so that the castle now shimmered ghostlike in green skies above sorrowful gray fields. He jumped up and put the candles out. "One puff," he said, "and it all disappears."

Halfway downstairs they passed a curtained door. Robert's curiosity overcame his manners and he asked what was behind it. "It is *Maman's* special room," Rupert said. "I've never been in it. Perhaps she keeps relics there and doesn't want me to remember all that *she* remembers."

Mrs. Medd met them and came to the top of the last flight. "To our next happy tea!" she said, and turned to go upstairs. But when Robert looked back from the street to wave good-by again, there she was, at the door, waiting for Rupert to come in, only now she had covered her head with a long black veil.

20

A.D. 1886–1888

SUNLIGHT AND STONE IN ITALY

WHEN Robert was seven, the Brents decided that the little boy could not survive in a town; they gave up their London house so that he might always live in the country. But before this an immense adventure had taken place.

The entire family emigrated to Italy, as an interlude between the emigration from London to the country. This was exciting enough, but also Robert's cousin Marcella Orwylstree was to be there, and from the age of four he had resolved to marry her. Her mother Caroline was his father's sister, and it was at Orwylstree Hall his own mother had died, only a year after her marriage; it was understood that she must never be alluded to — it would cause pain. Yet Robert had an elusive but vivid impression of her, in white, dancing among the daisies and clover and sorrel of the park, or again as just having disappeared into the rose garden amid heavy petals of crimson and copper-gold and cream.

But while it was very nice to have his cousin Marcella as companion — they were staying at Sorrento — when they daily went up into the hills and ate bread and chocolate while their nurses chattered, Robert was entranced to find violets and above all periwinkles growing wild. He rather perfunctorily made a necklace of them for Marcella, but she was not interested, and he didn't mind much. He was too absorbed in the different colors of the flowers and, above all, of the sea. He could not believe that he really saw such a blue. And while in London he had always had to *pretend* that there were mysteries — secret doors in houses, secrets in families — here *was* mystery: Vesuvius. He would have but to climb that cone to look into a seething world of lava, so much more convincing than the hell pictured in his Bible. He insisted, first, on lying flat on his face among the violets and ghostly periwinkles and then turning suddenly round to be confronted by the heaven-blue sea and the majestic mountain.

The day before they left, running home to the hotel he fell down by the statue of St. Peter seated close to the gate and cut his knee, so that he was in pain all the way to Rome and became pessimistic, especially as he had been brought up to believe that "little gentlemen never cry," so he had not that relief. He felt it was a good thing he had not looked down Vesuvius; probably he would have seen nothing: dreams never came true. Fairy tales had taught him to look for golden hair and deep blue eyes in his young princesses; but no, hair was never more than yellow; the blue was always greenish or grayish; even Marcella hadn't liked all the things he liked. He never told anyone about these secret hopes and griefs, certainly not Rupert, who would either not listen or would smile in a way that made him feel uncomfortable.

But Rome overwhelmed him. It was quite different from Italy. He had felt at home there over Sorrento; more at home, by far, than anywhere so far. When he thought this over, in later years, he saw that his impression consisted of dazzle: dazzling sunlight, dazzling tawny stone, and fountains. The city was pleased to see him because, along with the iron-hard stone, it provided him with a fountain round every unexpected corner: the tall pure jet of the Tritone; torrential outpourings like Trevi or San Paolo; gurgling, friendly little fountains on the top of hills among dark metallic trees. Of course the two sheaves of water rushing up before St. Peter's struck his imagination uniquely, just because everything else there was so immobile. It was such an enormous area of stone that pillar seemed clasped behind pillar, and the two sheaves of water rushing up, and then sending slow veils of mist drifting across the great piazza, were as living their own life, while the stone could, at best, only stay where it was.

He remembered that his grandfather looked at the Vatican, shook his head gravely, and said that there would certainly be no more popes when this one died. He did not know what the Pope was; but that did not matter.

When he went inside St. Peter's and under the cupola in the glory of the window of the Holy Ghost, it was like being in heaven, but not the heaven of the books — *his* heaven, his special heaven, built specially for him. And whenever he went outside it his eyes and then his memory went traveling back toward the Dome.

He said nothing about this, for he had neither the ideas nor the words for it, though he chattered freely about the fountains. So his people were surprised when his nurse, on their return, remarked, "Master Robert behaved very well during our little voyage, Mademoiselle; but, *chose bizarre,* it was impossible to keep him out of the churches."

"The *churches?*"

"Oh, directly he would see one of those leather curtains over the door he would cry, '*Mimi, Mimi, Mimi, faut y entrer!*' And he would *pull* me in."

Robert was sent for. "Of course, darling," said his aunt, "it didn't matter *so much* your going into those churches *abroad;* but your father wouldn't like your going into Roman Catholic churches here, even out of curiosity. Thank God, we have the open Bible, and we know *Who it is* who can forgive us our sins; we won't be forgiven because we light candles and bow down and scrape before images like the poor Romanists. Perhaps someday you will be called upon to help them to see the error of their ways, because there *are* some of them, even in England."

When Robert did not know what people were talking about, but only that they were talking "for his good," he sulked. And anyhow it was never any use trying to explain things to grown-up people — well, except Mrs. Medd, and even then you didn't have to explain, because she knew at once what you were meaning. So he didn't say that his nurse had taken him into two Roman Catholic churches even in London, when they had got caught in the rain. One had little windows of red glass all round, high up; the other was an enormous church and there certainly was a statue in it, of Jesus Christ, he supposed, because it seemed alive and smiled at him, almost as if it were amused; but Robert told himself to put away that thought, because you oughtn't to be amused about anything religious, and even a Roman Catholic church must be religious somehow or other, he considered.

He went to say good-by to Mrs. Medd before leaving for the country. She had said that this would be exciting for him. He answered rather priggishly that it would be not nearly so exciting as his visit to Italy. Then he found himself relating all sorts of details about Naples and Sorrento, about flowers and fountains, and how he had tumbled down before the statue and had cut his knee and *hadn't cried.*

"So you fell down before St. Peter," she said, smiling rather wryly, "and it hurt a lot, but you didn't cry! I wonder what will become of you!"

"My father wants me to go into the diplomatic service," he said. "It means that you become an ambassador, I think."

"That would be very grand," she remarked, "but it wasn't quite what I meant."

Robert was not used to being puzzled by Mrs. Medd

and got up to go home. But he made her promise to come and see them in the country.

Rupert walked with him round the square. "You stuck a knife into my mother," he said, "talking about those churches."

"What *do* you mean?" asked Robert.

"Of course," said Rupert, "she used to be a Catholic herself. I think she really is one still inside. She gave it all up because my father made her. My father gave it up himself, and that is why we are never asked to Medby. All the Medds are Catholics, and so they won't have anything to do with us."

"I don't think that's fair," Robert said. "Anyhow, now your father's dead, she can become one again if she wants to."

"Oh, she never would," Rupert said emphatically. "She is still married to him in her mind. He has put a spell on her. And anyhow *I* would stop her; I'm not going to have anyone saying that she turned Catholic again to sneak back into Medby that way, or to get *me* there. Not that I'd ever be likely to go there much. It was my great-grandfather, ages ago, who came south."

Robert, who had not understood much of this, said almost tearfully, "I suppose it's because your mother's French that you're so much cleverer than me."

Rupert thought it over, and said that it was probably true. "I never heard," he remarked dispassionately, "that the Medds were so very clever. Probably they've lasted so long because they've never allowed themselves to think. But don't you worry. I shall be far unhappier than you."

Mrs. Medd came to tea next day at the Brents' to make her own good-bys. "It will be sad for my young man to lose Robert," she said, "but after the summer he's going to Hutton Grove and I think you said that Robert was to go there, too."

Mrs. Brent agreed, but added that of course Robert would be waiting a year. He was much too small for a big preparatory school like that.

"We think," she said, "that he ought to go to a small school first, to make the change easier. He's a loving little boy, and we don't want him to feel too lost. May God keep him safe." She then said that they hoped to find something near Chislehurst where they had taken a house for a year at least. She hoped Mrs. Medd would come and spend the day with them and bring Rupert; it was lovely, unspoiled country though so near London.

And Mrs. Medd and Rupert did come when the summer was half over. After luncheon Robert took them for a walk and tried to make them catch up with his ecstatic delight in the little blue and copper butterflies, the silver-birch trees, the bracken which had so new a scent under the strong sunlight. But all the time he was guiding them toward his great "surprise," which was nothing less than the chapel where the Prince Imperial was buried. The Empress Eugénie had a house not far off. He thought Mrs. Medd would like it because it was French.

When she saw what the chapel was, she stopped short and her heart turned over. At first she could not speak, but Robert was tugging at her hand, and she could never have had the heart to disappoint him. She went in. Rupert, very angry, remained in the porch. Mrs. Medd forgot Robert and also the Prince Imperial, and walked forward as if she were being pulled, and then knelt down abruptly. Robert noticed that, a little way behind her, melting into the shadows, was another lady, also in black. No, it was not the Empress, as he thought at first. Robert knelt down, too, though he didn't know what to say. He turned to beckon Rupert in, but he scowled and turned his back. Then Mrs. Medd, white and shaking as if she were cold, was coming toward the door. She told her son to run on ahead; she wanted to speak to Robert.

"Are you angry with me?" asked Robert anxiously.

She took his hot little hand. "Has Rupert been talking to you?" she said. He turned red. "I see he has. He had no right to; but even if he hadn't, you'd have taken me to that chapel. So much, so much that I'd turned my back on! You've been in Catholic churches before. Do they seem very odd to you?"

Robert thought of the great, bare, fragrant Italian churches. He said, "I don't think I noticed anything much. They smell very nice and our English ones always smell horrid. And there were little lamps and candles. There's one special lamp — I don't know why it's special. But I felt at home there; I did really; it seemed so — *vulgar* going back to the hotel."

She smiled. "Don't let Rupert worry you," she said. "He's years and years older than you, really. I understand you much better than I do him. I'm *frightened* for him."

"Oh, *no,*" said Robert without thinking. "I'm sure the lady who took him across the street will take care of him.

Why! I believe it was the very one who was praying behind you in the chapel."

"What do you mean?" she said sharply. "There was no
one there but you and me." This time she did seem angry,
but she called to Rupert and they walked home to tea.
She was charming and gay and fascinated everyone as
usual, but when she left, they said, "How *very* French
she is! It's probably a good thing that Robert won't be
seeing very much of that boy. He's very old for his age,
and he certainly gets a lot of his expressions from his
mother. Well, no one could expect him to be quite English, poor boy."

The visit had been very different from what Robert
had looked forward to.

21

A.D. 1890–1892

AT ORWYLSTREE

AFTER the rather unfortunate episode at Chislehurst Robert saw very little of Rupert or Mrs. Medd, for in London
there might be parties in the pantomime season, and in

the country Robert's first experience of school life did nothing to increase his friendship with Rupert. He collected butterflies, birds' eggs, and stamps; read Hans Andersen, Grimm, and Harrison Ainsworth; developed a wholesome interest in ghosts, scaffolds, axes, and headless ladies; and drew gibbets with rotting corpses hanging from them over pestilential marshes; learned a few inaccurate immoralities and nothing else whatsoever.

In 1888 he went to his preparatory school at Hutton Grove near Richmond Park, where Rupert had already been for a year. The estate had belonged to distant forebears of his, so he felt a proprietary interest in it though the house was hardly older than 1750 and had been sold two generations ago for a school. But it was rather like Orwylstree Hall, gray, dignified, with tall windows some panes of which were a watery purple, and of course it had been much added to, till the original house was only the stem of a T.

The headmaster, Dr. Merton, was a clergyman who was never seen by smaller boys save at prayers (he was Low Church but discreetly so), or when boys periodically took their exercises to him to have mistakes marked and to be warned against conceit if he could find no occasion for rebuke. He gnawed his gray mustache while reading the exercises, grunting in a noncommittal way at intervals so that the wilting child before him knew not whether blame or grudging praise awaited him.

The study where this took place was adorned with engravings of the Acropolis of Athens, the Colosseum, and the Arch of Constantine, and busts of the more respectable Roman emperors, and a large, imperturbable photograph of Queen Victoria, presented by Her Majesty when some years ago she had visited the school: this sufficed to quell the most self-opinionated parent.

Dr. Merton's wife was seen but seldom at concerts and the like into which she sailed like a galleon attired in deep blue or green satins. She had two daughters: one was considered, without the slightest reason, to be rather fast; true, she went to the Royal Academy and took Robert there; her elder sister was shy but pious, and built a chapel, and put Robert into the choir where he wore a surplice — a different form of rapidity at that time, and not unsuspected of a leaning toward Rome. But Robert took not the slightest interest in church services except when they sang his favorite hymns.

Robert had not known what a gulf exists between a new boy and one a year older than he. He was hurt by a definite standoffishness in Rupert, but soon perceived that Rupert was unpopular. He did not disguise his distaste for ordinary games; he was discovered planning new "effects" for his theater and this was considered very girlish, though his complete detachment from public opinion and his occasionally very sharp tongue kept critics at a distance. Of course in this polite large school of some 120 boys there was no bullying, but a boy without a personal way of life could be very lonely. On the other hand, Rupert revealed himself as a marvelous actor, and could be both serious and extremely amusing. In a way, however, this isolated him still more; for, the boys argued, if he's got all that inside him, why doesn't he play the fool more? Why doesn't he get into any rows? No, Rupert was an alien among them; though when his mother came down for a garden party she was clearly so far the most elegant — all in black, but a filmy, lacy black — that her loveliness went to everybody's head, and for a time Rupert's stock rose, and also Robert's, because it was common property that Brent and Medd knew each other at home. . . .

For rather more than a year Robert plodded quietly at his work, and then both his imagination and his intelligence began to wake up and he always found himself first or second in his form and on what was called the "honors list." Rupert, on his part, began to feel the need of companionship, and since he could be brilliant when he chose, he got on the honors list, too. This meant that they were allowed to go round the grounds together. These were large. Immediately after the house came the headmaster's garden, with velvety lawns, cedar trees, and peacocks. To the right and beyond stretched playing fields, but still beyond and around these were the "grounds" properly so-called. These were quite densely wooded, and Rupert suggested that they should make secret lairs among the bushes from which they could watch other boys passing by and unaware of them.

Both he and Robert would have been horrified at the idea of eavesdropping on a conversation; but probably Rupert enjoyed hugging his private life to himself — no one else should know so much as that he was there! Robert, as so often, reached almost the same point by the opposite road. Once, at his little school near Chislehurst, he had been playing at hide-and-seek in a thick hazelwood copse. A boy called Young had called out, "Where are you?" Robert felt with a really violent shock that there was a "someone" hidden there: an "I" as real as he was an "I." He obscurely but very really felt that Young was the middle of his personal world and looking out at it through his own eyes. Rupert, in short, was never in any doubt about his being *he*. Robert began to realize that others were not just names attached to shapes parading before him, but selves, as truly as he was. He never needed much more philosophy than that!

One day Rupert announced that he was going to learn ancient Egyptian. "I really must know something," he said, "that my mother doesn't!" Robert thought he would like to learn it, too, because though he could now speak French and German he did not know Italian, and his aunts took refuge in it when they wanted to say something that he shouldn't understand. But he usually guessed. The boys therefore collected grammars, illustrated history books, and even a scarab or two, and in the holidays visited the British Museum together and looked at monuments and deciphered obelisks. Rupert took this very seriously, Robert more romantically. He could feel himself actually *in* the great temple colonnades; he drew picture after picture of the Sphinx; animal-headed gods stalked round his pillow and spectral bats with transparent wings flitted and flapped through his dreams.

On one of their London expeditions Rupert announced that they were going to make an escapade. "My aged kinsman, Medby," said he, "would have a fit if he knew;

but he has three sons, and one of them, my uncle Odo as I call him, thinks that this everlasting feud is silly and says I can always look in at their London house and have lunch or tea there if I want to. So that is what we'll do today. Museum now; then Medd House for lunch; and then you go back to Chislehurst."

"But Rupert," said Robert, rather alarmed, "if Lord Medby would object so much, d'you think we *ought?*"

"Oh, Robert," Rupert cried, "do *not* be so bourgeois! 'Ought, ought, ought!' If Uncle Odo says we can go, that's enough. Anyhow, I've arranged it all with Mrs. Blake. That's the housekeeper who's left in charge when the house is empty."

So they went to the austere house overlooking the Green Park. It had a well hall paved with black-and-white marble and going right up to a skylight. At the back was a superb staircase which divided after a short flight and swept up to the first gallery surrounding the hall. There were four of these galleries, and as you looked down from the top one the floor seemed fathoms deep below you. At the back, where the staircase parted, was the huge Medby scutcheon with all its quarterings. Otherwise, you saw nothing but ancestral portraits and, higher up, vast religious canvases too dark to be deciphered. All the furniture except in the little room where Mrs. Blake, who worshiped Rupert, gave them lunch, was swathed in dust sheets.

Inspired by the first glass of wine he'd ever drunk — white and dry — he liked it, which pleased Rupert who said that wine, after all, was part of civilization — Robert had a happy thought. "At Christmas," he said, "my Orwylstree cousins will ask me to Orwylstree Hall; they have theatricals for the village. Now *you* are marvelous at acting. I shall ask them to invite you, too."

"I'm not sure about deserting *maman*," Rupert said, "but Christmas is pretty grim anyway, and she has friends — she may like to be rid of me for once."

In due course Robert was invited and told to bring Rupert with him. But during the autumn he had a worse "feverish cold," as they called it, than usual, and was kept in bed in a special room. He was rather lightheaded; the fire flickered on the ceiling, and he thought he was back in his nursery. Then, on and off, he saw a lady sitting beside him, and he cried, "Oh, Mrs. Medd, how good of you! How kind of you!" The lady laughed gently and stroked his forehead, and his dreams quieted down.

When he got better, Rupert was allowed to come to see him. He brought him books, and made happy choices. One was Rider Haggard's *Cleopatra*, which gave him easy doses of Egyptian mysteries; another was *The Last Days of Pompei*, because that, too, mentioned Isis and would revive memories of Naples and Vesuvius; a third was *The Ingoldsby Legends*, which had a much greater effect than Rupert could have dreamed of. First, it encouraged the interest in heraldry which the great Medby coat of arms had lit up in Robert. He borrowed books from the headmaster and traced as much of the history of that great clan as he could, and was overwhelmed by the vision of its continuity. But he was still young enough to derive pleasurable qualms from the more macabre of the

Legends, especially the story of the murdered young Hamilton Tighe, after which each guilty conspirator "sees a man sitting there with his head on his knees. . . ." This would have sent his temperature up again had not the legend contained the lines: "Oh, the taper shall burn and the bell shall toll — And mass shall be said for my stepson's soul. . . . *Orate pro anima Hamilton Tighe!*"

Robert could not understand this, yet felt that he ought to; he seemed to be back in the scented air of Italian churches where tapers twinkled; he thought that perhaps souls were really flitting about him, real souls, not the painted Egyptian ones. He actually sat up in bed one night and said "God bless you" to any souls that might be within hearing; they flitted closer, but not in the least alarmingly. He lit his candle and then put it out at once lest its glimmer should be noticed, but he hoped it had shone into — *not* Amenti, the "Forgotten Land" of the Egyptians, but — but where? He didn't know, but he wasn't going to forget.

The Christmas holidays arrived. The two boys went off to Malton, the nearest station for Orwylstree. Robert was nervous; even the metal footwarmers could not take the chill off the railway carriage. He was afraid Rupert might not be approved of, or that everyone had forgotten to meet them. But there on the platform, protected by a tall footman, was his cousin Marcella, entirely self-possessed and very elegant in furs. Rupert was impressed and began to be on his best behavior. The brougham smelt pleasantly of leather and rugs; the horses clip-clopped rapidly along frozen roads, reached Orwylstree village, turned into the dark park, and drew up at the house.

They entered a semicircular hall, flagged with bleak stones, with nothing in it but coats and sticks and chairs that no one sat on. They passed here, too, through a well hall, and the staircase, climbing up to a gallery, was not without its dignity. But from the hall they were shown into a long library, tawny gold with the backs of unread books and vast leather armchairs. There were a lot of people there. The boys were tired and glad not to be expected to talk but to eat plenty of crumpets. Then they went upstairs to see their room; the house party was large and they had to share one. But it had a cheerful fire and was gay with chintz. They had supper early with Marcella, and found that when their elders came in from dinner they were expected to say good night and go to bed. Robert knelt to say his prayers; Rupert did not, but made no comment.

Next day they explored the house. Robert looked into the room where his mother had died; she had asked to see her baby, had sat up to welcome it; it had been too much for her and she fell back dead.

"You," said Rupert, guarding against emotion, "have no mother and I have no father. If people acted sensibly — they never do — your father would marry my mother; but I'm rather glad it certainly won't happen."

They spent the rest of the days before Christmas rehearsing intensively in the long potpourri-scented drawing room. Christmas Day arrived; there were presents; everyone drove to church.

"I," said Rupert to Robert, "shall do exactly what you

do. It would show great lack of *savoir-vivre* if I did not come."

So Robert sang the hymns louder than usual, and observed that there were two tall candles on the Communion table. There were none at Hutton Grove. He wondered if these were tapers that ever burned. . . .

Next day came the pantomime. *Cinderella* was acted for the first time in the village hall. All went satisfactorily. The hall was suffocating; the curtain seldom rose or fell without sticking; essential "properties" were missing till the last moment; nobody remembered his part except Rupert, who remembered everyone else's, too, and kept saving the situation. In fact, incredibly elegant as the prince's squire, he somehow stole the stage, was regarded with contemptuous jealousy by the men, and assured by the ladies that he must certainly come again next year.

The only incident was the visit of a cousin old enough to be called "aunt," a Mrs. Henry Orwylstree, a widow, dressed almost as exquisitely as Mrs. Medd, though she was so much older.

"*Quelle élégance!*" exclaimed Rupert under his breath.

But later that evening Marcella said to Robert, "Perhaps I ought to tell you: your aunt Anne has become a Roman Catholic. She waited till her husband died. We don't think it was very fair of her. But of course Romanists think differently about truthfulness."

"At least," said Rupert, "she doesn't disguise that her hair is *tout d'une pièce*." And indeed it was clear that she wore a quite charming red-brown wig. But Rupert's snub was so obvious that Marcella stared. Then she said, "I thought I'd better tell you for fear you might say something to hurt her feelings." And Rupert in his turn would have felt snubbed had he not reflected that Marcella was only ten and had been quick with her answer.

But Robert had now encountered a *living Catholic:* the mysterious thing had pierced his English armor; and as they drove to the station he hardly noticed the still, snow-covered world, the upper and lower lakes where Rupert had skated so gracefully while Robert hobbled clumsily around, and he found himself looking earnestly for the roofs of his Catholic aunt's house. She lived more modestly, nearer the town, and he wondered if he would ever see her again.

Rupert was very talkative and held forth on every detail of his delightful Christmas, though he never mentioned Mrs. Orwylstree. When he grew tired and stopped talking, Robert suddenly remembered his mother's room, and supposed that *she* must somehow be a "soul" . . . *"Orate pro anima."* He didn't know how to do that, or if he ought to — no one had told him to — and he felt uncomforted.

22

THE LADY AND THE LIAR

I

DURING Robert's last year at Hutton Grove he began to feel very lonely. There had always been a certain separation between him and Rupert, because Rupert was on the classical side and knew Greek while Robert knew only Latin. Still, Robert felt he loved Latin better than Rupert loved Greek; he wondered if Rupert really loved anything. Besides, Rupert, of course, had gone on to Barton School and even had got a scholarship there, a "special" one, because of his unusual proficiency in "general knowledge," which was just what Robert felt *he* had very little of.

Being rather unhappy, he began to say his prayers more carefully, but had a shock when a Bishop came and preached on the Psalm XV, which he called the Gentleman's Psalm. If you behaved as the Psalm said you should, you would be all that a gentleman should be and worthy of this school. Robert felt obscurely quite a lot that made him anxious. A bishop must certainly

· *189*

be very important, and this one looked benign and as if he would give you his autograph if you asked him for it. But Robert felt that most of the psalm didn't matter much to him: he knew he oughtn't to tell lies; you oughtn't to cheat — well, you learned *that* just by playing games. What *did* matter in the school, he began to feel, was exactly what no one would dream of mentioning: he could not remember that the bishop had mentioned the name of Christ — "Christian," yes; but because you must be a "Christian *gentleman*." But after the sermon they sang the hymn: "Love divine, all loves excelling — Joy of heaven to earth come down — Fix in us Thy humble dwelling . . . " That was more what he wanted, and he felt rather inclined to cry.

Afterward he went to a boy called Jordan with whom he was friendly and who, he knew, was the son of a clergyman. He asked him what he thought of the sermon.

"As a bishop," said Jordan, "of course he can't commit himself. Well, he can be as Low as he likes, but a middle course is better. My father is more advanced; but I mean to be still more advanced."

"I didn't know you meant to be a clergyman," said Robert, "and what's 'advanced'?"

"Well," said Jordan, "I haven't absolutely made up my mind. But it would be rather fun getting people to improve without their even noticing it. I suppose you have colored stoles in your church at home?"

"What are stoles?" Robert asked.

"I see I shall have to take you in hand," Jordan said.

"I don't suppose you've even been to a proper Choral Eucharist?"

Robert was getting annoyed. He hadn't the least intention of being taken in hand by anyone. But he'd seen the word "Eucharist" in a hymn and said that if Jordan meant Communion, of course he hadn't. No one at that school had been confirmed yet. . . . Jordan repeated that he must take him in hand and went away.

Robert began to wish he knew what Communion really meant. He knew that on some Sundays his people "stayed behind" after the morning service, and had been told that he would understand when he was older; but they said this also when he asked questions that obviously embarrassed them and made him feel that he had asked something wicked. But then, Communion in a church couldn't be wicked. He began to read the hymns "For Holy Communion" in his hymnbook: "Author of life divine — Who hast a table spread — Furnished with mystic wine — And everlasting bread . . . " "Draw nigh and take the Body of the Lord . . . " He could not tell why this seemed in keeping with the Italian churches and even the *Ingoldsby Legends*. Odd, but so it was.

But two events happened about this time. First, Rupert wrote that his old kinsman, Lord Medby, had died, leaving three sons — Cosmo, Yvo, and Odo — and that Cosmo, the new Lord Medby, felt as his brothers did, that feuds ought not to be kept up forever. Although he did not yet invite Mrs. Medd to Medby he increased her allowance, so that she decided to send Rupert into the diplomatic service just when Robert's family agreed that the poor boy would never shine there and that he had better go in for law. The other event was that while it had been intended to send him to Harlow, it was now considered that he would be better on the Barton hill than down by the river. Thus he was sure of meeting Rupert again.

But when he arrived at Barton next year, history repeated itself. Rupert was in the headmaster's house and even after a year had become so grand that Robert was helplessly shy of him. Moreover, Rupert already dressed with such perfection that one could foresee his splendor when he became two years older, whereas Robert's tie kept crawling up behind his collar, his trousers never kept their crease nor his Sunday tophat its mirrorlike shine. And he was naïve enough to be distressed that he was learning nothing; he came out top of his form simply because others did no work. Had he expressed what fascinated him in Latin poetry he would have deeply shocked his equals. Only when he had won some indisputable prominence would he have been tolerated had he displayed interest in schoolwork, let alone in beauty. So he slogged along uncomforted save by his prayers, which he began to lengthen.

In the evenings, when the talk about athletics and indecencies had exhausted itself, he used to go to his room, pull the top part of the window right down, and stand upon the sill with his elbows on the window sash and look at the shabby glare of London over the horizon. Though the vision of diplomacy and ambassadorial ribbons and stars had now faded, he knew he would be expected to get on in smart society and the "world" — he thought of theaters, parties, Piccadilly, clever talk — all that Rupert would be so good at and so effortlessly; no, *he* would never make a success of the life that he knew would be expected of him. And it was now that he read, in some sentimental novel, the second half of the Hail Mary: "Holy Mary, Mother of God, pray for us sinners now and at the hour of our death . . . " As he stood there, very depressed, on his windowsill, he felt he *must* say that prayer. But obscure inhibitions paralyzed him. It would be idolatry. Roman Catholics, he knew by now, prayed to the Virgin. But that meant putting her in the place of God. Night after night his soul ached to say the prayer, and yet he could not bring himself to say it.

About this time Rupert asked Robert to come for a walk. It was a Sunday afternoon, so, since there were no games, boys went for walks out of sheer boredom. After a long time Rupert said, "I suppose I'd better tell you: my mother's started being a Catholic once more."

"Oh, Rupert! how dreadful!"

"It's not in the least dreadful," said Rupert. "It's perfectly natural, and it'll do her a lot of good."

"Well," Robert said, "then I suppose that you will, too."

Rupert turned on him quite brutally. "If you ever say that again," he said, "we see no more of one another."

Robert saw that he meant it, and they made labored conversation till they reached home.

"Cheer up," said Rupert, "the world hasn't come to an end yet, worse luck."

But that night Robert gave in. Standing on his window-

sill, he put his head down on his arms and said the prayer.
All the motherhood he had never known surrounded him;
he felt as if a great cloak of dark blue velvet and warm
fur enveloped him; he was *enveloped*. He went on saying
the prayer till he noticed that he had climbed down and
was going to bed. It was long before he discovered the
first part of the Salutation.

II

During the next summer holidays Robert was sent to
Havre to relearn the French out of which his school was
sedulously educating him. At Southampton he had some
hours to wait for his midnight boat. At fifteen you may
feel, if left to your own resources, very grown up and
independent. Therefore he went to a restaurant and
ordered a grand dinner but would have been afraid of
asking for the wine to which Rupert had introduced him,
if only because he had forgotten its name. The waiter
suggested a nice bottle of strawberry champagne, and he
accepted this crimson and piercingly sweet beverage.

Then he strolled about and found himself opposite a
Catholic church, still open. In the porch he asked a
sacristan if Mass was going on.

The man answered, with a superior smile, "Oh, no.
Mass only in the morning."

Robert recovered face by examining a picture: Millet's
Angelus. He did not know what "Angelus" meant, but
perceived that here was Prayer — these peasants with

bowed heads were not just saying prayers, but praying. Something changed inside him, and he perceived he was putting up no more resistance. His heart began to pray. Inside, at the entrance of the sanctuary, he saw two statues, one of the Sacred Heart and one, he felt sure, of Our Lady. He felt as though thunderstruck. He remembered Longfellow's *Evangeline*, and the prayer: "Sacred Heart of the Saviour, O inexhaustible Fountain . . ."

After some time the sacristan wanted to close the church. Robert went down to the boat and remained on deck all night, sometimes sitting down to rest on a coil of rope, but on the whole staring at the two immensities of the water and the sky, and sometimes listening to sea rushing past and looking at the attentive stars. He said, over and over again: "Sacred Heart," and "Holy Mary, Mother of God." Thus the night passed.

On the quay at Havre a boy from his Chislehurst school, called Field, awaited him. They drove together to the upper town where they were to live with a "family," a "good" family (that is, a "de" family — by now "good" didn't mean virtuous), and, of course, Protestant. On the way Robert noticed a church with a tall cupola beneath which was inscribed "D.O.M." He knew vaguely that in Germany cathedrals were called *Dom*. While he and Field were having breakfast in a room of pale paneling and parquetry, of a new sort of bread, delicious butter, and unbelievable coffee, Mme. de Marchant came in to salute the newcomer. Robert asked at once how one descended to the Dom.

"*Nous n'avons pas ici de Dom*," said she coldly. "Why

should you ask? I am told you are *Anglocisant*. Me, I am Calvinist and without doubt predestined. It will be my joy in heaven to watch the papists burning beneath me; and you, still further down, since you are neither hot nor cold, will have been vomited from the divine mouth."

Robert was rather taken aback; he had heard much about the exquisite manners of the French but could not feel he had so far encountered them. He was then introduced to, and inspected, the three daughters of the house. He was more intolerant than he knew. He did not like these washed-out-looking girls, but still less the glossy young Englishman to whom one of them was engaged. He probably, thought Robert, spent his working hours oiling other people's hair as well as he obviously did his own. But the other English boy went away almost at once, and Robert felt independent.

The very first day he had gone to the terrace overlooking the town and at once descried the tall cupola. He went down by the lift and his sense of locality led him straight to the Rue d'Igouville, and there, at the end of it, was the Church of Saint-Michel, anemically narrow, forced by necessities of space to grow taller and taller, till its poor octagonal tower ended in the cupola like an elongated egg, and even this had weak little columns and a needle-thin spire above it. But even before he entered it Robert felt: "This is *at home!* This is natural!" Even the church in Southampton had felt — he could not have expressed it, but he meant "self-contained"; it did not join on to the world outside it. He suddenly felt as if he were looking at England as at something a long way off, where he had to play a part, where he was *not* at home. But by then he had gone in.

The church must have been recently redecorated, so smart and glossy was it. Behind the high altar was an apse with a statue of St. Michael on the left; the Angel, in a cuirass and kilt, was gracefully spearing a red-and-gold dragon with its mouth wide open; on the right was a highly groomed St. Joseph holding a lily. But at the back, in the middle, was an altar with a little cupboard over it, and above that, the Virgin Mary, he presumed, in white, with a blue sash, hands joined, looking skyward. The big altar now seemed to him negligible; here was something quite different. "Shield me in the shadow of thy wings," he said, not knowing why.

But as he turned back toward the door he saw that at the bottom of the church, on the left, was a great crucifix; he knew what it was, but felt he was not ready for it yet. On the right at the door was a chapel with the Sacred Heart statue above it, with two long strips of tapestry, red, with fleurs-de-lys inwoven on either side. Ah! this was the same figure as at Southampton. After all, this church had reached out into England. "Oh, inexhaustible Fountain." His heart beat quickly. He went into a little pious shop close by and bought some tapers; also a small metal object like a sun with rays upon a stem, and a piece of ruby glass for the heart of the sun.

"*On met un cierge par derrière,*" said the plump, benevolent lady who sold him this.

He discovered, on the way back, a confectionary where the most delectable fondants were available. The best were the coffee-flavored ones, and he asked for a *carnet* full of only these. Oh, no, he was told; they must be taken as they come. Now Robert knew that he could make himself very ingratiating when he chose, and he flirted so hard with the young lady behind the counter that he got just what sweets he wanted. Armed with these, he proceded to Saint-Michel, sat down before the Sacred Heart, and munched his fondants while looking at the statue. He did not feel it was in the least irreverent to do this, though it would have been out of the question before the great crucifix.

A fair was being held in the Grande Place on the way to this church. Robert haunted this, somewhat repelled by the pervasive odor of gingerbread, but uncomfortably fascinated by the peepshows exhibiting scenes of railway accidents, suicide pacts, and assassinations, of the lugubrious and the sinister that provided so much entertainment to the Latin soul. And here, to his amazement, he encountered Rupert.

"What on earth are you doing here?" Robert asked.

"I followed you," said Rupert. "I thought I might help in your education."

Robert told him where he was staying.

"*Des gens de rien,*" said Rupert. "*Viens avec.*"

He was living in the Hôtel de la Lune de Touraine, to be free, said he, from the English; he was using his French name.

"Which?" interjected Robert, somewhat sardonically.

"Festugières," said Rupert. "It is remembered despite the infamous revolution. I told *Maman,* who writes every day, that she must be careful to put it on the envelopes."

"But what do you do all day?"

"I improve my acquaintance with the proletariat," he said. "One of the dockers tried to throw me into the dock, but I tripped him and he went in instead. Of course I plunged in with the greatest intrepidity and rescued him. All applauded. Happily my money was in notes and well stitched into my shirt. I thought something of the kind might happen. Perhaps I'd been rather cheeky," said he reflectively. "But over a bock apiece we became friends from childhood. Even I picked up some expressions I hadn't known before."

Robert said that he was not surprised, and next day insisted on Rupert's visiting Saint-Michel.

"*Goût déplorable,*" was all the other said, but he condescended to come to the fair.

Robert was enchanted by a marionette show entitled the *Temptation of St. Anthony.* They paid two sous for the front seats — no one else was there, though the seats at one sou were packed. The saint was seated in his rocky hermitage. A lady in red satin appeared, offering the holy man a golden cup presumably containing champagne. The saint refused it, to the applause of the one-sou populace. Devils arrived, chanting "*Démolissons, démolissons son er-mi-tage!*" But the heavens opened and the saint went up in a glitter of pink fire.

Rupert by now was bored and stood up to go. "*Ce n'est pas fini! ce n'est pas fini!*" wailed the one-sou enthusiasts.

When Robert suggested sampling the next-door booth, Rupert said curtly that it wouldn't suit him; his education, apparently, must not proceed too rapidly. Afterward, Rupert showed him how he could easily climb out of his window of the house where he was staying and back again by means of the sturdy creepers, so Robert, who after all had an undeveloped spirit of adventure in him, performed this feat without disaster and went from time to time with Rupert to various cabarets where you paid nothing to enter but had to drink something.

After following Rupert's example once, Robert stuck to grenadine, save in a cabaret near the docks where the heavy atmosphere combined with an element that he did not understand — he never understood the rapid French of the performances — made him turn white. Rupert called for some brandy which certainly brought Robert's color back, but tasted so nasty that he managed to spill most of it on the floor. They took a cab back to the foot of the *ascenseur,* and Robert made his way home wondering what on earth was happening to Rupert.

Rupert, for his part, knew exactly what Robert was thinking, and their last night together in Havre he said, "I refuse to be criticized by you. Or by my mother. She has chosen to shut her mind up in a prison — perhaps she never really escaped from one. That is her affair. So far she hasn't attacked me and I don't think she will. She probably realizes that I am impregnable and that it's really she who has brought me up to be so.

"If you don't know what I'm talking about, remember that I'm years and years older than you, and I *must* know more things than you do. I know you will say I'm talking out of books. Perhaps I am, though I don't think so. But *you* can't do even that. Have you ever read one of Zola's books? Of course not. I've read pretty well the lot and find them shockingly dull. But, then, life *is* dull. What I object to is that he's got no idea that there's anything else. Now *I* know quite well that there's pure gold somewhere, and I'll test everything till I find it — not that I ever shall. I know that something or other should smell pure, but meantime, everything stinks. I find life disgusting and I don't like it. The only awful thing would be if I began to prefer corruption." He laughed. "Don't worry, *mon enfant*," he said. "You'll always go a steady second-class to — who knows where. But I shall go first-class — to hell, I suppose, since I can't see myself going to heaven."

As the boat drew away from Havre next morning Robert tried to catch sight of the tall cupola of Saint-Michel, but it was sunk in the mass of dockland warehouses and the smoke of the town. This daylight trip was very unlike the ecstatic night when he had come, able to think only of things beyond the seas and stars. Yet he was not unhappy. He still did not know what the Catholic "fact" might mean; but he knew he was not resisting whatever might lie ahead of him. He felt he had grown immeasurably older, what with Saint-Michel and this unknown Rupert. He felt, too, that in a strange way he was actually older than Rupert was and that somehow he must at all costs keep hold of him. And a challenge followed quickly.

On his return to Barton an older boy said to him, "It's not my business who your personal friends are but I may as well tell you that the house objects to your being seen about with that young swine Medd."

"What have you got against him?" Robert asked.

"That's the difficulty," said the boy. "No one can put his finger on anything exactly, but he's *all* wrong. Drop him."

"I can't," Robert said. "If he chooses to drop *me*, that's different. But if you can't give me a reason, the more he's disliked, the more I shall stick to him. I know him at home, for one thing."

"Have it your own way," said the other, "but you'll pay for it."

23

A.D. 1895

WATER FROM THE ROCK

As Robert expected, Rupert made no allusion at all to the explosive scene with which he had chosen to end their encounter at Havre, and Robert fully expected that their friendship would continue as before, punctuated with upheavals, after which life would settle down again. But an incident occurred that encouraged him to suppose he was not meant to let go of Rupert.

One day Mrs. Medd asked Robert to come to tea when he next was in London. He gladly went.

"Rupert," she said, "has gone out. I wanted to see you alone. It is for Rupert's sake. You will think this fantastic of me, but I ask you to help me to save my son. *C'est à moi la faute — ma très grande faute,*" she cried, and covered her face.

Robert had never seen a grownup cry, and he was appalled. But she recovered herself and went on without any apology. "You know," she said, "that I gave up my religion for my husband's sake. I adored him — too much. But I could not convince myself that it was really dead and you know that I have, very humbly, come back to it. But deliberately I allowed Rupert to be brought up without any faith. As a child he was lovely! *Un petit Stanislas!* Grace seemed to envelop him in spite of me, though I did have him baptized — I saw it was properly done. But now — look! Possibly a *Stanislas corrumpu.* How, I don't know. I don't really *know* him."

"No one does," Robert interjected.

"That may be," answered Mrs. Medd. "Nonetheless, it's to you I turn — a little Protestant — to rescue him."

Robert began to stammer. "*Mais, Madame* — he is still enveloped; and I am sure you are, too. It is that lady in black; I've never forgotten her; and so was I, that night at school; but then it was blue; very dark blue . . . "

She looked hard at him. "*Tu délires, mon enfant,*" she said very gently, and then stood up and took him by the elbow. "I don't want to be unfair to your family," she said, "but I think I might show you my oratory."

They went past the forbidden curtain. Robert was not much impressed. A crucifix over a sort of altar — a blue-and-white Virgin.

"I saw that statue, I mean one like it, at Havre," he said.

"It is Notre-Dame de Lourdes," said she. "But I won't tell you about that; that *would* be unfair. But no one can stop me asking her . . . "

"Who is that?" said Robert, pointing to a dark old picture.

"We think it is St. Luke," she answered. "My father-in-law was a doctor, and so was his father. And so, of course, was St. Luke."

"But why has he got that ring hanging round his neck?"

"I don't know," she answered, "but my intolerable young Rupert got in here one night and painted it, or repainted it when he was — so he says — asleep! Somnambulists in my family! *Ce serait vraiment trop fort!* But it's not always so clear. Some people don't notice it at all. *I* say that a chain is as strong as its strongest link. And there's something very strong about that one. Well, I'm glad you saw it." She looked at him and smiled.

Without noticing it, he knelt down, but had nothing to say. A prayer, not yet fully his own, was lifting him. Then they went out, and Robert felt that she had entrenched herself in her gay inaccessibility and he went away.

During the next term he worked as usual and said his prayers, including, of course, the Hail Mary and the invo-

cation to the Sacred Heart from *Evangeline,* but felt
fatalistic about the future, if he thought of it at all. He
felt helpless about what might happen to him, even
spiritually. He could not see himself *becoming* a Roman
Catholic, though he supposed he'd have to someday.
"What a weak character I must be," he thought. "I can't
even take hold of things the wrong way round, like
Rupert. Everything seems to be done *for* me."

In his home it was taken for granted that everyone
would behave in a particular way; at school, things were
still more rigid. The only choice he had made was to get
leave off football, which exhausted him, and to play
squash racquets instead; the game went fast; he could
always find a boy who didn't want it to last very long. As
for Rupert, he went in for fencing and gymnastics, which
he turned almost into acrobatics rather than feats of
strength. But this was only a breathing space.

One day Robert read in some illustrated paper an account of Lourdes. It was like a blow between the eyes, a
hypnotism. Havre faded, and Mrs. Medd's oratory; Robert
simply *was,* all day, at the foot of the Grotto with its pale
statue and the pyramid of tapers. He told Rupert, who
said, "*Quelle blague!*" and gave him a copy of Zola's
Lourdes. Robert left the story to one side, and the book
added color to his "background" of the pilgrimage and
taught him various prayers. Rupert also said that his
mother intended to take him away from Barton, where
he evidently didn't fit in, and send him to travel a little,
with a tutor, and learn about real things; but this wouldn't
happen for a year. Robert said that anyhow he must come

back this summer and see Orwylstree when it was not smothered in snow. Rupert saw at once that Robert meant him to meet the Catholic Mrs. Orwylstree and thought it would be rather fun to defeat her, wig and all.

Thither, then, they went, and the small park under the summer sun was lovely. The lake was on two levels divided by a transverse wall. The water trickled over it and clothed it with maidenhair fern; in the middle of this was a little island to which children liked to be rowed; they felt in a world of their own. Robert enjoyed showing Rupert also the long, narrow garden with cedar trees and lawns to the left, and old-fashioned flower beds to the right full of flowers such as snapdragons and sweet William and delphiniums exquisitely blue against the rose-red kitchen-garden wall on the right.

They went on through creaking iron gates, with the Orwylstree coat of arms interwoven, to a path fragrant with pine needles till they emerged at the foot of a small hill called The Knoll. Rupert sat down on a bench at the top, surveyed the scene, and approved of it.

"*Digne, mais pas trop grand,*" said he. He talked much more French here than in London. "In London," he declared, "I am still suffocated by the proximity of that abominable school. I cannot express myself."

"Perhaps," said Robert, "you haven't got a self *to* express."

Rupert stared at him. "That was clever," he said. "Is it possible that you *are* clever? I am, of course . . . " His voice trailed off.

"No one but you," said Robert, "would have had the cheek to say that!"

"Everyone does say it," Rupert answered, "to *Maman;* not to me, of course, for fear they might make me conceited."

"They needn't be afraid of *that,*" said Robert, almost acidly.

Rupert laughed charmingly. "I'm not exactly conceited. Proud? No, no. Vain? *A ma façon,* perhaps. But I have a horrible time ahead of me."

"I shall write your biography," said Robert, "and get my revenge."

"Neither of us would enjoy that," Rupert said. "Anyhow, no one will want to write yours."

One night they decided to go to a musical comedy called *The Pearl Girl.* Mrs. Henry Orwylstree asked them to an early dinner before it and to look in on their way home. This astonishing old lady came down to dinner in pure white, hanging in delicate straight folds, with her widow's cap and long white veil not hiding the auburn wig. Rupert was paralyzed with admiration, and gaped. To recover his poise, he plied her with compliments. "*Maman,*" he said, "*n'aurait jamais osé cela!*"

"I've been a pilgrim," she said gaily. "I've just come back from Lourdes. But you probably haven't heard of that."

Robert said he'd been thinking of nothing else for months. He asked if by any chance she'd brought back any of the water?

"If you ask me for it," she said, "I'll give you some. I wouldn't have offered it on my own account. But I don't suppose your grandfather could object to my giving you a little water! It'll be ready when you come back from the play."

Robert felt that his aunt, however charming, must be rather unimaginative. Or could she really have mentioned Lourdes without meaning to lead up to more? Anyway, he decided sooner or later he must take the initiative and settle for himself what he ought to do, whether or not others might object to it. But he was young enough to feel rather grand in the brougham, with Rupert and no elders supervising them, and grander still when they found the theater very empty and hardly anyone else in the stalls, so that they received all the *oeillades* of the chorus and even of the impressive lady to whom the tenor sang, "You're a pearl — little gurl . . . " Rupert covered Robert with shame by waking up and applauding vehemently, which made the audience in the circle laugh.

Robert could think of nothing but the miraculous water, and his aunt gave him a small bottle of it to take back to Orwylstree. That night he went to Rupert's room and said they must both drink some. Robert knelt down and drank from a wineglass he had filched from the dining room. Rupert did not kneel but looked at the water malignantly and put it to his lips. Then he cried furiously, *"J'ai voulu la cracher,* but I've swallowed it! Get out, Robert; get out!" Robert went to his room, bewildered. Neither of them mentioned this afterward.

Later in the holidays Mrs. Medd announced that the new Lord Medby had invited her and Rupert to Medby for as long as she liked. "I said I would not go if there was a party. I do not go to parties now. So you must come, too. Rupert must have someone of his age. You, of course, will be our guest. We shall travel first-class. To arrive otherwise would be *mal vu* by the stationmaster."

Rupert agreed. Robert thought this would have been rather impertinent had anyone but she said it; but her way of saying it seemed to make it inevitable. Then he was puzzled why any two people so serenely content with their own way of life should trouble about stationmasters. But he shrugged his shoulders and approached his grandfather.

The old colonel began by forbidding the whole plan. "The place is Roman Catholic," he said.

"Rupert isn't," interrupted Robert. "Anything but."

Then his grandfather said it might make Robert discontented to see life on so large a scale. "But he must someday," said one of his uncles who happened to be there; "to be in touch with such people should help in his career." "And," added one of his aunts, "I expect north-country ways are pretty rough; the life may harden him. We all think his mouth is rather *weak*."

Robert was at least hard enough to pay no attention when he was discussed in public; he also thought he would like to see Catholics who would be less — well, eccentric than Rupert and even Mrs. Medd, delightful and even dear as he found her. So off they went.

The express was stopped for them at Medby Station.

The youngest brother, Odo, met them on the platform.

"My brother Cosmo," said he, "is waiting for you at home. Yvo is dreadfully lazy, and so it's fallen to me to say how very welcome you are."

"Oh!" cried Mrs. Medd, "dare I ask — Mr. Medd, *may* I ask if the car may be opened? Such air! After London, unbelievable!"

Odo was delighted; he had been afraid that these southerners would be stuffy folks. But Robert himself was feeling intoxicated by this vigorous breeze and the mystery of hills such as he'd never seen save so long ago in Italy.

"This is our Beck," said Odo. "It's very empty just now, of course, but it can be quite a tumultuous little stream. And over there" — he pointed to a heavy patch of shadow near the top of a hill to the right — "*that* is Medby. Of course we live in only a little bit of it. You may find it rather grim at first, but you'll grow to love it, I hope."

After a while they passed under a very heavy gateway that was a whole house in itself. Somewhat further they turned left, climbed, and after passing two more gateways arrived at a door which, to Mrs. Medd's surprise, was opened by a young maid in blue and white; she had expected at least two footmen and a groom of the chambers. However, a housekeeper, voluminous in black silk, sailed down upon her and removed her heavy coat and then stood aside.

It appeared that the tower by which they had entered was far too old to have a "grand approach"; a flight of quite narrow steps led them up to the doorway in which

Lord Medby awaited them. This, Mrs. Medd felt, was right. To have come down to the doorstep would have been exorbitant: she was not royalty! But to have awaited her *in* the room would not have shown courtesy. "He has," she considered, "an exact sense of the order of things."

Lady Medby rose from near the chimney where even now a small wood fire was burning; she was tall, aquiline, and pale. Medby's two unmarried sisters, Maud and Beatrice, were also there, very plain, "sensibly" dressed, but entirely self-possessed; everyone would make way for them. . . . Yvo, a soldier on leave, hovered in the background and made no special impression.

Odo showed the boys to their rooms. Robert was puzzled by the shabbiness of his room and most of the furniture. Rupert's was just the same. Each contained a prayer stool with a lovely baroque crucifix above it; over the fireplace was a Madonna, and on either side of her, the portrait of a horse. It was still not quite dark, and Robert ran to his window and found that he looked down into a courtyard far below; high walls with narrow windows surrounded it. But they had been allotted, too, a day room in a corner turret from which the view would be wide. They changed, and descended when Odo fetched them.

"Dinner," said Lord Medby, "is always served, according to our custom, in the great hall. As my guest and kinsman, Rupert, will you take in Her Ladyship? I, of course, shall have the honor of escorting you, dear lady." This meant Mrs. Medd. "Robert, will you take in my sister

Maud? Yvo will follow with Beatrice. Odo, you must make your way as best you can."

The procession made its very formal way through a long corridor. The meal was set on a table across the great room on a raised dais. The table was lit entirely by candlelight, and a few more candles spaced along the walls failed to do more than reveal some shadowy suits of armor, and, higher up, some ghostly banners. There was an enormous fireplace with a coat of arms above it, and even the great window at the end of the hall admitted a twilight insufficient to make any real difference.

The ladies had transformed themselves into very dignified velvety personages. Robert was at first completely paralyzed, and even Rupert kept his eye, so far as he could, on his mother, who was very quiet, perfectly at her ease, and making even Lord Medby hope he was not too countrified. Mrs. Medd saw with approval that there was a massive and immobile butler in the background and *three* menservants in the Medby blue, with white gloves hiding hands no doubt of a most honest red.

After their simple meal their host announced that perhaps one glass of port would do the young gentlemen no harm. There would be coffee — my lady would escort the ladies — and at half-past ten there would be prayers in the house chapel so that the servants might come. "Mass will be at half-past eight tomorrow in the chapel; on Sundays we all adjourn to the church. After night prayers there will be tea for those who care for it. But probably these young men will want to go to bed after their long day."

During night prayers they knelt in a tribune. The earl read the prayers in a matter-of-fact voice but with manifest conviction. A candle shone by his prayer stool; two others, by a little shrine on the left. Robert was certainly very sleepy — the two flames riveted his eyes, they melted together and then parted into a ring of light which rotated, expanded, contracted, and kept pace with him all the way to bed and even while he had his bath before the fire. He tumbled into bed and slept soundly until the man called him next day with another huge can of boiling water.

24

A.D. 1895

THE WAKENING RING

DURING the following fortnight Mrs. Medd, one cannot deny it, did her best to establish herself in the good graces of Lady Maud and Lady Beatrice, and succeeded very well. They quite understood that her boots had never been meant for tramping over heather, bracken, or rocks, but were delighted by the interest she displayed in the house and their various recipes. She even tactfully alluded to one or two of her own. The earl, of course, was fascinated by her, and his brother Yvo even allowed himself to chaff him about this but was heavily snubbed. Rupert protected himself by a display of passionate inquisitiveness about all Medby history and was so adaptable that only seldom was it remembered that he was not a Catholic.

So Robert might have felt rather out of it had he not been able to browse about in the library and for the first time to read some Catholic books, in particular, Father Faa di Bruno's on the Catholic faith. He was reading a language strange to him. He thought the arguments inconclusive — not one of them would *convince* him. He believed in a mysterious something called "Catholic"; no argument would dislodge him from that and no argument drive him into it. He was not at home among arguments, but very much at home in the house chapel, and kept resolving to ask what was in the little reliquary before which a lamp burned in the daytime and two candles during night prayers and Mass.

Happily he found that he made friends with Odo Medd. One day they went for a walk and finally sat down on the stump of St. Paulinus's cross. Odo asked him if he liked being at Medby. Robert knew he could be frank. He laughed and said that in some ways he liked it very much.

"Not in others?"

"Well, I can't think why, but I'm happy in your chapel but somehow I feel uncomfortable down there where the water pours down behind those two holes in the rock. I

suppose it's always done it just like that — centuries before I ever looked at it. And I feel still queerer in that
little cave you've made a sort of chapel of. It feels —
inhabited, but I don't know what by."

Odo said, "I've rather wanted to talk to you, but I
didn't feel I had the right. Now I think you've given it to
me."

Robert said awkwardly that he was only sixteen; also
that he was still rather bewildered — he'd never lived in
a place like Medby before.

"Well, you have now," said Odo, "and you realize what
it means to us. And the point is that you seem to be the
only friend of Rupert, and I must say frankly that we
don't like him very much. He says he's terribly interested
in our family and the castle. But is he really? Or is he
putting it on?"

"He's ever so good an actor," Robert said. "But I don't
think he's putting it on. If he is, he won't keep it up; he'll
explode and say something frightfully rude. But Mrs.
Medd's all right, you know," he said anxiously. "She's
wonderful."

Odo laughed. "So you're under the spell, too? So you
ought to be. But to get back to my point. By now it's sure
that Cosmo won't have any children. Hard on my sister-in-
law: she feels she's failed in what was expected of her. As
for Yvo, he gets engaged twice a year at least but we never
dare to announce it in the papers because it never comes
to anything. And I can't see myself marrying. If I don't,
the succession will pass to the descendants of Rupert's
great-grandfather Cecil Medd, and that looks as if Rupert

is almost sure to inherit all this. I don't want to hurt your feelings — it's not only that we don't care for him personally — but the idea of a Protestant inheriting is appalling to us. I don't mean we're all saints — far from it. But we *have* got our faith. I'm not a very intelligent man, but I'm trying to talk to you as if you're grown up and all I can say is, do what you can for Rupert."

"It's very kind of you to talk to me like this," Robert said. "Mrs. Medd said practically the same thing. But what can I *do?* I'm — well, I'm just ordinary, not in the least like Rupert. Certainly I think he'll have a bad time — he'll get all the prizes and then chuck them all away, even if he isn't kicked out of everything."

"*That's* not an 'ordinary' remark!"

"But I mean it," said Robert, tears in his eyes. "I don't pretend to understand Rupert. I'm always saying that no one does. I'm sure he's got it in him to make good — be very much better than I am — but sometimes I feel as if he were possessed by a devil — I can't explain why. Even if I could, I don't think I ought to give him away, even to you. In spite of all, he's my friend, my only real one."

"And you certainly are his," said Odo, "and most certainly you mustn't give him away, to me or anyone else."

"But since we're talking like this," Robert suddenly said, "Rupert isn't the only thing. The worst thing is that I feel *doomed* to become a Catholic. That doesn't sound polite but I mean I can't help it. And I don't really know why. A lot of the arguments I've been reading wouldn't convince a cat." Odo smothered a grin. "It seems to me you can prove anything — I mean, the Church of England hasn't got anything better. Even in my own family they don't all think the same thing — at least I'm sure my uncles don't."

"I'd be no good at arguments myself," said Odo. "If anyone asked me anything, I'd refer him to our chaplain, or a priest I know in London who's well up in that sort of thing and also sensible."

"But *I* can't refer my people to chaplains or priests," said Robert desperately, "and there'll be a frightful row at home; everyone will say that Mrs. Medd influenced me and that my aunt, Mrs. Orwylstree, persuaded me, and my coming here will put the finishing touch." He began to cry.

Odo waited. Then he said, "You know that hereditary Catholics aren't always very sure of converts, as they say. But if you become one, you'll incline me to think better of them. Because you're young and you'll have a rough passage at home. You'll have to show backbone. I'm afraid I'm mixing my metaphors, so I'll add another — you'll have to plow a lonely furrow. After all, you're *in* your home, and Mrs. Medd and your aunt, to say nothing of us, aren't substitutes. But — and this is even more serious — I'm convinced that the world is going to be changed *altogether*. Who can tell what sort of man will be needed when Queen Victoria dies — if she ever does? Can Medby go on forever? I don't know. But I do know that the *res Catholica* will. That's about all the Latin I remember from school! And you may be the sort of man it'll need." There was a pause.

"I wanted to ask you," Robert said, "what you have in

the little reliquary in your chapel that you light two candles in front of. I don't mean on the altar — I know about that — but to the left."

"Well, all I can tell you for certain is that it's a ring. We've certainly possessed it since the fourteenth century. I've looked at it; it's clearly an original ring, but it's worn so fine that I think it must have been embedded in a thicker one; you can see it quite clearly outside. They've recently found some documents at Chartres about *a* ring which sounds certainly as if it might be this one. If it is, it was already connected with St. Bernard and even Alcuin who actually came here in 700 and something — there was still the wooden house then, but they were beginning to build the nursery tower — Rupert has shown it to you. But before *that,* well, there were a lot of old legends floating about which take it back to early Christian times, but there's no certainty. What is certain is the St. Cuthbert's St. Mark. You've seen that, too?"

"Yes, and it shows that Roman Catholics *did* read the Bible, and if I've been taught wrong about that, a whole lot more may be wrong, too."

"I'll leave you to think it over," said Odo, smiling. "*I* mustn't be said to have influenced you!" And he went down the hillside.

"I shall *have* to," Robert said to himself. "There'll be a horrible row, and I shan't be able to say why I *must* become a Catholic." No less than three people had given him *Plain Reasons against Joining the Church of Rome;* it *had* made him uncomfortable, but he learned several more prayers out of that, too. He did not try to find answers to the arguments, nor yet could he guess how dishonest a book it was. "But what would be the good," he thought, "of telling them I couldn't pray in any other way? Or that Our Lady *made* me pray to her? They'll say I'm sentimental and mustn't yield to impressions, but they never talk about that except when it's *this* impression. And they'll say that Romanism is un-English; but what could be more English than Medby? And what's good enough for your father and grandfather's good enough for you. But then the Medds would be right in not turning Protestant! And there's not a soul I can talk to about it."

The late afternoon was silent save for the clink of metal upon stone somewhere down there; he could see the old Roman bridge over the Beck — it must have sounded just like that when they were building it. And the westering sun sent level rays that revealed the outlines of the old wooden house that he'd taken for the trenches and ramparts of a Roman camp till Odo Medd explained it to him.

"I must read about Alcuin," he decided. "To think that he sat just here, just where *I* am." And again the mystery of "I-hood" welled up in him. He stood up and made his way down to the chapel cave, determined not to be scared by it. He went in. The sun shone straight into it and illuminated the stone built into the altar — *Soli Invicto . . .* To the Unconquered Sun? To the Sole Unconquered? Which had it meant at first? Robert knelt to examine it more closely. The little cross, crushed into the top, was clearly an afterthought; but at least it made it Christian.

· *219*

"The Lord is my enlightening — whom then shall I fear?"

Just then a shadow fell across it. Robert looked back; a priest in his cassock was standing in the mouth of the cave. "Don't let me disturb you," he said pleasantly. This was not the chaplain, who was old and seldom came outside the castle precincts. Robert got up off his knees and suddenly felt that here was someone he *could* talk to. "I'm staying here," he said. "I'm only a guest. I came with Mrs. Medd and her son. No doubt you've seen them."

"I'm a visitor, too," said the priest.

Robert was pleased. "I wanted someone to talk to," he said. "And I can't to anyone here. They'd feel it wasn't fair to my family. I mean, I'm sure I've got to become a Catholic, and I don't see how to. Well, I can't stop praying to Our Lady."

"I'm glad to hear that," said the priest. "Pray often to Our Lady of Medby. She has her special shrine in the castle chapel. Come with me." He kissed the stone altar and on the way down he taught Robert how to make acts of faith and contrition, and then a few lines of a prayer beginning: "Sacred Heart of Jesus, teach me the perfect forgetfulness of myself, since this is the only way of entering into Thee. Since all that I shall do in the future will be Thine, grant that I may do nothing that is unworthy of Thee."

They reached the chapel without meeting anyone, and after adoring the Blessed Sacrament they turned and knelt before the shrine containing the ring.

"I've never seen it," said Robert. "Lord Medby has the

keys." But the shrine appeared to be open and glowed interiorly. Robert could see a circle of shining gold, and a sweetly scented cloud enveloped him.

"Hold out your hand," said the priest, "and open your heart."

Robert's eyes were dazzled, but he felt that the ring was round his finger, round his heart.

"*Expecta Dominum*," said the priest, "*viriliter age, sed Ipse faciet.* I'll leave you here for a little." And he withdrew into the shadowy chapel.

Robert met Rupert in a corridor. "Where on earth have you been?" asked Rupert. "I've been looking for you everywhere."

"I went for a walk with your uncle Odo; after a bit he went away and I went down to the cave and one of the priests came and talked to me and then we went to the chapel —— " He broke off.

"What d'you mean, 'one of the priests'? There's only the old one, and he's enough for anybody. And I don't know why you keep going to the chapel. Your visits don't particularly impress anyone."

"I don't *want* to impress anyone," Robert said, "and you know perfectly well why I go there."

"It's bad enough," said Rupert, "to have to do the polite thing and go to Mass every day. I think that chapel simply stinks."

"Good heavens!" cried Robert. "I've never known any place to smell so delicious, not even the conservatory at Orwylstree." Then he felt he had been irreverent even to mention that conservatory, drenched though it were with fragrance, along with the chapel. Rupert turned his back and went off.

Next morning Robert asked Mrs. Medd if she knew a prayer beginning with the words he had learned. She said she thought she had seen it in a book by a Père La Colombière. "Where did *you* see it?"

"I didn't, but the priest who was here yesterday taught it to me, only Rupert said there wasn't anyone beside the chaplain."

"Well, as you know, I was driving out with *ces dames* and M. le Comte to Lavradale and so I shan't have met him; priests drift in and out. *Seigneur! quelle corvée que ces déjeuners!* What conversation — shorthorn cattle, *hein?* And enough food for a regiment. And what furniture! Some that is lovely, but how tolerate the mixture of old brocade with chintz and even horsehair? *Enfin*, I am glad you came. Such visits enlarge the views. But remember, *your* obol must be for your personal valet only. So, too, Rupert's. The rest is my affair."

Happily, the earl and Odo each gave the boys a golden sovereign so there was no difficulty about the obols, and indeed Robert had been worrying rather about whom he ought to tip and how much.

All the way home Mrs. Medd talked about the widening of views. "So far I have been right to stay at home to care for *ce cher enfant*. But now if he is to travel, how can I stay in that London house *à ne rien faire?* To think that in France there are women, old and young, who go sailing off to the Senegal, to Canada, to China, and become mis-

sionaries. But me, no. I don't see myself as a *nonne*. And
he will be back in time for the university. I must rearrange
my life, but you shall not have to be ashamed of me."

As they neared London, the train passed Barton on the
westward horizon, its spires and turrets black against
the angry conflagration of the sunset. "Only one term
more," said Rupert, "and the sooner and the further I'm
away from *that*, the better!"

25

A.D. 1896–1897

THE LAMP IS LIT

Mrs. Medd found it difficult to find a tutor who would
suit both her and Rupert, because if he objected to any
of the applicants he made himself so unpleasant that they
quickly withdrew their application, and it was decided
that he should stay at Barton at any rate till Christmas.
He did not quarrel with this because he was playing for
time and hoped that the whole topic of tutors would lapse
and that he would be able to travel by himself.

The autumn term began for both him and Robert in a

blaze of ambiguous glory. For royalty, having announced that it would visit the school during the summer term, had had to postpone that event owing to circumstances which even it could not control. It now appeared that early autumn, containing as it did an important school anniversary, would provide the auspicious occasion. The Earl of Medby, after a long discussion with his two brothers, had realized that Rupert, more likely than not, was to be his successor, and decided that he himself would come to Barton and effect a presentation, and, since he much preferred Robert to Rupert, gave notice that he, too, must be accessible as a sort of attaché.

The day came. The sun shone as though it were aware of what was expected of it. Flags fluttered; red druggets were unrolled; pinkish hydrangeas occupied every corner and disguised any unsightliness. All, down to the smallest fag, wore white waistcoats and blue-and-white buttonholes, and kept their tophats miraculously smooth. Exactly at eleven forty-five the illustrious party entered the assembly hall, the headmaster humbly grand in billowing Geneva gown, an inch or two behind Royalty yet managing to look as if he were well ahead of them and entirely responsible for their very existence. The organ crashed into the national anthem; the prince bowed with bluff bonhomie and the school uttered howls of welcome; the princess smiled and everyone immediately fell in love with her.

The head of the school, his knees turning to water, advanced and made his loyal speech and returned, dazed but triumphant, to his place. There were songs. The prince said he was very glad to be present; the princess waved her exquisitely gloved hand to right and left; "God Save the Queen" was sung, and the visitors, together with a privileged minority, were removed for luncheon in a marquee.

The world then emigrated to the terrace for introductions, and the earl was enchanted to behold Mrs. Medd, now dressed in elusive gray, close to the princess who, for the honor of Barton, wore blue. Besides, it suited her. The headmaster, torn between the magnificence of the moment and fury at the prominence of Rome, stared, bland but detached, at the sky.

The earl, his turn arriving, bowed, and the prince, unexpectedly but very warmly clasping his hand, said, "My dear Medby. I am very glad we at last meet. I cannot understand why I have not seen your wonderful house and now look forward to doing so."

"*Sir!*" gasped the earl, his head aswim at the thought of expenses. Then he said, "Our house will be very honored. May I present my young kinsman, Rupert Medd?"

The prince, who formed his opinions in a flash, nodded and had his hand shaken, but the princess, enthralled by Rupert's slim elegance, said with vague charm, "I hope you enjoy yourself here?"

Rupert, excited, lost his head a little and answered, "I do *now.*"

The prince's eyes narrowed. "And this?" he said to the earl, who was now holding Robert firmly by the elbow.

"My very good young friend, Robert Brent."

"Ha!" said the prince. "Brent? Excellent. Did I not stay

with your father? Your uncle? Someone of the name at Ajnaipur?"

"My father, sir," gulped Robert.

"Ha! Excellent. Following him? Too young to know yet." Then, suddenly bored, he began to twist his ring, and said, "I think, Medby, that this is enough. Bring this young man to tea."

So Robert went to tea, besides which the butler, with mixed emotions, for he was a strict non-conformist but duly bowed down to royalty, offered champagne. But Mrs. Medd sat on a bench on the terrace and laughed and laughed, but interiorly, while youth after youth rushed up to ask if they could get her anything — an ice? Coffee? Cucumber sandwiches? An ice, an ice, an ice? Rupert stood behind her, content with the court his mother was holding, till he allowed himself to realize that it was his fault that he — and, what was worse, that she — had not been invited to that tea.

That night both boys had their reaction. Rupert began to think that he had treated his mother very badly all his life. He put this down to the French in him; all French young men adored their mothers and treated them badly; they preyed on them; they were diabolically selfish, and shams. As he tossed about in bed, he saw himself as a sham, and that was pretty low. "*Low* is what I am," he said, and chewed the root of bitterness. He decided he must make up for it somehow. But how? And would he ever stick to that decision? "Good God!" he thought. "Am I weak as well as low?" Black devils gnawed at his brain, and he felt really ill next day, but settled down glumly to do some work for the rest of the term, and then he would trust to fate.

Robert was going through a reaction of his own. Once more he stood on his windowsill, but his room was different: tall walls of the houses opposite closed him in, and only through a narrow strip between them did he catch sight of the wide view and the rusty glare over London. He said the Hail Mary, but no warm, comforting mantle now fell around his shoulders.

He saw, more clearly than before, that he did not belong to the great and glittering world of which he had seen a highly artificialized version that day. He suddenly felt a lessening of Rupert's magnetism; after all, Rupert was destined, almost without doubt, to Medby; and there Robert would be at best a visitor. "Helping Rupert? Saving Rupert?" The words hardly made sense any more. Robert thought he had better lead his own life, not realizing that he visualized it as becoming as like "everybody else" as possible.

He took to playing musical-comedy tunes, like the songs in *The Shop Girl*, which made him quite popular in the house, since it did not mind inaccuracies provided it could shout, but which exasperated his family, since not only it didn't want to shout and was intolerant about mistakes, but had never really got beyond "Drink to Me only with Thine Eyes," or "Songs of Araby" — not that anyone, Robert thought, can really write tunes like that nowadays. And this made him see, with a shock, that he himself had really stuck fast at Gilbert and Sullivan, though even there he felt he wouldn't like things in the way other people did. They seemed to find the "Yeomen of the Guard" good fun, while he loved it but found it heart-breaking.

He even made a halfhearted attempt at being rowdy, but other boys, who rather liked him, said it didn't suit him, and he thought so himself. The "Green Carnation" version of life, popular just then, attracted him even less, though Rupert, despite his spell of studiousness, maliciously tried to indoctrinate him with some of its oddities. But the main result of these adolescent tumults was that Robert's heart grew hardened; he asked himself what was the use of all that praying and he pushed his crucifix and a little statue of Our Lady of Lourdes to the back of a drawer, under his handkerchiefs. After all, one couldn't exactly break them. . . . He frequently met Marcella in the holidays, but she was going through a phase of good works based on sound reason, and he refused to be improved, especially by her.

All the same, Robert knew quite well that he was trying to lead a life which was not really *his*, and that the experiments would come to nothing. This disheartened him, the more because he now had no one to talk with. Rupert had left, with the most casual of good-bys; in the house Robert was neither popular nor unpopular; in such a school everything was tolerated save extremes. He now was in a position of some authority and exercised it almost mechanically since no one troubled to resist him or did not do it twice. Equity, not strict justice, was the standard by which older boys were judged, and it was seen that he was neither lax nor tyrannical.

So his under mind began to function more freely; there was less to interfere with it. There was a song that haunted him, about the lights seen in the distance toward London. "Good night!" it said. "Sleep, and so may ever — Lights half seen across a murky lea — Child of hope, of courage and endeavor — Gleam a voiceless benison on thee. Youth be bearer — Soon of hardihood. Life be fairer. Loyaller to good, Till the far lamps vanish into light — Rest in the dream-time — Good-night!" He realized he was tempted to self-pity. Life's lea was murky enough, but what were the lights that he could honestly say he saw? "Half-seen — voiceless." He didn't want to live in a world of hints. He supposed that the author was a kind of trustful agnostic, asking him to be *content* with hints — to hope; but for what exactly? To be hardy, courageous, to "endeavor" — as if he wasn't always trying, and as if it didn't always come to nothing!

Once more he put his head down and said the Hail Mary omitted during these troublesome months. Turning to go to bed, he noticed that the drawer of his bureau was open and that the crucifix and Our Lady were lying on the top of his handkerchiefs

"Now who did that?" he asked himself. "One of the servants, rummaging around and prying?" But instantly he knew that this was ridiculous and that he must become a Catholic. In fact, that except for a short ceremony he *was* a Catholic.

He wondered how he should explain it, now that he must write home. He had read and reread the Catechism till it became like the rattling bones of a skeleton. He had

by now read different books that made excellent maps
of the Catholic country, so to say. His unforgettable visit
to Havre had left him with pictures, some ugly, some
amusing, some attractive, of a Catholic town. He had
seen the sturdy, unreflective life that was lived at Medby,
and Catholics as different as his aunt and Mrs. Medd.
But he felt that all of that was valuable and yet apart
from him. He *knew* that he was living by a Catholic life
as surely as his lungs were breathing air, even though he
breathed the Catholic "air" still through a barred gate,
but the bars would fall when he was able to ask them to.

He wrote home. After, he gathered, a blank of conster-
nation, contradictory but regulation formulas were expressed. "Who could have *dreamed* it? — I saw it coming! — The priests have got hold of him. — It's some
wretched girl. — He's caught by the glamor of Rome! —
He's a weak character and knows he needs a crutch. —
It's only a phase; lots of young men suffer from it. —
Dam' young prig; but he's obstinate enough to go through
with it. — Darling, why should you *change?* Haven't we
given you all you need?" He heroically refrained from
commenting on their having just sold two very nice horses
and bought one of the very first motorcars.

Meanwhile he settled down quietly to work and never
mentioned the subject save to say he would not promise
to wait till he was twenty-one "before doing anything
fatal." He said the date was perfectly artificial; he would
not be wiser one day after his birthday nor less wise one
day before.

Little by little his elders showed themselves kind but

mystified as good people must be who knew nothing at all about the Catholic Faith. Of course Robert must follow his own conscience. But couldn't he, above all, *wait*? Perhaps till he'd finished at Oxford? By the way, were Romans allowed to go there? Or could he try being a Catholic for, say, a year, without committing himself to anything? Then about his career . . . Perhaps, after all, diplomacy might be thought of? There was, said an uncle, something cosmopolitan about the old religion. This was hushed down; but it was admitted that there were some Catholics of good family and even talent in the Foreign Office.

About Christmas he caught a bad chill and stayed in bed, which saved him from hurting his family's feelings by refusing to go to Communion with them, which otherwise he would have had to do. Nor did he go to Orwylstree, but wrote to ask his Aunt Anne's prayers, leaving her to guess why. Next term he did not pick up, and was, though at first he did not know it, pining for confession and Communion. He was so obviously ill that he was sent with a tutor to the warmer climate of Torquay.

There he visited a priest daily, and at last wrote home to say that if this Father Smith were willing, he would ask to be received into the Church. They gave in, provided he took no vows or entered a monastery. An echo from childhood reached him: "It's never any good trying to explain! Grownups never understand."

Father Smith, clear that Robert knew what he was about and struck by his desire for the Sacraments, said he might be received in time for Easter. Robert wrote to his aunt, who accordingly transported herself to Torquay which she liked anyway.

Robert asked if they should invite Mrs. Medd. "She is very alone since Rupert went to Germany," he said, "and I used to see such a lot of them."

His aunt agreed without enthusiasm. She had not liked Rupert nor had she met his mother. However, when Mrs. Medd arrived only three days before the ceremony, she and Mrs. Orwylstree immediately made friends.

Mrs. Medd said to Robert, "I have had this little ring made. It has touched the one at Medby and I feel that it is somehow *that* that has drawn us all together. Wear it round your neck, if you like, but partly for Rupert's sake."

On the chosen afternoon Robert walked by himself down to the church; he had said he would prefer to be alone. He went through gardens sweet in this soft air with flowers and full of great rhododendrons, deep crimson and a very pure pink. Even at such a moment he saw, with astonishment and delight, that the world had come to life for him again. He knew himself surrounded with loveliness of color and form; that everything in this incandescent atmosphere was shining; that all the beauty that had beset him in childhood and that he had been forgetting was still there; why, the very fountains in Rome were now playing and singing for his sake. He reached the church.

The church was empty, he thought, save for his aunt and Mrs. Medd, but as he returned from making his confession he saw, under the shadows of the choir loft, another lady, in black, and kneeling; and, for a moment, on the other side, a young man standing. "But it's Rupert!" he thought. "Impossible!" Rupert looked angry and yet sad.

Yet when they went out he saw neither of these two persons. Mrs. Orwylstree was radiant, but Mrs. Medd looked white.

"Did you . . . ?" Robert began, but broke off.

"I think so," she said, but added nothing.

They drove away on pilgrimage to a convent beloved by Mrs. Orwylstree. Robert was duly exhibited. The nuns cooed and fluttered and provided an enormous tea which he couldn't eat. But that evening the three of them had a little festival dinner, and then Robert walked home slowly.

He had not felt excited, but now he felt free — in wide spaces of open air; he felt established and *in possession*. "This is *my* air! These are my flowers, my stars!" He knew he must not exult too much; in a sense, the "lights" were still "half-seen"; but the dark was full of light; the blessing was not "voiceless" — all nature sang a hymn around him. Then he said, "Come along, Rupert! You'll *have* to come!" And smiling at his boyish ritual, he said his last Hail Mary standing on his windowsill and prayed that the goal he had reached might be a true starting point — whither, he left to God.

26

CRIB AND CRUCIFIX

Robert, relieved of so great an anxiety, found that his
mind worked far more easily; he could concentrate as
never before and won quite a good scholarship at Oxford, though at St. Martha's, one of the smaller colleges.
At school Rupert had read only what interested him and
had crammed for his examinations and won quite a lot of
prizes, though he had done only a fortnight's work in each
term. But at Oxford it was harder to bluff, and his examin-
ers found him "unpredictable," a quality they detested.

"He is," they said, "not untalented; he emits unusual
ideas — no *harm* in that, but he fails to support them by
parallel instances."

So though he went to the much grander All Saints College, he could wear only the short commoners' gown, while
Robert floated around in the scholars' gown and could not
but feel a little exultation. He worked steadily at classics
and law; Rupert did languages and history. They saw
little of each other, as Rupert joined a hundred societies
where men discussed politics, art, socialism, morals, the

stage, and theology, which enabled him to argue for the opposition, irrefutably and quite unconvincingly. He made no close friends. During vacations he usually went abroad.

During their third winter Robert received an astonishing postcard sent from Sankt Markus in Tirol. Nothing was written on it save "Pray for me." Robert felt this was not mockery, and had a Mass offered for him.

Rupert had grown discontented with his rather spasmodic travels and judged that he had spent far too much time in social visits and tittle-tattle. In fact, he was annoyed with himself for talking so much and scattering his mental energies. He was rather surprised by this, because if the mood proved lasting, it might portend an embarrassing change in behavior. He had arranged to stay with a German family near Rankenheim where, he considered, he would not be likely to get into mischief and could seriously study German affairs. What exasperated him was the sense that he was growing up. He had always been inclined to jeer — not too unkindly! — at Robert who, he had felt, knew nothing of the world at all. But now he wondered whether Robert had not a far better head on his shoulders. Now that he was just twenty-one he could not shut his eyes to the probability of inheriting Medby and vast responsibilities. "And I never *have* been 'responsible,'" he glumly acknowledged. "I've left all responsibility to poor dear *Maman*."

Nor was he feeling comfortable in the German family with which he was staying. It was a large household, a most kindly home, very unlike the house that he had shared with his mother. It was lavish with coffee and cakes; Lutheran, but not argumentatively so. But he didn't like this self-satisfied middle classism mixed with sentimentalism; and while he was determined not to let the French in him prejudice him against these most unclassical Germans, he felt he was free to be in revolt against the Prussianism and the young army officers he met; and while among Catholics he might indeed count as an expatriate, Lutheranism, like Anglicanism, could never have been his "Father's house." He began to think that his own father had been blinded, but to what, he could not see.

At first he did not mean to go home at the Christmas holidays, disguising from himself his real motive, which was a wish not to meet Robert. But he was restless and wandered about the narrower streets, and two days after the feast saw a small Catholic church and entered it without knowing why. It was dark save for the altar lamp and seemed to him much larger than it had looked from outside. There was a crib, dimly illuminated within. He peered into it to see the figures more clearly, and thus first stooped and then found himself kneeling at the wooden rail in front of the crib which filled a whole side chapel.

Then he began to feel that this was the most beautiful thing he had ever seen. He remained quite unconscious of the almost uncouth simplicity of the figures; but they *were* "figures." He could not have explained even to himself why there was also a "fact" there, beautiful beyond words or even thought.

He had not noticed that a workingman and a woman

had knelt down beside him. The man turned a little toward him and said, *"Ostende mihi faciem tuam; sonet vox tua in auribus meis: vox enim tua suavis et facies decora."*

The woman said nothing, but remained bowed in prayer, her head covered with her shawl. If Rupert had thought at all, he would have assumed that all sorts of Catholics might quote bits out of the Latin liturgy, but he seemed to be outside of thought, save that a kind of echo circled in his head: "Show me thy face — for thy face is fair. . . . Let me hear thy voice, for thy voice is very sweet. Show me thy face!"

After a while he felt giddy and stumbled toward the door. Turning, he looked back at the crib. In the dim light the man and the woman seemed to have got inside it — at least he could see no other figures; the small image of the Child was invisible from that distance. He felt really ill and hoped he had not caught a chill; but on arriving at the house he felt, on the contrary, astonishingly well, and, on an impulse, wrote to his mother that he would come home to celebrate the New Year.

The visit was the greatest success. Mrs. Medd had longed to have Rupert at home with her, but would not ask. Of course they were called upon by the Brents, who came up for a pantomime or two. Robert appeared, but always in a crowd, and he felt as nervous of Rupert as Rupert did of him, though in different ways.

Left to themselves, Mrs. Medd and Rupert had a joyous week. They invented a play and acted it to themselves with great vivacity. One evening Mrs. Medd decided she was a north-country chatelaine and talked steadily about shorthorns and mangel-wurzels and Rupert retaliated by becoming a German *Hausfrau*. They had never felt so close together as during those days. In fact, Rupert, suddenly serious, said one evening, "I'm sure, *Maman*, that you've made a crèche in your oratory. May I see it?"

Mrs. Medd, without comment, took him into the tiny room. Rupert knelt down to peer into the crib. "I'm getting too shortsighted for words," he said apologetically. "*Ostende mihi faciem tuam,*" he uttered, half in a dream. "*Sonet vox tua in auribus meis,*" he went on unconsciously. "For thy voice is sweet, and thy face most fair."

He rose abruptly. He looked at the murky picture of St. Luke. "There is that ring that I painted in my sleep," he said, laughing. "It does not rhyme with the rest, *Maman;* it is far too crude."

"You see it like that?" she said. "*I* think it is getting mellower and will harmonize very well."

It was decided that Rupert would conclude his stay in Germany by a tour, part by train, part on foot, which would take him by way of Nüremberg and Munich and so into the Austrian Tyrol. Lord Medby gave him a few more letters of introduction which he was not eager to use. He went, in fact, rather hurriedly till he reached Innsbruck and then felt that his tour had somehow properly begun.

It was a temptation to turn aside through the Brenner Pass toward Italy, but he knew that it would not be wise just now to mix memories, and he tramped steadily eastward, for the winter even here was very mild, till he came to Sankt Markus in Tirol. He wondered how the baroque-topped tower of the church seemed so perfectly in place inside these ancient walls and heavily scutch-eoned gateways till he realized that it could but mean a continuity of culture, of Catholic culture, and that any-one with a sense of history, such as he rather plumed him-self on having, ought to feel at home there.

He had been tired after his tramp, and slept late. He went into the church; only a very few old people were there, and the priest, old, too, but rugged as an oak, sat there saying his Office. But the priest felt Rupert's pres-ence and came to him.

"It is very late," he said. "Mass is over many hours ago, but possibly the young gentleman wishes to receive Com-munion?"

Rupert said awkwardly that he had already had his cof-fee. Then, feeling this dishonest, but also conscious of an unbridged gulf between himself and everything around him, added, "I have no faith."

The kind old faded eyes looked steadily at him. "Is it possible," said the priest, "to look at these great moun-tains and the fields, and to listen to the waters, and also look into the good faces of my dear people, and not to know that our Father both made them and is keeping them?"

"I have made myself unworthy," Rupert replied, "so much as to know about God, if there is a God; and cer-tainly He cannot want *me*."

The priest took him by the arm and walked him, un-resisting, round the church. "Here is the chapel of St.

Mark, our patron," he said; and Rupert remembered the little gospel, St. Mark, at Medby, written by St. Cuthbert all those centuries ago. Then there was a Calvary chapel.

"You cannot reach higher than the cross," said the priest.

Rupert said that he was of the earth, and earthy.

"But where," said the old man, "is the cross rooted, if not in the earth? And its arms embrace the world."

"I know about these things," said Rupert, melancholy. "But knowing *about* them is not the same as *knowing* them."

"That will be given you, my dear young man — at a cost."

Rupert said, "Even if that is true, and even if I had the courage to pay the price, what *is* the price? I've no idea."

"Is there nothing," said the priest gravely, "that you know you are resisting?"

"I suppose," Rupert answered slowly, "that I will not give in to my mother, who stopped being a Catholic and has become one again; and I have a friend who has already become one. He is much better than I, but he has no experience of life."

The priest smiled broadly and then grew grave again. "Perhaps he is not less wise than you, though he may not be so clever. Do you think that possibly there is a little pride in you? Do you ever pray?"

"Pride, yes; pray, no," said Rupert rather rudely.

"Try to pray, or, rather, do not try; but if the Holy Spirit makes Himself heard, praying within you, do not defend yourself. Do not use words, but wish that the dear

Lord may show you his face and make his voice heard to you."

Rupert's mind was full of echoes; he was frightened, and said violently, "I hate the whole thing. Thank you very much, but I *will* not have all that!" And he marched out of the church.

"He hates," the priest reflected. "That may be very good. For if he could not hate, how could he love? But how will love come to him? Perhaps with one great wrench, as the sickness is torn out of a man at Lourdes? Or with a very slow and weary convalescence? I think it will be slow, and then will come the wrench; but not too hard, please God." And he knelt to ask that he might draw off some of the guilty world's pain into himself.

That afternoon Rupert walked up through the fields and the austere setting of firs and glacier streams and rocks. He halted by a crucifix, haggard beneath its little wooden penthouse, and just as it struck him as ghastly beyond endurance a tiny child ran up and standing on tiptoe tucked a bunch of winter flowers between the feet and the cross. She did this most gaily, and stroked the wounded feet and ran away, catching hold of Rupert's hand and kissing it. He stood appalled. "She loves — both of us!" he thought, trembling.

Next day he left Sankt Markus and proceeded by Salzburg as far as Ischl. He went one morning to inspect the tall church there and found Mass just ending. The priest as he came out bowed to a lady kneeling in the stalls. Presumably one of the imperial family. And in fact, having presented a letter of introduction to a neighboring

Schloss, and being bidden by its owner to call next day at five, Rupert found the lady already there. It was the Archduchess Eugenia, and he clicked his heels and bowed quite successfully.

"You like Austria?" she said.

"It is a most beautiful country," he replied.

And she, to his surprise, said, "A very tragic one."

The Graf implored her not to mention tragedy — especially to this young visitor. *"Gaudeamus igitur juvenes dum sumus!* You have seen our wonderful Vienna? When in Germany you spent time at Heidelberg, no? You have joined in the singing —— "

"My dear Franz," interrupted the archduchess, "it is quite useless to speak to this young man like that, or for me *not* to mention tragedy. The Mother of Sorrows has looked into his eyes, and *Gaudeamus* is not *his* song. My young Mr. Medd," said she, "you will see much lightheartedness in our land, and you may think of us in terms of pastry and cream-tufted coffee and waltzes; but believe me there is little gaiety at court and it is because I shall not see you again that I can speak to you like that. This poor imperial fabric is too frail for the great crown that rests upon it; the feathers are falling from our eagle. But *Stat crux dum volvitur orbis;* nothing but that stands firm."

Rupert, alarmed by what seemed to him too rhetorical as well as so very unexpected, murmured that he had seen some very beautiful crosses in the fields, and was almost as relieved as the Graf was when she said she was so pleased to have met Mr. Medd, which meant that he must make his bow. For the old diplomat never knew what indiscretion she might perpetrate next. "After all," he thought, "what with etiquette and assassinations and never expressing an opinion if by chance you have one, no wonder the family brain sometimes rocks!"

27

A.D. 1902–1908

AT BETHLEHEM

By 1902, when Robert and Rupert were on the eve of going down from Oxford, the Boer War had dragged its dismal length along and Rupert had become notorious for the outrageous views he aired in the Union. But he spoke so extremely well and was so imperturbable that few debates could dispense with him though he was usually howled down. Just now he exasperated everyone by calling Kimberley and Johannesburg cancers in the midst of South Africa, that the native races could not forever be kept under anyone's heel, and that the future of South Africa would be neither black nor white but various shades of brown. This was too much for either side, and Rupert could not finish his speech, but draped himself in smiles and awaited the ragging of his rooms. But nothing happened; perhaps just because he put up no self-defense he was felt to be intangible. And he made men nervous.

But the war had not only developed his mind; it had changed his not-distant future. His uncle Yvo had gone out to Africa and died of enteric. It was certain that Odo did not mean to marry. The Countess of Medby had died, and the earl, a good deal older than his brothers, became still more of a recluse. Rupert seemed bound to inherit.

Just before they left Oxford the two friends went for a long walk above Marston and looked down upon the gray towers among their trees.

"I don't suppose I shall ever come back," said Rupert. "I've been in this place but never really of it, and in ten years' time I'd be even more out of place. Even you don't really *belong*."

"Of course you'll come back," said Robert. "We both will, on all the official occasions. It'll be just as it was except that no one will be in the least interested in us — or anyhow in me. We really shall be outside!"

"You English!" exclaimed Rupert. "Everything just as it was! You thought Queen Victoria was immortal and now you probably think Pope Leo is. You're so dreadfully innocent — so innocent and unimaginative! I tried to make 'em see that the Boer War meant the end of an epoch. Walls are cracking everywhere; and don't imagine that the Oxford walls will last as they are, nor will anything that's inside them. I tell you, a world is ending. Three quarters of Europe are a pot coming to boil."

"Cracking walls, boiling pots, ending worlds!" said Robert, rather stung. "I didn't expect you to mix your metaphors. And I do wish," he said with some heat, "you wouldn't say 'You English'! What's more English than Medby?"

"We're all of us mongrels," said Rupert. "Even Medby wouldn't have got its 'by' if it wasn't for the Danes. And as for me myself, I'm English, but I'm also French, and that means Gallo-Roman-Frankish. Amuse yourself disentangling the threads in my character! Meanwhile, I'm going to spend as much time in East Europe as I can. That'll be where the explosions will begin. I've been there, but I'm not *in* their skins, and I want to be."

"That," said Robert gravely, "is already very Catholic."

"Why did you have to say that?" cried Rupert. "Can't even you see that why I'm not and never could be *of* Oxford is that it's agnostic and is comfortable about it, and I am, too — don't interrupt yet — but I'm in anguish about it. *Omnis consummationis vidi finem* — yes! I'm perverse enough to read the Psalms, too," he said, smiling wryly, "and at times I really do feel that there's a limit put to every perfect thing — in fact, that there *is* no perfect thing; nothing is all-inclusive, though that's what the *res Catholica* claims to be. You wouldn't expect me to hand myself over to an ism; *a* way of looking at things; *a* code of morals — or immorality, if you prefer it. It can't be 'a' anything; it's got to be *the* thing."

"I think," said Robert diffidently, "it's a mixture of waiting for God's touch and *letting* yourself be touched."

"But," said Rupert, almost feverishly by now, "I don't believe I'm resisting His touch any more. But there's a pane of thick glass between myself and all that you mean, and if God won't break it from His side, I can't from mine; I see everything quite clearly, but I'm on the other side. Or there's a pebble in my heart, and *I* can't grind it away, or dissolve it. And what do I mean when I say 'I'? For the glass and the pebble *are* my 'I,' or part of me. How can I pray, if there's part of me that simply isn't praying? What rot I'm talking!"

"No," said Robert, "you're not. But you have a harder job than I. Perhaps God put me down on His side of your glass from the beginning. Or Our Lady came and pulled me through. Don't let's analyze too much. But God will melt your pebble when you're both ready for it. *Expectans expectavi!* I know some of the Psalms, too!"

They laughed and went back good friends.

Not long after this Odo Medd wrote to Mrs. Medd:

My dear Cousin: As you know, Yvo's death has left me the next heir to Medby, which Cosmo, who practically never appears in public now, has made over to me legally already. But since I shall not marry, Rupert will succeed me. This is where you can be of great help. Since Mary's death there is no hostess here. Will you act as chatelaine on my and Rupert's behalf? Will you transfer yourself to Arlington Street at least for the season? — What a blessing that despite the feud you were presented, so you can take all our debutantes to court if it doesn't exhaust you.

But then you would always be welcome here and, if I may say so, needed, for I don't intend to let Medby go on being a mere hermitage as Cosmo did. I don't expect to expire just yet, so Rupert's career needn't be interfered with. What is settled for him? I hope he goes on meeting that civil young fellow Robert Brent, who will be a steadying influence if he needs one. Do you think he will become a Catholic? He mustn't be pushed, and anyhow that would only have the opposite effect. Still, it would be appalling if the tradition here were snapped. I do hope you will see your way to making the sacrifice I suggested. Your affectionate cousin, Odo Medd.

Mrs. Medd replied:

My dear Cousin Odo: I foresaw, and feared, that something of the sort must happen, and for Rupert's sake I accept. I shall be sorry to leave my poky little house here and shall feel very lost in Arlington Street and shall be a very dull maman to these alarming young persons. Rupert is at the moment in Hungary, but he will come back to help me move. The Boer War upset him seriously — he still thinks the world is coming to an end! But I think he is really gaining — how shall I say — poise. He does not see much of Robert Brent who is, I half think, or was, entiché of a young cousin of his at Orwylstree Hall; but who can guess what these young men, so modern, have behind their foreheads? Rupert is at least less exotique than he was. We never speak about religion, but he has not that terrible hate in his eyes that he used to.

With my best wishes; your affectionate cousin, Marie-Claire.

During the next four years time seemed to stand still. Rupert went to South Africa, but no one seemed to have learned anything from that war. He even went, one year, to China, but he knew that that was useless: the Boxer rising of 1900 did not appear to have affected the Europeans nor the Chinese save that their immemorial art was vanishing; even the missionaries still seemed to want to introduce a European culture into a world which, if it lost its own, would gravitate only toward chaos. And he knew he, mere visitor that he was, would never get "into" the Chinese or even the true Indian.

It was now more or less settled that he would live at Medby and learn about the estate that would be his. Before going there he went, without telling anyone, to Palestine. He traveled straight to Jerusalem, but, in obedience to an obscure instinct, refused to enter it. He excluded from his mind all archaeology, all history, especially what was ecclesiastical. He felt that some crisis was approaching and sat upon the Mount of Olives allowing it thus to approach. He watched the enormous stones that were the bastions of the city, and then felt he must turn his back even upon these. He had still been looking at reality through the thin, impermeable glass. He felt paradoxically that it would be sacrilege to sit where Christ had sat and see Him with something, however transparent, intervening.

He went to Bethlehem, still without entering it, and

arranged with his guide that they should make for some accessible point of the bleached and barren land not far from it whence he could look two ways: westward, and to an eastward point where the Dead Sea should be visible. He continued to sit there, alone, during the night. There was but little moonlight, but the stars were brilliant. And during the night he saw, behind no glass, the meaning of evil. He looked straight into the eyes of evil and knew that it was now possible for him to make a choice. He did not know that he made it, but he must have made it, because when the dawn rushed up over the hills of Moab he told the guide to take him back, aching in every limb and stunned in soul, to Bethlehem.

He went into the Church of the Nativity and stood waiting. He found himself thinking of the ring. "I must come full circle," he said to himself. "I must become a child again; 'but how shall a man be born again, once he is old?' I am alive, but not yet born." He went into the cave itself and knelt. Three old Arabs were standing near him, constantly bowing low, and sprinkling the floor with spices, very sweet and glittering. One of them held out an old parchment to him. He looked at the strange characters and then found he knew what they meant. "The Vision is still for its appointed time: it hastens toward the end — it will not lie! Though it tarry, wait for it, for it will surely come, and not delay."

The old men took the parchment from him and went away. Rupert brushed his hand over his eyes. Well, something had happened: he supposed there must be a space of incubation before the next thing happened. . . . he could not feel excited, nor romantic, nor devout. He visited respectfully the chief places in the Holy Land, repeating brief night and morning prayers, with a special memento for his parents.

Next summer Robert visited Medby and was sitting with Rupert by St. Paulinus's cross. The clink of metal could again be heard from far below; something was being repaired. Construction, repairing, ever since Roman soldiers had built that bridge nineteen hundred years ago!

"The bridge is very frail," said Robert. "Any shock might destroy it. Don't repair it into being a sham, Rupert! May the men who built it rest in peace!"

"At that time," Rupert said, "not one stone of Medby had been laid upon another. Yet Jerusalem was old already by a thousand years and more. The foundations still are there. What will be built on them? You know that my uncle has made Medby over to me legally? Shall I see the end of it, and will someone build on its foundations in another thousand years?"

Robert said that he was sure, now, that the stone in the altar in the rock chapel *was* first carved in honor of Mithra and that a Christian added the cross, and, "May I say something now?" he asked half-mischievously.

Rupert nodded.

"It's possible, you know, that your descendants may swing full circle and become just farmers once more. Let's hope not cattle thieves! But you've got to come full circle yourself, Rupert, and you're doing it! I've been watching you doing it! The water down there has been pouring behind the rock for centuries, but what did water mean till it became baptismal? And you *are* baptized! You are a Catholic, and really you know it. Up to now you wouldn't — yes, I dare say you couldn't — but now you can, Rupert, and you must!"

As he looked at Rupert, he could almost see the hard, transparent glass dissolving, becoming a mist, a light: the stone in the heart melting, reddening, becoming pure blood, Christ's Blood poured into the living soul.

Rupert bowed his head. "*Credo,*" said he.

Just then the great Medby bell began to toll, majestic, slow, sending out waves of solemn music from its silver bronze. Other bells chimed, too, echoing melodiously from tower to tower.

"What is that?" asked Rupert. "What are they ringing for?"

The two young men ran down to the castle. In a corridor they met a footman.

"What are the bells ringing for?" asked Rupert.

The man looked blank. "The bells, sir?"

And in fact the music had faded away over the fells and resounded only in their minds. By an immediate instinct they made for the house chapel. No one was there but Mrs. Medd, kneeling before the shrine of the ring. Apparently she had lit all the candles, for the chapel was full of light. Rupert and Robert genuflected to the tabernacle and then knelt down on either side of her. After a while Rupert bent and kissed her hand. She embraced him, and then, half-turning, gave her left hand to Robert and smiled. He, too, smiled, and went out of the chapel.

"All this," said Rupert afterward, "shows that you cannot resist God's hand in the long run and that He won't force yours. What do I see now, that I didn't see years ago? Why have I, or something in me, been praying, Show me thy face; let thy voice sound in my ears? And why did nothing happen? The final touch must be God's."

"And the first touch, too," said Robert. "It's a ring! Only you've seen it as an enclosure you wanted to get out of; but a circle *isn't* a mere enclosure! The radii start out from the center and then move on and on into the infinite."

"Here!" said Rupert. "I can't have you turning into a mystic. I must settle down and become one of the *bon petits bourgeois* of the Church and not provide you and poor *Maman* with any more agitations."

"Well," Robert said, "I've never seen you so lighthearted and almost frivolous before, not even at Oxford when you played the fool so much! But yes, I expect the ring will go to sleep again for quite some time. We must do our job: you here, and I in London, I suppose."

28

THE CROSS OF UMBRIA

W<small>HEN</small> Robert was twenty-eight he married — not the Orwylstree cousin, but, to everyone's satisfaction, an outlying Medd. At first they lived in London, but when their second son was born they took a pleasant house in Surrey, where, their origins having been duly tracked down, everyone called on them, tactfully passing over the regrettable fact that they were Romanists.

Lord Medd died rather suddenly; Odo left everything in Rupert's hands, and discovered in him an unexpected genius for finance. Time passed so rapidly that the 1914 war was declared, they felt, almost overnight. Robert, considered too old for this massacre of the innocents, was suddenly seized upon for the decoding of intercepted enemy wireless and was so miraculously good at it that, oddly enough, he was kept on at that work.

Rupert began by wondering if he should not be a conscientious objector and seek a job in some minesweeper where he would have as much danger and discomfort as anyone and yet not be asked to kill. But this raised such a storm that he revived a long-dormant "Medby's Own," ran such fantastic risks that he became known as Madby, was covered with decorations, but, half to his annoyance, was never hit. Afterward he was so strongly urged — not least by ecclesiastics — to marry, that he did so. But almost immediately his wife died in the great influenza epidemic, so there were no children. His uncle Odo also died, and so did Robert's younger son.

Rupert, now head of his family, considered that he had yielded to others long enough and that a new world must be prepared for. He began by changing Medd House in Arlington Street into a residential club for people who had gravely suffered in the war, specifying further uses to which it could be put when that generation had died out. The simple and dignified exterior and the view over the Green Park remained unchanged; but most of the *objets d'art* went to America. Indeed a charming million-airess bought the grand staircase just as it stood and put it at one end of her dining room; it led nowhere, but had the vast Medby escutcheon still above it which she came to hold must be hers by ancestral right. At the opposite end of her room was an organ on which Lohengrin, Tristan, and muted jazz were played during dinner, the keyboard and organist behind a fence of lilies till one evening the scent overpowered the poor man and he fainted, so the flowers were replaced by a gilded grille from a Spanish convent adorned with emblems of the Passion.

In the spring of 1921 Rupert asked Robert to come with him through Germany to Austria. He wanted, he said, to obtain a personal perspective of the results of war. "The

Germans," he said, "have always needed a Siegfried, a magic sword, a shining shield. For a while the Kaiser served as a mystic figure. Now there is none, and *we* certainly can't supply one. Just compare the Rhine and its legends and our Thames which never has created any! Who could *sing* about the Thames? Can we offer the Germans a *personality?*"

They found the poor country a prey to devastation, desperation, and anger — anger, when the people were not too hungry. They hurried on toward Austria, expecting to find it still worse, but determined for all that to visit Sankt-Markus in Tirol.

Naturally no one now remembered Rupert. The church was still there, though the roof leaked, and the priest was different. The crucifix in the fields was there, but it had slipped crooked and no one had straightened it. They were putting up at the old guesthouse, but there was no more joy there, nor atmosphere of innocence.

"We must do something about that leaking roof," Rupert said, "but how many roofs in this one little town must be leaking! Are there men or money or materials to mend them? Is there the will? They see our car and ask themselves how much they can make out of two more invading plutocrats."

"They aren't just greedy or surly," Robert said. "Deep down they remain Austrians; they're lovable and feel love themselves, if only we gave them the chance."

Rupert growled, and they went off to see the priest. He was young, bewildered, and suspicious. Finally Rupert's charm made him open up. "In old days," he said, "we were poor, but we did not starve. Priests were servants of the state; they had to say what they were told to say, and looked forward to pensions. But what chance has any Austrian now? There is no fuel; hardly any trade; no opening to the sea. One third of our population is in Vienna. Wait till you see it!"

Rupert offered the priest some money which he took dubiously.

"I think," said Rupert, "you might say that it comes from two Englishmen; but do not say — do *not* say it is meant politically. It is meant lovingly! I would like you to repair the roof of your church with it, but you are free to do what you think best."

"Sir," said the priest, his eyes suddenly full of tears, "your visit has made me believe that there is still some Christian love left in the world."

Their visit to Vienna seemed to sadden them less than the sight of the stricken countryside, though they felt heartsick at the sight of horribly rich people gorging in restaurants while young men and women in the streets were forced to every degradation if they, or their parents, were not to starve. Rupert afterwards made some crashing speeches in the House of Lords which were listened to with due politeness but added to his unpopularity. They turned back toward Italy.

They went by way of Cremona, giving no thought to Stradivarius or more than a glance at the Torrazzo of which the Cremonesi were so proud because it was the tallest tower in Italy. But they did stand and stare at the battered statue of St. Omobuono.

"To think," said Rupert, "that if the legend is true, that old merchant once possessed the ring! We know its history for certain back to old William Flete, who lived near Siena and knew St. Catherine. We might find out some more about it there. Earlier than that, one has to trust to tradition which takes us back to this old saint and possibly to St. Hildegard." But they made no discoveries and drove on to Assisi.

One evening — it was now early summer — they were sitting on a terrace there overlooking the great Umbrian plain. The Porziuncola was but a shadow far below them, almost lost in the splendid glow.

"What peace!" said Robert.

"Romantic as ever!" Rupert said. "Umbria was a very quarrelsome world. But its wars were better than ours. I believe that cruelty exists in all of us, bottled up either by faith or by law. And the less faith we have, and the more scientific we are, the more easily the seal of law will crack and the savagery will come spouting out — but a cold and calculated savagery such as has never been possible before." The white eyes of insanity seemed to stare at the two Englishmen.

"It's very odd," said Robert, "that it's you, who are so much more sensitive than I —— "

"But I'm much more realistic!" Rupert interrupted. "But go on."

"That's because you're really Latin. Well, it's odd that you should have been the one called to see all the horrors of the war, and I only to guess them. Still, my particular horror was that just because the young men one met *were*

· 257

young, *therefore* they were likely to die almost any day. It wasn't so much the collapse of morals that alarmed me — that had begun well before the war — it was the masses of men who came home and had been *taught* to do what was necessary, or expedient, at the moment, so a generation has grown up to which 'right' and 'wrong' just don't mean anything, but only what pays or pleases. We've learned nothing, but unlearned a lot."

Just then a Franciscan approached them, heavily hooded, his hands deep beneath his cloak.

"Young gentlemen," he said, "you must beware of sitting out in the brown of the evening. It grows cold suddenly. Let us walk toward our convent. Would you perhaps be English?"

Rupert said "Yes," and they followed the friar.

"The Franciscan family," said their guide, "has had so much to do with England! We have a very old tradition that our 'Brother Jacopa,' as our Father Francis called her, was caused to preserve an ancient ring which came into the hands of an English hermit, and he in his turn gave it to an English traveler."

Rupert smiled. "It is not lost," he said. "That traveler was an ancestor of mine. His name, like mine, was Medd. And since I am now head of our family, the ring belongs to me. Or I to it. The center of my home is the shrine where the ring reposes."

"Bravo!" said the friar, laughing gently. "Many of the noble Casa Medana, as we call it, have visited Assisi in times past, but I doubt if there has been mention of the ring. God be praised. You see how closely we are bound

to one another. But, as you sat, you were talking and seemed sad."

They told him as well as they could.

The friar, too, seemed sad. "You do not dream," said he, "that the war is yet over? As the Lord said, these are but the beginning of sorrows, or, as I am told the words mean, the beginning of birth pangs. We poor friars do not make politics nor are we prophets, but anyone can see that a new world is being born — a bad world, at first, where Caesar will enthrone himself as God. You have seen only a rehearsal. What can we do? At present nothing but devote ourselves to the relief of suffering, the suffering of Christ still wounded in His brothers and sisters, and, if He is to be recrucified, ask to share with Him even in that." He sighed, and drew his hands still farther beneath his cloak.

Robert asked if he lived in Assisi. The friar answered briefly that Assisi was the home of all Franciscans, older and younger, but that his own convent lay farther south, under Monte Gargano. "We must pray," said he, "that St. Michael may spread his wings and unsheath his sword. It sheds no blood but carves its way into the prisons of the spirit."

They had reached the great churches and entered the lower one. In the dim light of the lamps they seemed to see the walls melt; Francis was no longer buried deep beneath iron bars, but was moving about, gay and wounded, frail but immortal. They did not know how long they knelt there, but at last the friar touched them with the extremity of his fingers and said, "Now come."

They walked on either side of him to the doors and went out.

The Englishmen turned to look once again into the church, but the heavy doors had swung shut. They turned to thank the friar, but he had vanished into the dusk. They looked once more at the doors. "*Signori*," said a passing laborer, "you are too late. The doors were locked after the Angelus — an hour ago. Only the angels could make their way in now!" He saluted and passed on.

For a moment or two the friends stood silent. Then they began to talk rather breathlessly. They passed the façade of the pagan temple on the way to their lodging.

"How insane was our education," said Robert. "To think that in all my years at Oxford Assisi was mentioned only once — *scandentis Assisi;* even before Christ it was climbing up this hill; I suppose Propertius saw that temple? He and his Cynthia! Let us say a Hail Mary for them."

"I wonder," Rupert answered, "if anyone in the world has thought of doing that! They will be grateful for your education, after all!" They said the prayer, but then Robert could endure it no more.

"Rupert! I shall never forget what he said about the birth pangs of a new world! *We* are between worlds. Who can tell how much more suffering will be needed before the new one really comes to birth! What will it be like? A new sort of laity. A new kind of priest. A new going out of our Upper Room in which we've huddled ourselves so long! What can we say? And how can we make people hear?"

"I expect," Rupert said, "that the friar was asking us to accept a new crucifixion. Then we may trust that souls that look so dead may rise again!"

29

A.D. 1930

"THE OWL AT THE WINDOW"

BY the summer of this year Robert Brent's own family was dead or dispersed save for two old aunts who disapproved of him on principle. His surviving son was finishing his years at Oxford, where he was allegedly reading law, but talked vaguely about "writing." Robert had almost given up going there; he was treated politely by the young men he met, but they talked to him in a language which was not really their own. The university itself was no more sure of itself: its buildings began to seem like a native city engulfed in a town insufferably overcrowded and vulgarized. Oxford no more had its "secret": its Triple Crown was discarded; its Book was closed; the Lord was no more its "Illumination." And Robert had no call to return there when within only a year his son, who had gone to Uganda to study native conditions, died of snakebite. It became then more and more a custom for him to stay at Medby whenever his work in London left him free.

Rupert was more than ever convinced that an era, even a world, had ended; but as long as Medby existed and as he was head of the family, he had no hesitation about living *en grand seigneur*. His flag floated over the great tower; he always dined in his place at the high table, looking down the shadowy hall to the tall window at its far end where so much history could be read in the stained-glass coats of arms.

Robert went straight to Medby after visiting his son's grave in Africa. Rupert naturally had refrained from inviting any guests, so at dinner there were only himself, with Robert on his left and Mrs. Medd, as she wished still to be called, on his right; she wore a mantilla of black lace over her thick white hair.

Robert was suddenly overwhelmed by feeling so absolutely part of the place that he exclaimed, "It's amazing of you to have adopted me like this!"

"It was the house that adopted you," said Rupert. "When we first came here, it said to me, 'I am yours,' but to you it said, 'You are mine.' And you fitted in; you always did, even in London, though we were always — well, fencing with one another."

"I never fenced with *bonne Maman!*" said Robert indignantly. It was she herself who had said he must call her that. "*Maman,*" as such, belonged to Rupert; but she

... *vous allez bien ensemble!*" But no questions
d be asked. At a certain point he always retired be-
a wall of reticence. He wouldn't speak. But no, she
after all he wasn't dull!

ell, she had realized that if she was to be associated
that motherhood, she must fully live by Mary's life;
vent to the Carmelites and made her confession and
second and truer first Communion. She found herself
ng gently an old hymn — "*Astre propice au marin —
e ma barque au rivage* . . .*"

st then the two men came in. "*Singing, Maman?*"
Rupert. "Splendid! Let's have some music."
The Owl,'" Robert said. "Do please sing 'The Owl!'"

*and la nuit fait tout disparaître,
l'hibou chante à la fenêtre,
sur la tour d'un vieux château sans maître* . . .

his childhood, when Robert had learned that, rose
arm and friendly round him; and here actually was
ight flooding the vast countryside, here was the old
e, happily with its master, but for how long?
ey shivered, and Rupert jumped up. "Now me!" he

tinkled maliciously into Offenbach. Mrs. Medd
d, but could not resist, and floated off, light as ever,
ing all by herself. Rupert kept lapsing from key to
inserting shocking disharmonies, and then carica-
his own tune "according to" Mozart, Chopin, even
ner. Mrs. Medd parodied her own dance accordingly

had always needed a son, and Rupert year by year had
seemed to be growing away from her.

"Nor I with you," she said, smiling. "But I was very shy
of you — of both of you!"

They both turned to look at her. It seemed impossible
that this serene old lady could ever have been shy! Yet
they perceived that she had changed less than either of
them, save that the skin was drawn more closely over the
delicate bones.

She answered Robert's thoughts, as she often did.
"You've changed a little, Robert; but it's quite right that
you should be a trifle — weightier; and your face so much
firmer, and your hair only a little less unmanageable than
it was."

"Here!" cried Rupert, alarmed. "We seem to be getting
very personal!"

"But I haven't nearly finished," said his mother. "I wonder, *mon enfant*, whether you any more need to see things
as magical!"

"But did I ever?" Robert had always thought of himself
as quite commonplace.

"But of course! You always had to transfigure everything! You loved flowers, but you wanted the sun to shine
through them! Even your little theater, when you lit it up,
became a magical cave. Fountains — you wanted to see
them magically begin to play. Then you had your 'secret'
period — secret doors, sliding panels — you always
wanted *something else*, and you sometimes succeeded in
seeing it."

"But this sounds as if I was always pretending."

"No, no! You wanted everything to be a parable, and to mean something, even if the meaning wasn't clear. And that wasn't due only to your little Scottish mother, it was your *mère du ciel.*"

This came too near forbidden ground, and Rupert quickly intervened. "After this raking up of infantile memories and the public vivisection of my guest, I *think,* Madame . . ."

She laughed and said gaily, "Don't sit too long over your port. I shall be in my tower room. There's a fire there." She curtsied to Milord, and made off.

The two men sat down again, and Rupert said that she was quite right to have a little fire; even in summer the evenings up here could be chilly. Then they discussed a little house that Robert proposed to buy, behind Gray's Inn.

Mrs. Medd turned on no lights, but sat, hands clasped, watching the red glow of the wood. She knew that while she was talking about Robert her son had been thinking, not of magic, but of his own explorations into what she called *la mystique noire, le culte d'en bas.* An old ghost came up: where had responsibility begun? Not, she thought, in her old French ancestry, when court ladies had sought escape into satanism — she could not see that her home had ever suffered from that taint or had any of it been bequeathed to her soul. What of her childhood in that impoverished royalist family, where all was so rigidly formalized, even religion? As a girl, she had always been willful, she remembered all too well; and when that red-headed Englishman arrived, with all the vitality of the

Medds but without their faith, ostr
father's jettison of that belief, she h
ostracism, imagining that she could
faith. Even when he died, it was
that made her feel still bound to hi
ring I thee wed . . . "

But then Rupert began to get big
like her, not like those redheads!
she felt that Medby ought to be h
that picture of the castle, so inapp
had made so French, and almost in
her little oratory. And how often s
eyes turning first to the picture t
many lights in his model theater, a
curtain over the forbidden door
always felt at cross-purposes with

But then Robert had appeared,
who never made friends, so close
that dull little boy, even though
him? Dull? But enigmatic, too. W
that she had led Rupert across th
really upstairs at the window al
what had happened to Robert
which brought him so much ne
Rupert was becoming — yes, cru
off into a dark world where she v
low him? This was when she had
must mother Robert, too. "*Je sui
maman,*" she had said, and he h
mais, voyez-vous, madame, j'ai

till she cried enough. They followed her to the chapel, said their night prayers, paid homage to the ring, and kissed one another good night.

Rupert said he didn't feel like bed yet; the moon was full; why not make their pet pilgrimage to St. Paulinus's cross? They pulled on heavier shoes and went out.

"I'm not sure," Robert said, "what your mother meant about magic. The only idea that occurs to me is that I never feel sure about *time*. Here are we, two fairly elderly gentlemen, having just behaved like children, and now *I* don't feel myself any definite age. At the moment I simply *am* what I was when I first came with you to Medby. But I doubt if you could be that 'you' any more."

"I don't want to be. But, as I said, this house incorporated you. It has lived through so many selves. It took much longer to be sure of me than of you, and no wonder! But since you are incorporate in it, can you *be* at the time when each of its selves were alive?"

"I really think so," said Robert, "and if I knew a lot more history, I'd do it better. And at any rate since the ring came to live here it ties the whole thing together."

By now they had climbed to where the water fell steadily behind the rock face.

"What sort of magic did this have for you?" Rupert asked.

"Some, certainly. But I was gravitating toward the Faith, I suppose, and so I didn't need magic so much. But if I hadn't had a sort of film of faith protecting me, this old waterfall would have been terribly haunted — or haunting."

By now they had climbed to the cave chapel. "Now here," Robert went on, "there was neither magic nor haunting. It had been soaked in prayer far too long. Your castle has, too. It's grown up — so had the Saxon house — in the hands of men who prayed. Mystery, then, if you like, but not magic."

They looked down at the enormous mass of buildings over which the moon was drawing delicate veils, opalescent, silver-gray, changing the castle into something transparent, ethereal, as if it might float away with the streaming water and the moonlight. But away from the moon the stars shone steadily.

"*Noctis signa severa — austera silentia noctis*," said Rupert. "That's Lucretius, isn't it? This is what I take it as meaning: There *are* stars, and they're meant to serve as signs. But they're grave — not threatening — but terribly serious. And anything that interferes with the silence of the night is a desecration. This is what makes me less hopeless about myself. How many *signs* of the Faith were given me, but I did nothing about them. In that German church . . . that crucifix in the Tyrol . . . and in the church at Bethlehem . . . and I could tell you more things like that. Why didn't I act on them? Why were there those long silences? I can only hope that God meant that there should be long gaps. I assure you I was very conscious of the 'austerity' of them. And even since my being received, I feel I'm in another gap. And that friar at Assisi didn't — well, throw any new light onto it."

"I expect," Robert said, "we shall always have to wait for an indication of what's to be done next; you never *have* seen any ending to any perfect thing, because there isn't any. And it's false to talk of 'hopeless.' "

Rupert leaned forward, his face blanched in the moonlight and the shadows under his eyes and cheekbones very dark. He said, "Yes; I shouldn't have said 'hopeless.' Still, *you* can go back and back and find yourself at home in history; but can either of us go forward? No one knows what'll happen, and so they don't know what to say or do. I'm not totally inactive; I take the chair; I make speeches, but I cut no ice."

"You do and you don't. You puzzle people. You make one speech, and they think you're a black reactionary. You make another, and they think you're a red revolutionary. And that is simply because you *are* consistent; you stick to Catholic principles. You won't condescend to be partisan. You refuse anything that's merely decorative. That's why the clergy aren't content with you. You don't shout!"

"Good Lord!" cried Rupert. "Decorative? Didn't I consent to have a whole pageant of Medby under my very walls? In aid of — I forget what."

"You did," said Robert grimly. "And you refused to take the part of successive earls, suitably made up, and make speeches into microphones."

"The fact remains," Rupert said, "that neither you nor I are prophets, and a prophet is what is wanted. But prophets have usually had to be martyrs, too."

"Wait till that happens to you, you have to carry on with your job here, and I, I suppose, in London. I could really retire now, but I don't mean to till I'm sixty-five.

Meanwhile, short of direct inspiration, we can't do better than to pick up more facts. I think the best terrain for that just now isn't your far-east Europe any more, but Spain perhaps, and Portugal certainly."

"It's attractive," Rupert said. "I had an ancestress not very long ago who had to be fetched back from Toledo; that's when her nephew met Marie-Geneviève at Festugières who became my great-grandmother . . . and before that another ancestress went with Queen Philippa to Portugal."

"And *that*," said Robert wickedly, "was 'not so long ago,' either? My dear old feudal lord, what a perspective!"

At that they both laughed and went home, and did in fact go to Portugal in time to witness the beginning of her resurrection.

30

A.D. 1946–1950

FULL CIRCLE

ROBERT BRENT had indeed meant to retire when he was sixty-five, and had thought he might have ten more years of reasonably active life after that. After his visit with Rupert to Portugal he found he had fallen in love with the country and tried to go there yearly.

He loved especially the desolate southern part of the land and even went as far as Cape St. Vincent and looked out toward Africa, and felt that there was little around him that Henry the Navigator had not seen. He liked to help to restore in small ways the churches he encountered. Such poverty! So much broken glass, tattered linen. "I think our friar would be pleased with me!" he said. And he liked to share simple meals with peasants by the road-side or under the olive trees, making the sign of the cross and saying the Hail Mary in Latin, and they found them-selves doing so, too, and followed him to Mass — so rare in the terrible dearth of priests.

This stood for him as a symbol of apostolate in coun-tries other than his own. At home he had to be content with visits in the evening to Dockland, though he knew what dreadful poverty existed in respectable parts of London, too, hidden behind a façade of genteel houses rapidly turning into squalid nests for verminous inhabit-ants. He noticed, first, how shallow was the entry made by the official teaching into youthful minds, even though priests and nuns wore themselves to death over instruct-ing their children who so often escaped them the moment they had left school.

But again, piercing through the godless cement that seemed spread so thickly over minds that nothing above or beyond it seemed even imaginable, sprang suddenly pure jets of what could only be the Spirit at his mysterious work within. Robert never could recover from the night when a young man said to him, "If Jesus Christ was the son of God, same as they tell us, how could God go and kill Him? *I could never kill the child of me own brain!*" Who could ever guess what went on in these confused young minds? Who could dare say that heavenly things were *not* lurking there? How fumbling were the most honest of his efforts! "Commit thy way unto the Lord," he kept repeating to himself, "and he shall bring it to pass."

Rupert, on his side, seemed to have come to life. He spoke more trenchantly but was far from ingratiating himself among the moneyed classes of the north, though he had practically conquered the obstinate suspicion with which he was at first regarded. All the same, as a man said to him: "We like you all right, but when the revolution comes, you'll be the first to go — you an' your priest!"

But the revolution came first in the shape of the second great war, and Robert Brent kept on at his solicitor's work, fitting in such war work as he could manage. His wife had not long survived the death of her second son, and he lived in a small Georgian house hidden behind Gray's Inn. He had furnished it perfectly, and it had a small garden behind it where he could sit under a plane tree. He liked to drive his small car to different parts of London, and thus it was that he had discovered, south of the river, an almost unknown little church, built during the early Gothic "revival" and never readorned. It was dedicated in honor of Our Lady and St. Peter.

He used to sit far forward, where he could see the high altar and the tabernacle, but also, on his left, look into the Lady chapel where the Mother of God and her Child were seated in their niche, painted with crimson and blue that had turned almost black, and everywhere the gilding and brass had become rusted and grimy. The church itself was very dark, for huge warehouses had towered up around it; it huddled itself deep between them. But Our Lady had come out of her chapel, and stood, a humble Virgin of Lourdes, in a little cave of cork against a pillar. And suddenly he realized why he liked coming there! Two strips of tapestry, faded blue with fleurs-de-lys in-woven, flanked the statue. They were just like the red-and-yellow ones which, so long ago, had hung by the Sacred Heart in Saint-Michael's church at Havre. He felt himself back there, and reviewed his conscience. Well, he wasn't munching coffee fondants any more! But that visit hadn't been wasted. Despite the bleak Calvinist house-hold, the fair, the apparition of the worldly-wise Rupert, the cabarets, and the bad brandy — no, it hadn't been wasted; perhaps none of his life had been altogether wasted.

After the war he returned to the church, which was un-harmed. But in what setting would his last years be spent? Orwylstree Hall had been sold, to become — a school? a golf club? Better demolished, he thought, like Hutton Grove. No, that was selfish.

But Medby! It had received two direct hits; the whole of the domestic wings were in ruins; only the heavy old tower at the corner remained intact. Happily, the church, the hospital, and the school were uninjured and could now in fact be extended on the tremendous foundations that nothing save an earthquake could destroy, and the deep dungeons where most of the treasures had been stored. But an imaginative and zealous ministry had been sure that the park must be a mere sheath for surface coal and plowed it up. They found a few shovelfuls and then realized that they were attacking rock. The outlines of the Saxon house were obliterated; a reservoir had been built up the hill. It was now empty, but somehow it had drained off the water into a different direction. The Beck had almost ceased to flow; no stream now fell behind the rock face; no fairy, no saint, now peered out through the orifice. The passing of heavy lorries had shaken down the Roman bridge. The chapel in the cave had been dismantled, but the ancient stone had not been dislodged and Mass might be possible there again someday.

Robert went to Medby as soon as he could extricate himself from the thousand duties in which the after war entangled him. He was anxious to be near Rupert, who had remained there all the time, serving in the hospital and managing the refugees who came at intervals imagining that the castle at least would be safe; and in fact its subterranean labyrinths protected them as long as it was necessary.

They went out on the second evening after Robert's arrival, past the blackened stumps of the eight great yew trees, past the dried-up hollows hard to detect now under a tangle of briars that veiled them, and past, even, the cave where Our Lady no more sat. Even there only the massive altar remained in place. They sat down on the step of what had been the cross of St. Paulinus.

"I am now going to tell you," said Rupert, "what may astonish you, and you may disapprove of it. You've seen yourself how unsettled I've been ever since I became a Catholic. That was because I felt sure God was calling me to a special vocation — I didn't know what. Of course I thought it might be the priesthood. That is why I put off marrying till so late. But Mary died, and we had no children. So that wasn't to be the road. What I've done is this. I've arranged for my cousins from Avondale to occupy the old tower for as long as they like; there's plenty of room. Then the school and the hospital already serve half the countryside, and if they choose to build we can have a research center and all sorts of enterprises."

"But what about yourself?"

"Well, I'm making some final arrangements, and then I'm going to Russia."

"Good God!" said Robert, startled out of himself.

"I've no idea what I shall do there, but I'm sure that that is my vocation. I can read Russian and I'll soon speak it. One might rescue people . . . get into jails . . . anyhow, learn the facts. And I'm taking the ring with me. I'm sure it has a meaning, and that's *not* being superstitious! God will see that it's kept safe. In fact, if I were — er — killed or anything like that, it would make its way back to *you*."

Robert was silent for a long time. Then he said: "Your mother is a very old lady indeed. Oughtn't you, perhaps, to wait?"

"No. She wants me to go. She is too old to become a

Poor Clare, as she would wish; but she will go to Rome and live in a sort of annex to one of their convents. I've inspected it; it's poor, but healthy and clean. And we both have a lot to expiate."

"Oh, my dear Rupert!"

"Well, we have. And certainly the world has. She and I are perfectly clear that we want to finish our lives penitentially; and you know her well enough to be sure she's perfectly gay about it. She's an extraordinary person."

Robert reflected that Rupert wasn't so very ordinary himself. They went to Communion next day at St. Etheldreda's in the ancient crypt, and this was their good-by.

Robert Brent, now almost quite alone, but not lonely, reflecting on Rupert, found himself murmuring Vergil's lines: "*Sancta ad vos anima* — a consecrated soul, with never a thought of cowardice or betrayal, shall I descend to you, not once unworthy of my high ancestry — *magnorum haud umquam indignus avorum*." Well — cowardice? No, that never had been Rupert's. A traitor? Even in his perversities he had not been treacherous; had been openly fighting against the mysterious power that was drawing him to Itself.

The solemn music of the Latin sent Robert's mood back to that first school and its velvety lawns where first he had heard that music. *Tendebantque manus ripae ulterioris amore.* "Poor little chaps," he thought, "there we all were, reaching out our hands in longing for the further shore. But," he thought, "it was the further shore that reached out and laid hold of us and wouldn't let go." He smiled to think of those old novels, and how mysterious hands had reached forth from across the Thames, the Seine, the Tiber, even the Nile. But those were not hands that could pull him very far forward; still, he had paddled out a little way and then drawn back, shivering, to his own familiar bank. Yet he *could* not stay there!

"If I go to sunset or to sunrise, up to the heavens or down to the abyss, *there* art *Thou;* it is Thy hand that has hold of me — Thy right hand that is holding me." It was against that hand that Rupert had fought, with his dark, inverted mysticism. Robert remembered how he had meant to spit the Lourdes water out, but had swallowed it. And he recalled his own fierce fight against praying to Our Lady; then his intoxication with Lourdes. No, he would not go back there. "There is no going back." Never back to Orwylstree; never to Medby. So much of life had been simply swept away from him. But after all, here was still Our Lady of Lourdes in her humble grotto made of cork.

It was three years later, about Christmas, that a Hungarian refugee called and gave him a little packet. It was the ring. Apparently a Pole had given it to him and the Pole had got it from a Ukrainian. Before that its history was lost. This must mean that Rupert was dead! How? when? None would ever know. He wrote to Mr. Anthony Medd, now of Medby:

Dear Mr. Medd: The ring, which was Medby's greatest treasure, has come back to me from Russia, as Lord

Medby said it would if he died. I do not know what you will do about "presuming death." Meanwhile, will you kindly tell me what you want done about the ring?

Yours very sincerely,

Robert Brent.

Mr. Medd replied:

Dear Mr. Brent: Thank you for your letter. I am not taking up the "presumption" of my kinsman's death, if only because my wife and I are going to Australia where a friend of mine has a large estate and it would be awkward for me if I were anything but Mr. Medd. I retain the tower we at present live in; the rest is now the property of the hospital and school, etc., which I think may quite likely be nationalized. I have given them our relics for their museum, the only valuable one, so far as I know, being a small book said to have been written by St. Cuthbert. I have no sentiment about your ring; please keep it or dispose of it as you will. If my children like to claim the title and come back here, they must do as they please.

Yours very sincerely,

Anthony Medd.

Robert Brent, much upset, took a taxi — he no longer drove — to his church and showed the ring to Our Lady. "What shall I do?" he asked. "If I keep it, to whom shall I leave it? Hadn't I better give it now? But to whom?" Mrs. Medd had died, the nuns felt sure, in the odor of sanctity. To Tours? To Chartres? To Lourdes?

No answer came from the cork grotto. Suddenly the name "Jerusalem" came into his mind. But who could guess the future of that distraught city? Just then a lady dressed in deep mourning came in and lit every candle she could find round the crib. As she left, she smiled and made him a little bow. He was feeling extremely tired and his mind was confused. He half-rose, but she smiled again and went out of the church. "Bethlehem, I think," he said to himself.

He had a chalice made, and the delicate, frail ring was embedded in the stem. He confided this to a priest on his way to Palestine and felt that he had finished his vocation. He had always loved the Advent prayer which asked that these holy things may cause us — made, by Thy mighty power, ever more pure — to return to their First Beginning. And, without knowing it, but with much prayer, he had restored the gold to the place where it had first been offered.

In February he caught pneumonia, and his doctor told him he must have a day nurse, and, after a while, a night nurse, too. He handed his few personal possessions to such old friends as were allowed to see him; and, when the nurse protested against his rooms being thus stripped, "My superfluities," he said.

He was tempted to think of his life as ineffectual; nothing had been finished — not even by Rupert. But he turned his mind from that to Claude la Colombière's prayer: "Teach me the perfect forgetfulness of myself." And when the days closed in he said, "The darkness is not darkness with Thee, but the night is as clear as the day."

He was brought Communion twice a week, and once he watched a priest in red vestments saying mass at the foot of his bed. Then it was Rupert himself saying, "Show me Thy face, let Thy voice sound in my ears, for Thy voice is sweet, and Thy face most fair."

The firelight flickered on his ceiling; he was back in his nursery again. Then Rupert helped Our Lady to spread her dark blue velvet mantle over him; they both smiled at him, and he went to sleep.

Cathedral of Christ the King
714 King St. West.
Hamilton, Ontario

Cathedral of Christ the King
.714 KING STREET WEST
HAMILTON, ONTARIO